THE SUITABLE SUITOR

Henry Hartnell was a fond mother's ideal match for a headstrong daughter like Jessamine Dalton. He was honest, honorable, and wealthy enough to provide for the upbringing of Jessamine's brothers and sisters and the comfort of Jessamine's mother, all of them exiled by poverty from their aristocratic world.

In Jessamine's eyes, however, Mr. Hartnell had one flaw. He was the dullest gentleman in England.

Still, he had to be better than the insufferably arrogant, shamefully faithless Sir Ivor Bellamy, now preparing to house a London beauty in the mansion the Daltons once called their own. That, at least, was what Jessamine told herself—as she tried to heed the voice of reason and not hear the siren song of love. .

D1738981

About the Author

Vanessa Gray grew up in Oak Park, Illinois, and graduated from the University of Chicago. She currently lives in the farm country of northeastern Indiana, where she pursues her interest in the history of Georgian England and the Middle Ages. She is the author of a number of bestselling Regencies available in Signet editions.

A Signet Super Regency

"A tender and sensitive love story . . . an
exciting blend of romance and history"
—*Romantic Times*

The Guarded Heart

Barbara Hazard

*Passion and danger embraced her—
but one man intoxicated her flesh
with love's irresistible promise . . .*

Beautiful Erica Stone found her husband mysteriously murdered in Vienna and herself alone and helpless in this city
of romance . . . until the handsome, cynical Owen Kings-
ley, Duke of Graves, promised her protection if she would
spy for England among the licentious lords of Europe.
Aside from the danger and intrigue, Erica found herself
wrestling with her passion, for the tantalizingly reserved
Duke, when their first achingly tender kiss sparked a
desire in her more powerfully exciting than her hesitant
heart had ever felt before. . . .

The Lost Legacy

by
Vanessa Gray

A SIGNET BOOK
NEW AMERICAN LIBRARY

NAL BOOKS ARE AVAILABLE AT QUANTITY DISCOUNTS WHEN USED TO
PROMOTE PRODUCTS OR SERVICES. FOR INFORMATION PLEASE WRITE TO
PREMIUM MARKETING DIVISION, NEW AMERICAN LIBRARY,
1633 BROADWAY, NEW YORK, NEW YORK 10019.

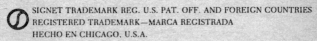

SIGNET, SIGNET CLASSIC, MENTOR, ONYX, PLUME,
MERIDIAN and NAL BOOKS are published by
NAL PENGUIN INC., 1633 Broadway, New York, New York 10019

First Printing, December, 1987

1 2 3 4 5 6 7 8 9

PRINTED IN THE UNITED STATES OF AMERICA

1

The family group in the green salon of Oakminster sat as though posing for a group portrait by Sir Joshua Reynolds.

So thought Jessamine Dalton, indulging in one of the irreverent thoughts that had long provided annoyance both to her mother, sitting across the room near the fireplace, hands folded in her black merino lap, and to several of her governesses, now thankfully long departed.

Mrs. Elizabeth Dalton, long a widow, was surrounded by her four children, all handsome but stiffly uncomfortable in the mourning clothes newly acquired because of the death of her father, Sir Mumford Bellamy.

All that Sir Joshua would have found lacking, Jess told herself with an inner smile, was a small lapdog or two to complete the arrangement.

There had been few occasions in recent weeks for Jess to entertain any sort of personal reflection, to say nothing of giving way to amusement. That first moment, when Silas, old Sir Mumford Bellamy's groom, had galloped up the drive, bawling for Lister and Doughty to help his master, whose overturned chaise at that moment pinned the mortally injured owner in his own ditch, had opened six weeks of grave illness for her grandfather, ending three days ago with his death.

Now, the funeral over and the guests departed, the Daltons were alone. Jess, on whose slender shoulders most of the sickroom care had rested, was fagged beyond reason. She longed for nothing more than a week in bed, eiderdown pulled up around her ears, relieved only by an occasional refreshing cup of tea placed gently in her hand. Such a hiatus in her life could not be accommodated at Oakminster—not at the moment.

The atmosphere of deep mourning added to the depression that wrapped them all. Even Althea Dalton, having reached the advanced age of thirteen, was constrained to don the regulation garments of adult gloom. Jess, watching her young sister, felt a jolt somewhere in the region of her stomach. Althea in her black alpaca gown, devoid of ruffles and without jewelry except for a row of jet buttons from waist to chin, seemed transmuted from hoyden to young lady —moreover, a young lady with whom Jess was not acquainted. Her hair a little darker than Jess's blond curls, her eyes a lighter blue, her nose a trifle tip-tilted—all these were familiar to Jess. But the girl's unconscious elegance as she smoothed her skirt was new. Althea was on the verge of growing up, and somehow Jess was sad.

But suddenly the illusion was shattered. Jess saw the mutinous glint in her sister's eyes. *That* expression Jess knew full well.

"I shall not wear this black again!" Althea said stoutly, but fortunately in a voice too low for her mother to hear.

Jess murmured, "No need to, Althea. You won't be out in even local society for a year yet, you know."

Althea's lower lip jutted out obstinately. Her dramatic defiance had collapsed around her, but at only thirteen she lacked experience and resolution to revive it.

Her mother, besides, was occupied with her own unsatisfactory thoughts. "What will become of us all?" inquired Mrs. Dalton, plaiting a fold in her skirt. Her voice was querulous, carrying an overtone of bewilderment which Jessamine recognized with sinking heart.

"Mama, you know we shall deal very well. Fortunately we are not dependent upon Grandpapa's money." And a good thing, too, she thought morosely, since their distant cousin, Ivor Bellamy, the heir to the great estates of Oakminster, was not noted in Jess's mind for generosity. She had good reason for her opinion.

Silvester Dalton, a young man with, surprisingly, no pretensions to a career as a dandy even at fifteen, was too restless to sit still. The funeral of his grandfather was the first ceremony of the kind he had witnessed, and while he was not bowed down with grief, since his grandfather's commerce with him had been nearly entirely along the lines of severe criticism and even contempt, it went hard with him to pretend a solemnity he did not feel.

"I suppose," said Silvester, his voice too loud in the sober silence, "that the heir will not consider buying my commission?"

"If justice were done," remarked Mrs. Dalton, looking fondly at her elder son, "you would be the heir. But of course that would not bring you a commission, for you would be obligated to stay here and run Oakminster. I am persuaded you would like that much better than running off to sea. I cannot understand all the legal business, for dear Papa said that no woman had a head for business, except you, of course, Jess, and I do think it is most unbecoming of you."

Mrs. Dalton's voice trailed away, and she had recourse to her black-bordered handkerchief. Jess sighed quietly. There was no way to mollify her mother, as she had learned to her repeated sorrow.

Mrs. Dalton was possessed of several fixed ideas, and one of them was that Jess was taking on regrettably unladylike habits when she had required Acton, the farm manager, to present his books to her at the end of last quarter. But since at the time Sir Mumford was lying in his great bed upstairs, waiting irascibly for death, someone had to take over the running of the estates. At fifteen Silvester was too young, to say nothing of his firmly held conviction that the only career even worth his consideration was that of a *sea captain*.

Mrs. Dalton continued. "Why the estate should be settled only through the male line, I cannot see. I have two fine sons, and what is to become of them? If Sir Ivor Bellamy does his duty by us, and I am sure it is not my fault that I was my dear father's only child, he should see my sons settled. Although I do not quite know what Philip should wish for."

Jess answered for Philip, the ten-year-old who was edging, book in hand, toward a window where there was light to read. "He wishes only to live in a library."

"You see, Mama?" exclaimed Silvester. "I would not need to stay home after all. Philip can run the estates."

"But he is not going to," objected Jess. "Ivor is perfectly capable of managing Oakminster. It is only a small addition to his holdings, you know."

Too late, she realized that she had opened another of Pandora's boxes. One of her mother's close-held grievances was that Jess should have married her one-time betrothed, Ivor Bellamy. With the passage of four years, however, Mrs. Dalton had given up trying to make Jess see reason over the broken engagement. Now, Jess feared, the conversation would run again along well-worn grooves. But to her surprise, her mother only said mildly, "I suppose we shall hear soon that Sir Ivor wishes to evict us. What is your thought, Jess? You know him better than we do."

Well enough, thought Jess, to have developed a strong and irreversible aversion to him. And richly deserved, too! "I doubt he has any interest in . . . in Oakminster." Or in any of us, she added silently. "He has no understanding," she added with barely suppressed emotion, "and little human feeling at all. He is outrageously puffed up with his own importance, and is not likely to pay any heed to aught but his own wishes!"

"Jess, my dear!" exclaimed her mother. "I did not know you felt so strongly against him. You know you never explained anything. I wish you had confided in me before, instead of acting like the heroine of a novel, so silent and martyred, you know."

"What good would that have done?"

"I would have told you that all men are so, and you must ignore their faults for the advantage of setting up your own establishment." She sighed. "Of course the situation does not always work well. But your papa did not know he would die so young and so deeply in debt."

Jess was struck by the notion that she might, in her own unhappiness, have grossly underestimated her mother.

"No, Jess, I would have been of more use to you if we had talked about . . . about your troubles. You should have married him when you had the opportunity. Now, of course, it is too late, and who knows what will become of us!"

Anger and dismay rose abruptly into Jess's throat, so that she could not have spoken had there been anything she wanted to say. She had gone over this matter of her onetime betrothal to Ivor and the subsequent quarrel so many times that it was engraved upon her memory. Time is supposed to heal all wounds, she thought with a touch of bitterness, but there was a regrettable lapse in the healing process in this case. Her mother's words put the cap on it. *It was too late.*

It was of course to be expected that her mother's lament would be for herself, and not for the misery that had enveloped Jess for that first year after the break with Ivor, before she began to climb slowly out of the pit. The pit, according to Scripture, was one that she had dug for herself and fallen therein. The thought did not help.

"Could you write to him, Jess," demanded Silvester,

"see what he says about purchasing my commission?"

"You are too young to go to sea," said his mother firmly. "I should not sleep a wink knowing that you were out on a ship on that terrible ocean, always soaking wet if you were not washed overboard—I know you, Silvester, and I know that unless I keep after you, you will not take care of yourself. But if," she added thoughtfully, "I wrote a letter to the commodore, or whatever you call him, he would see to it that at least you put on dry hose."

Silvester squirmed, his face reddening. "Mother! I would simply die if you did that!"

"Then you must promise me that you will pay close heed to your health."

"For goodness' sake!" exclaimed Jess, losing patience. "Silvester has not gone to sea yet. He does not have a commission, nor any hope of getting one, at least not from . . . from the heir."

She found to her surprise that this time she could not speak Ivor's name. It had been so long since she had thought of him as anything but that Monster of Unfeeling, that his name did not come trippingly to the tongue, as once it had. Silvester's talk of the sea brought her a quick memory—she and Ivor face-to-face, Ivor's ordinarily dark complexion bleached by fury to the color of wood ashes and his eyes narrowed to slits, exchanging mutual vows—not of affection, truly. As she recalled, they had each sworn that they would not care if the other drowned, and would grant succor to the sodden victim only to the extent of proffering a totally redundant glass of water.

And Silvester wanted Ivor to help him go to sea! More likely the heir would send Jess—in a leaky boat.

But she became aware of the anxious faces turned her way. Her mother, of whom she was truly fond, brushing away a tear while she sent a speaking glance at her daughter, and Silvester, the light of hope dying in his face as no reassurance came his way.

Jess roused herself. No bridge could be crossed before one reached it, and in the meantime, there was no advantage in guessing what Ivor's reaction might be.

"He does not need Oakminster, Mama," said Jess pacifically. "As I recall, he dislikes the country excessively. I should imagine that we will receive a short note from his man of affairs, telling Acton that he should present his accounts to Ivor's own man of affairs from now on, and that will be the end of it for us. He won't care what we do, nor where we live. I doubt we shall be disturbed at all."

In fact, she was of half a mind to believe that Ivor would not even remember her name. She had not heard that he had married, but certainly a man of such wealth and presence could not resist the determined efforts of mamas and daughters for the four years since she and Ivor had parted forever.

"Well," said Mrs. Dalton comfortably, "that is all right, then. And, Jess, of course you have Henry. As soon as the year is out, and we may wear colors again, it may be well to make the announcement at once."

"Announcement! Of what, pray?"

"Your betrothal to Henry Hartnell, of course. But if Henry's grandfather dies, I do hope it will be soon. Not that I wish him any hardship, but it will be too bad if we have to undergo *another* year of mourning!"

Jess, shocked into reality by her mother's clear expectation that there was no alternative but that she marry Henry Hartnell, surely the most deadly bore in the north of England, fled out-of-doors to her favorite refuge.

The herb garden, originally designed and planted by Great-Grandmother Bellamy, was placed out of sight behind a rose arbor of particular magnificence. Jess often wondered whether her ancestor too had found reasons to remove herself occasionally from sight of the house, and had made for herself a charming and fragrant haven of quiet.

There, in a spot unhallowed—what a mistake! she should have said *undefiled*—by the memory of Ivor's presence, she sank onto a marble bench and considered her future.

At one time, that prospect had been, to say the least, pleasing. She had gained the attentions of one of the foremost beaux of the day, a man of wealth and address, and a distant cousin. She had not then thought about securing the future of her own family, since the legal entanglements of an entailed estate were completely absent from her mind.

Instead—and today, to her regret, she recognized her fault—she had thought only of the excitement of her betrothal, her pride in arriving at, for example, Carlton House or Devonshire House, on the arm of a handsome gentleman, and knowing that all eyes, and some of them satisfactorily full of envy, were on her.

How disgustingly young and shallow she had been! she thought now.

She realized that she really knew very little about her onetime betrothed. She knew his features well: those gray eyes that could be warmly comforting, or—at the end—had turned cold as The Wash in winter. His straight strong eyebrows, dark as his hair, and the well-shaped lips that could, on occasion, smile in a way that turned her heart over. She remembered *that*!

She had tried, with some success, to erase those final quarrels from her memory. She convinced herself that she would never set eyes on Ivor again, totally forgetting over the years that he, as the grandson of Sir Mumford's younger brother, would inherit the Bellamy estates.

A sound of a twig breaking underfoot startled her. Looking up, she saw Philip standing shyly at a little distance, watching her hopefully. For once he did not have a book in his hand.

His dark blue eyes, so much like hers, were fixed anxiously on her, and with a rush of affection she welcomed his company.

"Philip!" she exclaimed with pleasure. "Come sit with me. Did you get tired of all the gloom in the house?"

He came hesitantly. "You don't mind?" She made room for him on the bench. He looked so downcast that she was minded to put an arm around his shoulders, but fortunately thought better of it. He was no longer a little boy. At the age of ten, he was shooting up in height, but he was still so thin he appeared to be put together, and hastily at that, from a supply of sticks.

They sat in companionable silence for some little while. Jess was content to let the fragrant breeze come to her across the herb garden and forget the uproar back in her mother's drawing room. It was of course to be expected that her mother would be upset over the prospect of being removed against her will from the house in which she had been born and had lived until her short and ill-starred marriage. When Jess's father had come to his untimely end, hastened by an over-indulgence in the more debilitating ways of society, and it was found that except for her mother's untouchable settlement the family was without funds, it was only natural that Mrs. Dalton should bring her four children home, and home to her meant Oakminster.

Now the future had clouded again, and Mrs. Dalton fretted. Jess dearly loved her mother, but there were some occasions on which it was more prudent, in the interests of her own sanity, to remove herself from an active discussion—as now.

This was the first time that Philip had joined her in her harmless escape. She glanced sidelong at him, wondering whether he had come with a message or to seek compatible company. She soon found out that neither explanation fitted.

"Are you going to marry Mr. Hartnell?" Philip asked bluntly.

"Mama seems to think so," said Jess, dealing with Philip as an adult. "But I shall not agree. At least until I have to."

"Why would you have to?"

"Oh," she said lightly, "if we lost our money, or were put out into the road. Something like that. You don't like him?"

"No. He always looks past me," explained Philip simply. Jess understood him clearly. Henry paid attention to Henry.

Philip continued. "Besides, if we find the treasure, we'll be all right. For money, I mean."

"Treasure?" Jess repeated idly. Then, with more attention, she repeated, "What treasure?"

"The Bellamy treasure. They said that the Cavalier Bellamy, the one who fought for the king, buried all the family gold and silver someplace, and if we found it, it would be ours, wouldn't it?"

"I never heard of a treasure of ours being buried. But I suppose . . ." She stopped short, unwilling to disillusion Philip with his comforting dreams of a treasure trove.

But Philip was not stupid. "I know. Even if we found it, I suppose it would go to the heir." Sighing, he stood up and stretched, his thin body all sharp angles. "Why didn't you marry him when you had the chance, Jess? It would have saved us a lot of trouble."

2

At the same time that Jess was reviewing her past life, with particular attention to the errors she had made which were now past recovery, Sir Ivor Bellamy stood in the well-furnished library in his small but elegant town house in Brook Street.

As Jessamine was in company with her brother Philip, so Sir Ivor was in company with his sister, Cleo, Lady Chichester. Cleo was making an unexpected morning call. Ivor's surprise at seeing her at this unusual hour, for she very seldom appeared in her own morning room before noon, was equaled by his instant surmise that the coming interview would not be to his taste.

Today Lady Chichester had much on her mind, and she had so far unburdened herself to her brother as to reach the point where action was to be recommended.

"I must urge upon you—"

Her brother interrupted her. "Must you?"

"Don't try to put me off, Ivor. I know your temper, and you do not frighten me. Chichester says that the rumor is all over town, and I am most upset."

"I wonder at your husband. Surely he did not need to inform you of mere rumors, especially if he knew you would be distressed?"

Diverted, Cleo followed the new trail. "He did not know it would upset me, of course. He takes the greatest care of me, and although I know you do not like him overmuch—"

"Agreed," murmured Ivor.

"Yet at least he is cognizant of his duty, and he does it."

"Are you in a delicate condition? Again?"

"Don't be common." Cleo returned to the attack. "I refer to the news that everyone is talking about."

"Not quite everybody, dear sister. I for one do not know what you are talking about. Surely no one objects to the new way I tie my neckcloth? I myself think it quite becoming."

"You idiot! You know Charles cares nothing for fashion! He would not even notice if that were the fault."

She smiled in spite of herself. She owned a great fondness for her brother, since they two were more of an age than the younger children who had blessed the Bellamy nursery after them. It was a source of unhappiness to her that her dear Ivor had taken such a dislike of her husband. Charles was perhaps a bit dull, she thought honestly, but he was a good man and she had a great affection for him. It did not occur to her that Ivor deliberately held himself aloof from her Charles so as not to be seen to interfere in his sister's life.

"What does dear Charles dislike?" encouraged Ivor. "If it is not my neckcloth, then I confess it is quite beyond me to fathom his mind."

"It's this business about the Bellamys," she told him. "The *other* Bellamys, I mean, of course."

Ivor was barely able to prevent a startled expression from appearing on his handsome features. The Bellamy "business" had been the subject of his entire morning's musings. The letter now on his desk had brought home to him the inescapable fact that the Bellamy affair could no longer be postponed. He was not pleased to learn that the other Bellamys and he himself were the subjects of rampant gossip.

"And what," he inquired, "do the rumors say?"

"That you are still angry with Jessamine, although I never understood why you jilted her—"

Between clenched teeth he said, "I did not jilt her!"

"Well, my dear, that is only one of several conflicting rumors," she said apologetically. "And when you inherit Great-Uncle's estate, they say you plan to turn her out into the street. Although I suppose it would be the road you turn her out into, being in the country, wouldn't it?"

"And Chichester believes that? Then he's more fool than I thought possible!"

"I did not say that!" she cried, wounded. "I said only that he was concerned about your reputation—"

"My thanks to him!" said Ivor savagely.

"—What with such ugly things being said about you."

"Ugly things?" repeated her brother in a quiet, and therefore dangerous, voice. "I am sure you cannot wish to keep me entirely in the dark?"

"Oh, dear, I knew I'd make a mull of it!"

"And so you have."

Lady Chichester quite properly ignored this remark. "They're saying that our Great-Uncle Bellamy—"

"Sir Mumford," offered Ivor.

"—is getting ready to die. And what will you do about it?"

"Since I am not a practitioner of the art of medicine, my dear, I fear my hands are tied."

"Ivor!"

"However," he continued blandly, "your concern is too late." He indicated the letter on his desk. "A message from Acton, who appears to be Uncle's estate manager."

"Then Uncle Mumford is dead?" she said in a stifled voice. "But what will happen to . . . the Daltons?"

Suddenly amused, he told his sister, "You may speak Jess's name, you know. I am not so tender as all that."

"I am sure I do not wonder," said Cleo with returning spirit, "that you will hear her name again and again when this news gets out. Mark my words, Ivor. Your reputation will be in shreds!"

"Because of the 'ugly things'?"

Lady Chichester was on a tangent of her own. "I

know you will not take your revenge on Jessamine out on her mother."

"Good God, is that what they expect of me?"

She nodded. "But I know you could not make her leave her home, for what would be the use of it, when you have more manors and places to live than you could ever use? And even if you had no roof in the world to call your own, you are never cruel, Ivor."

Cruel? It was surprising to hear the same words from his sister's lips that had run through his thoughts all the morning, ever since the moment he received Acton's informative letter. Although the word had been in his mind, the only source of cruelty he knew had not been he himself, but a golden-haired, blue-eyed miss named Jessamine Elizabeth Dalton!

"Why you don't marry is something I don't know!" exclaimed Cleo. "If you were betrothed, there would be none of this gossip."

"How would my commitment to marry stop the many mouths of Dame Rumor?"

"Because they would all know that you were not cherishing the idea of revenge on the poor girl— Jessamine, I mean, of course—and you would not be delighted at the opportunity of making her life miserable." She watched her brother through narrowed eyes. Knowing him so well, she believed she could read the processes of deep thought on his features or, more likely, the impact of a new and, she feared, unholy thought.

"What is it, Ivor?"

He did not answer for a moment, his gaze directed inward on a prospect that slowly began to please him. "Cleo, you've done it! My thanks to Chichester!" She noticed a glint in his eyes that caused her uneasiness. "I feel sure that you have a myriad of things to do, Cleo? Places you must go? I do not wish to keep you a moment beyond your wishes."

So saying, he escorted her into the black-and-white-tiled foyer, took her furs from his butler, Benton, tucked them closely around her throat, and held the door for her.

"Ivor! I cannot understand you! I do not even think I trust you! Whatever shall I tell Charles? Have you gone quite out of your wits?"

Handing her into her carriage, he said, with the sudden smile that could make any female heart thump alarmingly, "My dear, instead of losing my wits, I think I am in a fair way of regaining them!"

She looked at him from the carriage window, a troubled smile on her face as the vehicle drew away. While she did not understand the sudden alteration in her brother's usually somber spirits, she rejoiced in the change. He had been out of sorts, even savage in his moods, for more months than she could count. Ever since, she realized, his betrothal to Jessamine Dalton had been broken.

She had not become well-acquainted with Jess, since she had been at Chichester Manor awaiting the birth of her older son during the Season when Ivor had finally decided to marry.

She settled back against the squabs. Whatever thought had taken possession of her brother just now, and whatever consequences it might have for them all, at least he was once again cheerful. No matter how short a time it might last, she was grateful for the moment!

For the moment, Ivor was held in thrall by the momentous idea that had come to him, inspired by his sister's remonstrances. He had been of several minds, during the past weeks since he had been informed by his uncle's legal representative that Sir Mumford could not recover from his injuries, as to what to do about the Bellamy legacy, entailed on him.

His own father had told him that the senior Bellamy estates, those recently in the hands of Sir Mumford, had dwindled over the years until they were hardly worth thinking of. Ivor's father and grandfather had prospered mightily, as had Ivor, and he was far from requiring any additional income.

There had been, at one time, a tale of Bellamy jewels, said to have disappeared at the time that Oliver Cromwell and his lieutenants—some of them with very odd names indeed!—had ranged the countryside pillaging the Cavalier families. The Bellamys of course had been loyal to the king, but at least the lands had been retrieved from the Commonwealth by an ancestor of considerable deviousness. Ivor hoped devoutly that he had inherited enough of that quality to serve at the present moment.

He had, upon first receiving the message from Acton, decided to renounce the inheritance. Then, upon sober thought, he realized that there were legal reasons why he could not simply dismiss the Bellamy estate from his mind and his purse.

However, one of the main factors which guided his thoughts was not of a legal nature. Without old Uncle Mumford, there was now no one to manage the estates. Jess's brother—Silvester, was that his name? —could not be more than fifteen now, and hardly able to take over the task of providing good care for the tenants and especially, in Ivor's mind, of providing comfort for Jess.

He could picture Jess beset by farmers, factors, creditors, angry tenants—no, it simply would not do.

And while he was thinking about the best way of providing for Jess, he realized that the emotion that he had buried, and buried deep, for the past four years was shouldering its way to the surface of his mind.

He wanted Jess!

There had been a time when he could remember every word she had said to him—words that seared, and words he thought would scar him indelibly. He was less sure of what he had said to her, but he knew now he had been wrong. He had been insanely in love with her—the first woman he had ever wanted to marry—and he had wanted to possess her, heart, mind, soul, and behavior.

He still wanted her—God, how he wanted her!—but he was far wiser now than he had been then. The intervening years—years at first of savage and bitter anger, and then of beginning to assess his own faults, and finally of despair at the loss of the happiness he had so lightly valued—had brought him to this point, this very day.

The Bellamy legacy was in his hands, and perhaps he could entice Jess back into his arms.

A very subtle plan, that was what was needed—that, and the enormous self-control that would be needed to carry it out. Could he?

He *must*. The alternative, a life without Jess, without sunshine, without warmth, was too miserable to think about.

Her brother was miserable, thought Cleo on her way home. If he were only not so *stubborn*!

Shedding her furs as she walked into her husband's library, she said, "I could just shake him!"

Charles was a quiet man, possessed of quiet humor and of a great tolerance for his charming wife, fueled by a strong affection for her. "I suppose he threw you out?"

"Of course not! Why should he? I'm his sister, after all, and I had an obligation to fulfill."

"Somehow I should not expect Ivor to give much thought to your obligation. I should imagine he would call it interfering, an intrusion he has never taken to."

"But he is so exasperating! I simply told him, Charles, and in the kindest way possible, that he ought to offer for someone, and then the rumors would stop."

"Rumors are not known to stop until they are ready.

I suppose," he added with a great air of cooperation, "that you mentioned a name or two?"

"Well," she said, not meeting her husband's eyes, "I did just refer to Angela Trompion. He has paid some attention to her, you know."

"If you call two dances at Almack's in the last month paying attention, then I must assume you are correct. But it didn't seem to me that he had the slightest interest in her."

"Or anyone!" Cleo thrust out her hands in a gesture of despair. "What is to become of him?" She stumbled forward and was caught reassuringly in her husband's firm embrace.

"Here, here. Don't cry! Ivor is well able to manage his own affairs, you know. If he wishes to wed, then he will do so."

After a few moments of enjoyable comforting, Cleo drew away from her husband's arms and wiped her eyes. "Come to think of it," she said with rueful humor, "I shall quite simply die if he offers for Angela. I cannot abide a woman with a slavish devotion to convention."

Secretly amused, Charles said, "And that is the woman you wish Ivor to wed?"

"No, truly I do not. But I do not know quite what to do. If only he hadn't taken such an aversion to Jess . . . I wish I knew what they hare quarreled about."

With more accuracy than he knew, he answered, "I warrant they themselves have forgotten by now."

"What shall I do?"

"Nothing. That is my considered advice, and while I should not like to be more firm with you than I must be, I shall have no hesitation in forbidding you to meddle in Ivor's affairs."

She laughed merrily. "As if you could forbid me to do anything—that is, with any hope of obedience on my part! And especially to do with my brother!"

Still in good humor, Charles murmured, "There is that, of course."

Although Cleo left Charles without confiding further in him, the matter was not settled in her mind. How could she explain the sinking feeling in her stomach when she saw that glint in Ivor's eye, when she had mentioned Jess, at the end? He was, she was sure, about to do something quite outrageous, and she could only hope that he would not find himself too deeply entangled in his desire to revenge himself on Jess for jilting him—if indeed that was the truth of the matter. Cleo supposed he felt vengeful, for he was a man of pride.

She could not hope, she knew, to bring Ivor to reason, or to convince him to give up whatever scheme lay at the back of his mind. She dared not interfere too much, since dear Charles did not wish her to do so.

But if Ivor Bellamy was capable of forming outlandish schemes to gain what Cleo assessed as revenge, his sister was not devoid of deviousness herself.

It was, she thought, perhaps time to spend a fortnight at the spa in Scarborough. Bath was, besides, becoming quite tedious, being full of the same people one saw daily in London. It was only a coincidence— at least so she would say if the subject were broached to her—that Oakminster, the present home of her and Ivor's cousins the Daltons, lay a very short distance off the road to Scarborough. She could leave in a sennight, and she would be very much surprised if she were required to spend the four days it would take to drive from London to York. She could reach Oakminster by midday on the second day.

She would inform her husband of her plans to visit Scarborough, but not until she was almost ready to start.

3

Life, thought Jessamine, was too quiet, too calm. Almost, she decided, like the oppressive quiet before a storm.

She had entertained some unpleasant speculations about the effects to be expected upon the reappearance in her sphere of her onetime betrothed. Those conjectures had included hopes that Ivor might renew his attentions—only, of course, so that she could refuse him again. There had even been a few moments, more than she liked, of true regret that she had, four years ago, been so unreasonable.

In the first flurry of confusion after Grandpapa's death, and the stark realization that distant cousin Ivor Bellamy was indeed the heir to the Bellamy estate and therefore in a certain degree in charge of her life, Jess dreamed of Ivor's riding up—for some reason peculiar to dreams—on a white horse and scooping her up to carry her off. Or, on gloomier nights, she saw herself in rags in a ditch, and Ivor, still on his horse, spurning her with a wicked laugh.

She woke often from her troubled sleep, startled to find herself still in her white-and-pink bedroom, and knew she would not be able to get back to sleep. It was on those nights that she crept to the window and let the cold night air blow gently on her face. Too bad, she thought, the breeze could not cool her fevered thoughts as easily!

Ivor could at any moment instruct his man of affairs to put the Daltons out of the house. Oakminster had never belonged to Mrs. Dalton. Indeed, she had, newly widowed, brought her family to shelter only on the sufferance of Sir Mumford.

Where could they go? There were several houses on the estate which could be put at their disposal, but none that Jess thought desirable. Besides, wherever they moved on the estate, they would still reside there at Ivor's pleasure.

Wryly, she thought, she had been a fool to dismiss Ivor only for her own reasons. But she was never accustomed to look with cold calculation upon the uncertain future!

During the day she was able to keep a tight rein on her thoughts, determined not to give her mother the slightest cause for uneasiness. True, Jess spent much time in the garden, pruning her roses savagely, and lopping the heads of noxious weeds, as well as, blindly, some promising new Michaelmas daisies.

Fred, the gardener, held such an affection for young Miss Jess that he said nothing about his ruined herbaceous border. Ah, he thought, she's a troubled woman, needing children about her knees. As an afterthought he added: and o'course a man to take care of her.

Outwardly, at least as long as she did not have a pair of pruning shears in her hand, she appeared serene. As indeed, she thought, she had no reason not to be. There had been no alteration in her circumstances, except for the absence of Grandpapa, not an unmixed sorrow.

Even her mother seemed easier in her mind, now that there was no expectation of ferocious paternal roars emanating without notice from the library, followed by a distressingly frank appraisal of her failings. If Mrs. Dalton entertained a secret burden of guilt over her improved comfort of mind on that head, she did not allow it to show. As the days wore on, with no word from the man she called in her mind The Heir, her optimism bubbled up like a spring when the leaves which had choked it were cleared away.

Following Jess into the drawing room on a particularly fine day in May, she said, "I do think we have nothing to worry about, Jess. You were quite right. The Heir has too many engagements to occupy him, and in truth I doubt we shall hear from him at all."

"Probably we shall learn that Acton has had his

instructions. I do not think that Sir Ivor will overlook
receiving the income from this estate."

"Oh, dear. I never received the impression that he
was careful about money. Why, my dear, do you not
recall how openhanded he was to us in London? His
carriage at our disposal whenever we wished for it,
and fresh flowers sent to the house nearly every day.
The most delicate attentions—of course, after your
marriage had been fixed. I vow I do wish you had not
cried off, Jess. We would have no worries at all."

"We have none now, Mama. Until Ivor evicts us
into the street, we shall simply go on as before."

"You do recall the Bellamy rubies, do you not?"
Mrs. Dalton sighed, lost in recollection. "Too bad you
returned them."

"They were not mine," said Jess crisply. "Besides,
they did not complement my complexion. I looked
dreadful in that ornate Georgian-designed parure."

"But," pointed out her mother in a surprisingly
practical turn of mind, "you would have known you
had them—that is, of course, had you married them. I
mean of course *him*. You would not have needed to
wear them often. I suppose we shall expect to see them
on another Lady Bellamy someday."

Tightly Jess retorted, "I shall hope she is a
brunette."

Mrs. Dalton cast a sidelong glance at her daughter.
She had never understood the cause of the quarrel
between Jess and dear Ivor. At least he had been "dear
Ivor" to her then. Thinking that she was watching
from a distance a simple lovers' quarrel, she had made
no effort to intervene until it was obvious that she was
too late. Jess had retreated into a forbidding silence,
refusing to meet Ivor in public or in private, sending
the ruby parure—only one part of the fabulous
Bellamy jewels dating from the last century—back to
its owner.

Mrs. Dalton had entertained hopes that the quarrel
would be made up, but as months, even years, went by
and there was no sight of Ivor, those hopes gradually

faded away. Now, since Ivor had not taken the opportunity of his inheriting Oakminster to come down and renew his acquaintance with this branch of his family, she believed all was lost. And what she would do with Jess, since from all indications the girl was determined to remain a spinster, she did not in the least know.

In the hall, Mrs. Dalton met her younger son, Philip. "What are you doing with those books?"

"I just want to read all the books in the library," pointed out Philip with some impatience, "before we have to leave."

"Leave! There's been no mention of leaving. If your cousin Ivor ever does write to give us his direction, then I am sure you may apply to him for liberty to use his library as much as you wish."

"But," said Philip gloomily, "what if he comes here to live? I can't take the books with me."

"Nonsense. He has several manors that are far prettier than Oakminster," said his mother cheerfully. "The one he owns in Wiltshire, I vow, is one of the loveliest places in England. I visited there once, with your father, when we were first married. Of course, Ivor was only an infant then, but his parents were most gracious. No, Philip, you may rest assured that Ivor will not turn us out, especially since he has not done so by this time."

As a seeress, Mrs. Dalton failed. Two days after this stoutly optimistic declaration, the blow fell. It came in the form of a letter addressed most courteously to Mrs. Dalton herself.

"I wonder who is writing to me," she murmured, setting down her breakfast coffee cup. "The writing is not familiar to me."

Jess smiled. "The best way to find out, Mama . . ."

"Goodness, I know *that*. But . . . well, I suppose it is an invitation of some sort."

She opened the missive without misgivings.

Jess, whose suspicions about the letter were very

near the surface, watched her mother. That lady turned white, gave a choked sound, and fell back in her chair.

"Mama!" cried Jess, springing up to ring the bell vigorously. She sent Meggie for restoring salts and a cold wet towel. Not until her mother had returned to herself, apparent from the sputtering sounds from her lips and the spirited way in which she pushed the maid's supporting arm away, did Jess pick up the letter, still lying on the table, a hairbreadth from the marmalade jar.

One corner of the letter had fallen into the jar, and absently she picked up a napkin to wipe it clean. She read quickly, and then, more slowly, read the letter again. It was heavily formal, written—not, however, in Ivor's hand—in the third person, and carried a message of significant import.

Sir Ivor Bellamy presents his compliments to Mrs. Dalton. He wishes to inspect Oakminster, with a view of establishing residence within the month. He understands Mrs. Dalton's situation, and will be pleased to consult with her on the subject of alternative accommodations for her.

Good God! thought Jess, her speculations whirling like dead leaves in October. What on earth are we to do?

She did not know she had spoken aloud until she heard her mother's answer. "We will quite simply follow Sir Ivor's wishes," she said with great dignity. "He is, after all, The Heir."

Mrs. Dalton rose, motioning to the maid to support her, and went up the stairs. She would not cry, she would *not* cry, until she reached the privacy of her own sitting room. Then, she suspected darkly, she would merely throw herself on the bed in a monumental fit of hysterics.

In the meantime, Jess read the fateful letter again. Just like Ivor! He did not even deign to address her mother in his own hand! Now that she remembered it, his arrogant way was one of the least attractive of his manners. Since, at the time of their betrothal, he had been all kindness and courtesy to her and her family, she had not noticed his odious condescension to everyone else. Now . . . How dare he! To treat my mother in such a way!

How like Ivor! Just when we thought we were settled, he stirs everything up—and we shall never be comfortable again!

4

Jess knew it was too late to keep the contents of the fateful letter from the knowledge of the servants. She had seen Meggie's bright gaze fixed upon the offending correspondence. Although Meggie could not read, she was adept at recognizing a crisis and winkling out information from her mistress. It would take the smaller part of an hour for the news to percolate through indoor and outdoor servants.

But in the meantime there was Doughty, fairly itching no doubt to clear away, and the letter plain to view. Jess picked up the note and folded it into her pocket. If the message had been in Ivor's handwriting, she might have thought twice about that. There is something very personal about a man's handwriting, she told herself, that could bring his person closer to her. If the letter had borne the intangible imprint of her onetime love, she might have recoiled from such a personal gesture.

But it was written by his secretary, or his agent, or even a friend, and thus had nothing of Ivor about it. Yet, although she would not have admitted it under pain of torture, she could not leave Ivor's message lying there on the breakfast table in the marmalade, for all who entered to read.

She heard the expensive paper crackle in her pocket as she crossed the lawn toward her herb garden. Fred was working at the far end of the garden, hoeing the row of cabbages set aside for his personal use. She sank onto the bench and covered her face with her hands. She could not control her thoughts, and let them therefore roam at will.

She had really believed, she admitted, that Ivor might one day come back into her life. There was no doubt now that he would not. Such a cold, arrogant letter! She resented too that he sent such an unfeeling message to her mother, who had not hurt him in the least. In fact, if Ivor had ever wanted an ally in his pursuit of Jess four years ago, Mrs. Dalton was willing and at hand.

But Ivor, in his self-satisfaction—an assessment of his character that Jess had made after the break—had never needed any advocate with Jess. She had been so much in love at first that he would have had to grow two heads to make her even hesitate in agreeing to marry him.

And then had come the breakup. Even now she turned away from thinking about it. He had said such savage things to her, accused her of flirting with other men, with ignoring her betrothed, with—

What was the use of thinking of it all now? The betrothal was dead and buried, and only the faint remnant remained of a sweetness that could never in this world have its equal, like the unmistakable scent of lavender on linen sheets.

A voice spoke near at hand. "Jessamine?"

She looked up quickly. "Oh, Henry. I didn't see you coming across the lawn."

"I feared to disturb your innocent meditation," said Henry Hartnell. Catching a glimpse of Jess's high color, he added, "I perceive that something has sorely troubled you. Is something amiss?"

"No."

"I beg leave to doubt that. Surely you have not quarreled with your mother? Doughty told me she was not receiving. I hope nothing is amiss between you? I do think there is nothing more displeasing than to see members of a family fall out with one another."

"Oh, Henry!" She gave a sputtering laugh. "How can you think so?" Especially, she thought, when his own mother and father had at one time not spoken to each other for two years.

He possessed such a literal-minded, truly stodgy

character. It occurred to her that he deserved a little teasing to set him down a peg. Remembering a subject he had explained at length on more than one occasion, she said, "Surely you must dislike even more the prospect of the millworkers destroying the looms?"

Henry's face darkened, and Jess at once was sorry she had brought up a subject so painful to him. Henry's maternal grandfather had been "in trade." Old Mr. Wickes had by native shrewdness and a good deal of luck prospered to the extent of owning several large and productive mills, using Sir Richard Arkwright's invention for the production of thread. The beautiful Wickes heiress had captured Henry's grandfather's fancy, as had the enormous fortune that came with her, and "trade" for the first time entered the Hartnell family. A matter of shame, possibly, for some proud families, and Henry was no exception. But he held firm Tory views on the status in society to be occupied by the millworkers, and that place did not encompass protests against mill conditions, to say nothing of armed rebellion.

There were mill owners who basely truckled to their workers. Henry was not one of them. The burden of his conversation for some months now fell into two parts. On the one hand, the devil-inspired ingratitude of the workers was examined, and on the other hand the failure of the government to see its clear duty to oppress the rebels was condemned.

Henry at this moment was pursuing a different trail. "I perceive that something out of the ordinary must have occurred to distress you, Jessamine. Your remark about the millworkers is proof of that. I shall of course overlook your playfulness, since it is obvious that you are too perturbed to think before you speak."

Henry was at it again, thought Jess. With only a word or two, he was able to infuriate her and at the same time amuse her with his pompous manner which surely could not be equaled anywhere in England.

Henry, by virtue of his proximity across the fields, and of being the only eligible gentleman in the vicinity, was the only candidate for Jess's hand. He would inherit the lands and the title upon his father's death, as he now owned the mills bequeathed him by his late mother. He had long been an escort of Jess's to the various social functions that cheered the days and evenings of the gentry of the surrounding neighborhood.

Now Jess saw that he would not give way until she confided her current distress to him. Besides, he would have to know sooner or later that the Daltons were leaving Oakminster.

She pulled the offending missive from her pocket and thrust it at him. "There! See what the beast has done!"

He read it carefully, and a puzzled expression appeared in his eyes. "Beast? Jessamine, this letter simply tells you that Sir Ivor will come to inspect his manors. Oakminster is his property, you know. Surely you recognize his rights. You knew this could happen any moment."

"Of course I did. But I didn't, if you understand me."

"No," said Henry slowly. "I don't think I do."

"He has let us alone for weeks. He gave us no acknowledgment that he even knew he was inheriting Oakminster, and what that might mean to us. And now . . . he's coming within the week, and throwing us all out in the road, and I've lived here most of my life!"

"But," said Henry, rereading the letter as though he must have overlooked the menace that Jess had seen in it, "he will find you another place to live. He says as much, right here."

Unreasonably, Jess cried, "Or his secretary says as much. Ivor didn't even write it himself."

"I suppose," said Henry judiciously, "his hand is not

legible. So many gentlemen find it hard to write clearly."

Stung, Jess retorted, "He has an elegant hand!"

Henry had not been made privy to Jess's quarrel with Ivor. But after Jess returned unwed to Oakminster, he had spent an unhappy year in London to acquire what his father called "town bronze," and he had heard a good many rumors. Most of the gossip had blamed Jess; since no one could credit that a lady of no great fortune could spurn a gentleman of title and considerable wealth; therefore the rift must be attributable to some wrongdoing on her part.

Henry had met Sir Ivor Bellamy on several social occasions and had quite liked him, save for the possibility that he had made Jess in some way unhappy. But Henry had not traveled in Sir Ivor's circles and did not get to know him well.

By mischance, Henry now put a foot wrong. "I hope you are not refining too much, Jessamine, on the possibility that Sir Ivor will renew his attentions to you. As a man of some experience, I can tell you that you have nothing to fear. *Nothing.* Sir Ivor will not lay himself open to further rejection, you may rest assured."

"Rejections?" echoed Jess in a wondering tone. Suddenly the possibility opened a grand vista of promise before her. She would indeed reject him. It was the best way—in truth the only way—that she could make Ivor atone for some years of wretchedness.

Not that she was miserable now! she told herself with a fine disregard for the truth. It was only that she yearned to avenge her mother's present distress and future unhappiness in being exiled from Oakminster.

There was a way at last to bring Ivor to his knees.

Although she needed to work diligently on the details of her scheme, she was well aware that Henry would play a major role. She smiled sweetly at the man beside her on the marble bench and told him,

"Oh, no, I am sure Ivor would not be so unaware of his own consequence as to renew his attentions to me. Pray do not be anxious for me."

Henry said, unconsciously digging a pit before his feet, "He will not force himself on you, Jessamine. I shall see to that myself. I may be a trifle premature, since you will be in mourning for some time yet, but you may be sure I shall not stand idly by while he annoys you. I may not yet have a right—"

With alarm, she interrupted him. "Henry, pray do not say another word. I regard you as a good neighbor . . . and friend. Nothing more."

To her relief, he smiled. "And so we shall always be." Then, as though he had listened to his own words and found them lacking, he added with heavy humor, "At least friends. Not always neighbors."

She chose to misunderstand him. "I know. We shall have to see where Sir Ivor chooses to move us." She stood up. "I begin to feel a chill. Let us go back to the house. Unless," she added hopefully, "you must return home at once?"

She longed to be alone with her proposed plan, and steal a few satisfying glimpses down the vista of fancy to the far end, where Ivor, once more rejected, stood in abject humiliation.

"I shall escort you back," said Henry. As they strolled toward the house, he inquired, "What kind of alternative accommodations do you think Sir Ivor means to offer?"

"I can't think," said Jess truthfully. "But he surely would not offer us another manor of his. There is no sense to that. If he expects to give us a house, then why not leave us in this one?"

"Surely he could not mean the dower house? That is much too small for your family."

"And where would Philip put his books? Silvester has some idea of getting Ivor's backing for a naval

commission, although I doubt Ivor would do anything
for us. But there are several houses on Oakminster
land, none very pleasant. There is, as you say, the
dower house, and the old rectory that is vacant now
that Father Claridge has retired and moved to Scarborough to live with his daughter. And perhaps that
small cottage that Grandmother Dalton was given
when she was widowed."

"None of those sounds desirable."

"I suppose none of them is," said Jess. "If a house
stands empty for too long, it is fit for nothing but cob-
webby spiders and mice in the wainscot. I shall have to
make inquiries to find a large cat!"

After a few moments Henry resumed. "I recall there
is a house nearer the river, but I have see that recently,
and in truth I wonder that the walls hold up the roof."
He glanced furtively at Jess.

"You must mean Oaklane!" cried Jess, struck by
memory. "I have not even thought of it these long
years. Acton should not have neglected it, for I believe
it was a handsome structure at one time. I wonder
why it has not been repaired and let to some one. I
must speak to Acton—"

Hastily Henry pointed out, "Is not that Sir Ivor's
province now?"

Sadly Jess agreed. Sir Ivor was now in charge of the
least facet of her life.

But only until she had accomplished the planned
denouement of her newly born revenge!

5

When Jess, with Henry in tow, returned to the house, she found that Mrs. Dalton had recovered sufficiently to come downstairs. She now sat stiffly erect in her favorite chair in the green salon. Only Jess, who knew her mother well, had a fleeting fancy that Mrs. Dalton resembled nothing so much as a dowager queen embattled, preparing to resist to the death if need be an enemy of prodigious power.

Even the chairs, the small tables, her favorite footstool, and the militantly stiff green brocade draperies seemed to array themselves in support of their mistress.

Jess's fancy was shattered when she caught sight of Althea, sitting forward on her chair like a bird on a perch, alert and in a way apparently ready to fly.

Their mother had found a captive audience for unburdening herself. She was midway through imparting her news, which she clearly regarded as catastrophic.

"To think that just as a whim on the part of some distant cousin, who has small reason to regard us with favor, I admit, I shall be required to leave the home where I have lived in happiness—well, perhaps not always entirely in happiness, not that there haven't been a few good times, or really more than that because my children are a joy to me—"

"I am glad to see you looking more the thing," Jess said as she entered, recognizing that in this mood her mother would have to be interrupted sometime, and now was as good as any. Besides, she was convinced that the next complaint on the tip of her mother's tongue would be on the subject of Jess's inexplicable jilting of The Heir. Jess thought she could not bear hearing the familiar words again. "Mama, here is Henry come to call."

Mrs. Dalton smiled upon Henry Hartnell, who was after all a gentleman and therefore superior in understanding, and abandoned her monologue to Althea. The conversation became general for the next half-hour, and finally Henry rose to take his leave with expressions of civility and sympathy.

Henry found himself alone in the foyer with Jess for a few moments. "I cannot refrain from telling you how very well I understand your position. It saddens me to see your mother so greatly distressed. It is too bad your grandfather did not attempt to break the entail. I understand that at times this contract can be set aside if there is sufficient reason."

"But it is too late, Henry," said Jess, a bit crisply, adding, "Besides, we all knew the estate would pass to Ivor. He does not surprise us."

She was far from considering Henry an intimate, to whom she would impart confidences. A good friend perhaps, primarily because of his geographical proximity, but his plodding intelligence often moved her to unladylike impatiences.

However, she must quell whatever tendencies she had to dismiss Henry with a sharp word. Her new plan must be worked out carefully, but it must involve Henry, even unwittingly.

Henry lowered his voice to a confidential tone. "Pray do not be dismayed over this development. Of course this was to be expected. I quite agree with you on that head. Knowing Sir Ivor as you do, I wonder you can contemplate his arrival with equanimity. Surely you must dread the sight of a man who has treated you in such a dishonorable way."

A sharp retort sprang to her lips, but unfortunately the approach of the butler to open the door prevented the words from utterance. Really, Jess thought, Henry takes too much upon himself!

But Henry was not finished with her this day. Drawing her through the open door to the porch, he told her, "You are not alone in your trouble."

Oh, dear, she thought. I believed I had effectively

diverted him from declaring himself there in the herb garden! Surely she had not given him any encouragement.

He continued, "I will see that Sir Ivor—no matter how grand he considers himself—will do you no harm, nor will he distress your mother for long. I shall see to that. In fact, I hope soon to be in a position to make plans of my own for your family."

"Pray do not concern yourself on our account, Henry. You bear no responsibility for us. I beg you, do not continue."

"I suspect that you consider me no match for that wicked man who once had the temerity to spurn you, but I assure you—"

Driven beyond endurance by his determination to forge ahead in his unflattering remarks, and forgetting that only an hour ago she had decided to smile excessively upon Henry as soon as Ivor arrived at Oakminster, Jess exclaimed, "Do not assure me of anything, Henry. I am quite able to deal with Ivor myself."

Her voice had risen, and she suddenly became aware of Doughty hovering in clear hopes of hearing more. "Come now, Henry," she said on a coaxing note, "let us not quarrel. We are old enough friends to know better." She smiled winningly at him, and he grudgingly agreed.

"No quarrel, Jessamine. But I do ask a favor. Convey word to me, if you will, as soon as you know Sir Ivor's plans for . . . for which of the estate houses he chooses for you."

"Of course."

Mrs. Dalton came out to stand with Jess and watch Henry ride off down the graveled drive. "Henry," said Mrs. Dalton at last, "will make a good match for you, Jessamine."

"Not for me, Mama. I would die of ennui in six months. Not so long, I think. Three months would be the limit of my expected survival."

Mrs. Dalton did not seem to have heard her. "Now that Sir Ivor is no longer eligible."

Touched again upon a sore place, Jess cried, "Why not? He has not wed that I know of."

"No gentleman ever comes back to someone who jilted him. Make sure of that."

"But I didn't—"

This gentleman might well be an exception, thought Jess without the slightest reason for hope. He had given her no attention, not even a word, for four years. Indeed, he now seemed intent on an ungenerous disposal of her family. But Jess believed that somehow her dream of final revenge must become real. And as part of it, Ivor must be attracted to her again. But perhaps she no longer allured him. Doubt of her own charms assailed her for a moment, and she sighed heavily.

Mrs. Dalton sent an inquiring glance at her daughter. Is it possible, she wondered, that at last I am to hear the truth of that dreadful quarrel? At least of this moment, no it was not possible. Jess was silent. Whether Jess jilted Ivor, or whether the reverse was true, Mrs. Dalton feared she would never know. What she did know was that she did not ever wish to see her dear daughter as wretched again as she had been in the aftermath of that quarrel.

Although Jess's mother was willing to let the question of that broken engagement die a natural death, if it could do so with Ivor's arrival so imminent, the elder of Jess's two brothers, in the event, was not.

Silvester, having gone out as was his habit in the early morning to ride through the misty lanes of the estate, returned to the stables totally unaware of the events of the morning.

Coming into the house from the rear, he came upon Althea emerging from the green salon, intent upon escaping before her mother returned.

Althea, disinclined to deal in details, favored her brother with a pithy sentence before she vanished into the kitchen for a slice of bread covered thickly with damson-plum preserves to stay her hunger until time for luncheon. Unfortunately, the message was unclear. Something about being sent into exile, like Napoleon? He shook his head. His younger sister took some queer notions! But obviously something had happened.

He burst onto the porch to join his mother and Jess, full of fifteen-year-old impulsiveness and awkwardness. Jess spared a thought to his ungainly figure, wondering whether she had ever, at that age, been so immature. She decided not, even while her mother was commiserating with her son.

"Have you had a nice ride, Silvester? Who knows but what it may be your last one here at Oakminster! I should not think that The Heir will allow the use of his stables. I must say that I had thought better of him than to let us take comfort in his absence and then overthrow everything so absolutely. Although, of course, the way he and Jess—"

"Mama," interrupted Jess with desperation, "Silvester does not know what you are talking of. He was not here when the letter arrived, you know."

Turning with relief to his sister, Silvester burst out, "Then that's all right. If it's a letter that's at bottom of all this, I didn't write it, that is sure."

Refraining from commenting that he in all probability had already forgotten his tutor's careful instruction—indeed, she wondered if Silvester still remembered the proper use of a pencil—Jess forestalled her mother's explanation, and told her brother, "Ivor has written to say he is coming down to live here."

Sheer disbelief appeared in Silvester's tanned features. "Here? With us? Mama, you said he had many estates better than this one!"

"And that is true!" exclaimed Mrs. Dalton. "Jess, do you think he might send us to the priory in Wiltshire? I recall that house has a lovely prospect, and is most comfortable. Of course, that is the house where Ivor was born, but this after all is the Bellamy seat. But perhaps there is a house nearer to Scarborough than we are here that he might have in his gift."

"I think," said Jess unhappily, "we shall just have to wait and see what he has in mind for us. Unfortunately, we have no recourse against whatever he plans."

Although they did have some alternatives to agreeing to whatever Ivor demanded, Jess knew very well her mother would not agree, for example, to hiring a reasonably large house in Scarborough, much as she sighed for the excitement of town life.

Her mother was essentially a countrywoman, and while she did not ride, nor did she garden, she took pleasure in looking through her broad windows at her velvety lawn, her venerable trees providing comfortable shade for the house, and her well-placed and very well-kept flowering borders.

Suddenly Jess was seized by an unreasoning and white-hot anger against the man who was responsible for upsetting her mother, and for speaking, with such calm arrogance, about removing Mrs. Dalton from the house she had grown up in. She did not even have the satisfaction of believing that Ivor was in some way retaliating for her refusal to marry him. If that were so, she might have some means of influencing him— such as promising not to reveal some of the very uncivil things he had said to her, words that still burned dangerously when they came to her mind.

Her plan which had seemed so practical—the scheme that would bring Ivor to offer for her and receive her contemptuous refusal—paled and disappeared.

"You don't mean we're going to move?" cried Silvester, aghast at the first real change that had entered his young life. "But we can't! I mean, this is home!"

Poor Silvester, thought Jess. Inarticulate, terrified of giving vent to his emotions, embarrassed by the intensity of his feelings, he could only stand, his jaw sagging open, while a myriad of thoughts raced across his mind.

"Silvester," said Jess in an attempt to soothe, "all he said was that he was coming to inspect the house with a view to living here. He may not like the place at all."

"He said," pointed out Mrs. Dalton with an air of settling the entire discussion, "he would discuss with me an alternative place to live. Now, what else can that mean? Jess, it's your doing, you know. If you had married him, your mother would not be evicted from the only home she has ever known."

Stung, Jess retorted, "What about Beech Manor? That's the first home I knew. And we lived there for fifteen years until Papa died!"

"But I was not happy there!" wailed Mrs. Dalton into her handkerchief.

Since Mrs. Dalton had never given any sign of being unhappy in the home she lived in after her marriage, Jess was encouraged to take her present complaint as being of no importance. Besides, Jess was old enough —although Silvester was not—to recall her mother's extensive complaints when, after her father's debts were paid, they had been required to move back here to Oakminster.

Fortunately, her father's debts had not eaten into Mrs. Dalton's jointure, nor was she bereft of certain other legacies that had come her way over the years, so that they were not, as a family, verging on penury. But of course, the funds at their disposal did not run to purchasing a naval commission for Silvester, although in all likelihood Philip might count on his university studies to come.

"Where are we to go then?"

Jess said, although it galled her mightily, "That must depend on . . ." In the end she could not speak his name. ". . . on The Heir."

6

The Heir arrived promptly upon the heels of his shattering letter. He came modestly for a visit of such consequence, thought his onetime love, being content to appear on the gravel sweep before the entrance of Oakminster in a modest carriage, black with yellow-pricked wheels, and an unassuming team, driven by an elderly coachman, and only two servants up at the back.

But the knowledgeable onlooker would observe that the four black horses, chosen no doubt to match the vehicle they pulled, were of a quality to excite envy in the heart of any notable whip, and groomed to a shine no duller than the coach itself. The coach was well-sprung, and larger than it first appeared.

Jess was forced to agree that Sir Ivor Bellamy did not come with an arrogant flourish to deal with his homeless relations.

When Ivor stepped down from his carriage and advanced toward the several Daltons who were gathering on the porch to greet him, the most grudging spectator could not fault his manner.

Ivor was a large man, broad of shoulder and powerful of limb, as many an opponent at Jackson's had learned, but his great charm lay in the sudden smile that could, when he chose, light up his broad, dark face. With the smile, which he now bestowed upon Mrs. Dalton, came a smile in his gray eyes, under straight, strong eyebrows.

Jess was all too acutely aware of the magnetism that emanated from him, in all likelihood without his conscious knowledge. She herself had been the prime victim of his charm, she reflected, but that was when she was young and foolish. Now she was older, but as she watched him cross the gravel drive toward her, she realized that she was just as foolish as ever.

Foolish! What an inadequate word! She had lost her breath, primarily because she was aware of a large and very tight band around her chest. The unbidden and unwelcome thought teased her that he could have been hers had she given in. And for the moment, regret was bitter on her tongue.

But, she vowed, he would never know it. She would treat him as though he were the merest of acquaintances. She would even receive Henry Hartnell with grace and friendly charm, as she had planned, even though an imp that sometimes pointed out flaws in her reasoning told her that probably Henry's reception would be warmer if Ivor were within sight.

She was stiff with sudden apprehension. What would he say to her? The last words they had spoken were heavy with animosity. What would she say to him? Nothing, she realized, because her mouth was dry as the sands of Arabia, and words would not come.

Fortunately, words were not required. Sir Ivor mounted the steps and bowed low over Mrs. Dalton's hand.

"I must offer my condolences on your recent loss," he said in such a kind, civil manner that she momentarily wavered in her hostility. "I trust that time will work its healing on your grief."

Jess watched with some awe the clear melting of her mother's sentiments toward the man who had once been almost her son-in-law.

"Thank you," said Mrs. Dalton, looking up at him with soft admiration. "Already in these few weeks I find myself easier on that head." Her tone was dubious. Clearly she was thinking that they had been so comfortable that she hardly missed her obstreperous father, until here came Ivor with the clear intent of turning them all upside down.

She turned to go inside, expecting her family and their guest to follow her. Suddenly aware that they

were not doing so, she hesitated. Then, seeing that The
Heir was not intending to take possession of
Oakminster at once, and was waiting meticulously for
her to invite him in, she was covered with confusion,
and stumbled over her words.

Without knowing quite how it happened, they
found themselves together in the green salon, comfortably seated, and Cross approaching through the
entrance hall with refreshments.

Althea hesitated to sit down, not because she was
too well-brought-up to sit until her mother bade her,
but because she was holding a half-eaten apple behind
her and feared to bring it to her mother's notice.

To his credit, Ivor did not glance around him, as
one might in someone else's home, at his surroundings.
Such an action could be interpreted only as the heir
assessing his new acquisition, and Ivor was far too
well-mannered for that.

Besides, he had a well-thought-out scheme in mind,
one that had been examined carefully both by him and
by his lifelong friend and onetime schoolfellow, Giles
Leighton.

"Only one objection occurs to me," Giles had said at
the end of a long evening in Mount Street, an evening
replete with discussion and brandy.

"What can that be? We've cudgeled our minds—I
conceive to good effect—and the only possible snag I
can see is if Jess will not credit the Lady Dorine. I
surely feel a nonexistent Lady Dorine would serve my
purpose better than an actual person." Harking back
to his conversation with his sister, he said, "No one
would believe that I had offered for someone like . . .
well, like Angela Trompion. Besides, I do not choose
to be trapped by Jess in that way!"

"Even I would not believe that if you told me to my
face!" laughed Giles. "But will Miss Dalton make
inquiries?"

"Why should she? She has been away from London

so long that it would be amazing were she to know everyone in society. The Lady Dorine—does she have a last name?—might well be a young miss just out of the schoolroom. But, on consideration, why would I want a schoolroom chit?"

Giles laughed. "So you can mold her to your taste, of course! That is why most men marry very young ladies."

"I can think of nothing worse! No, I prefer a woman of some intelligence, with some common sense as to how to go on. I have no intention of playing tutor to a child."

They sat in companionable silence for some time. The brandy was passed again, and finally Giles repeated, "Only one objection."

"Very well. Out with it."

"Pray do not vent your anger on me, Ivor, but I suspect that you yourself will prove the sticking point."

"You mean," said Ivor, overly honest in his cups, "that Miss Dalton may no longer favor me?"

"Well, after all, she said as much, did she not? If she did, you would likely be married with half a dozen infants by now."

"In four years?" murmured Ivor. "I think you over-estimate me. As well as, of course, Jess." He stared at his brandy glass as though he had not seen one like it before. But his thoughts were gloomy. Suppose Giles was right. Suppose she did not still cherish a *tendre* for him, to say nothing of still being headlong in love with him. Since his own feelings had not altered, he had not given thought to the possibility that hers had. He did not like what he saw in his fancy.

"One word of warning," said Giles at last.

"What?" demanded Ivor, frowning.

"See that your vile temper does not overcome your scheming. She may feel jealous, as you hope, at the thought that you may be planning to wed our mythical

Lady Dorine—why 'Dorine,' I wonder?—but you may set all at naught if you shout at her again."

Recalling the years of misery behind him, and recognizing how much his future was worth—nothing at all without Jessamine—Ivor said slowly, "I wonder if you are not right, Giles. However, I think my reputation lags behind the truth. Once being famed for bad temper, one is always expected to burst forth with invective and intolerant speech. Giles, my friend, have you seen me in temper, at least in the past year?"

"No," Giles said slowly. "But I've been in Paris, you know, helping to get fat Louis settled!"

"I do not suffer fools gladly, I admit to that. But such are the uses of reputation that now a raised eyebrow sends everyone into flight." Ivor's voice was rueful.

Giles left the house on Mount Street and stopped on the doorstep, he and his friend looked toward the east, where a thin hint of gray indicated where the sun intended to rise before long.

"Giles, I see only one solution." Giles looked apprehensively at his friend, having known him well and long. "You'll have to come down to Oakminster and keep me in line."

A herculean task," laughed Giles, "and one I shall never attempt!"

That very day Ivor had instructed his man of affairs to write to Mrs. Dalton, announcing his impending arrival. Now, at Oakminster, sitting apparently at his ease in his own drawing room, though presently in the possession of the Daltons, Ivor set himself to charm, not his darling Jess, of whom he was quiveringly aware out of the corner of his eye, but Mrs. Dalton.

An empty-headed woman, as he remembered her, with now and then such flashes of shrewdness as stunned the listener. Now he answered questions about the drive up from London—of course he had had cattle sent ahead, and he was not driving his curricle because he intended to stay in the area for some time and believed the carriage would be more appropriate for his use.

His answers were automatic. Jess was a bit paler than he recalled, and even thinner than before. But she had recently lost her grandfather, and Ivor had no illusions about the effect on the family of his letter to Mrs. Dalton suggesting that a removal to another house was imminent. An uprooted family might well have given way to stormy emotions.

Jess had appeared flushed when he arrived, but now so ashen as to give rise to some anxiety. She was even lovelier than he recalled, and with a new air about her that he could not quite identify. Perhaps she was more vulnerable than before. Or perhaps lonely.

He felt a pang of guilt over the scheme that he had with Giles's help hatched in London. His dearest wish at this moment was to scrap the scheme and quite simply take her in his arms and pour out his heart to her, could he find the words. Of course, he dared not give way to impulse.

By this time, the refreshments Cross had brought in were demolished. Jess had not touched the tiny sandwiches, and Mrs. Dalton's appetite had been restrained. Young Silvester had eaten his share, as became a young lad, but Ivor, who had met none of the younger Daltons before, was astonished to see that at least half of the cakes and sandwiches had vanished into the custody of young Althea. Hadn't he seen an apple in her hand when he arrived? The girl was voracious!

He hoped whimsically that before the child was old enough to be married she would satisfy her overweening hunger, or else she must find a wealthy husband. Preferably one with a large estate of gardens, orchards, and edible livestock!

7

While Ivor Bellamy during his years in the *ton* had perfected a particularly charming stream of small conversation, adroit and increasingly cynical, and designed to put both belle and dowager at ease without in any way committing himself to the slightest obligation, he found that his experience served him ill at this time.

How could one say to a widow: What a fine painting that is! when it was most likely that it belonged, not to her, but to the estate one had just inherited, and from which residence it was planned to remove the lady?

In fact, nothing looked as though it belonged to Mrs. Dalton herself. The furnishings and even the draperies at the windows were more suitable to a bygone age—sort of a house frozen in amber. But he could not comment on the slightest object. Even the expansive view from the windows and the excellence of the sandwiches might suggest that The Heir was judging the outside prospect for his own later viewing, and considering whether or not to retain the Dalton cook.

Nor could one suggest to the daughter of the house that she stroll with him in the grounds, at least at the same time that one felt waves of sheer desire sweeping over one like a spring tide at Fastnet. Indeed, Ivor was stunned by the intensity of his desire for Jess, the more surprising since he had held it in check for four years.

Fortunately, Mrs. Dalton had never recognized an embarrassing conversational lull in her life. "I have been hoping, Sir Ivor, that you would bring to us a bit of the gossip from London. I vow we are sadly out of things here, and with Papa ill for so long and now gone . . . But of course you would know that," she said in pretty confusion. "I was speaking, you know, of mourning, for we cannot be seen at any but the most

50

private parties for months yet, till we put off our black gloves . . ." Mrs. Dalton took a breath. The sight of such an elegant and sophisticated man in her drawing room spurred a small scheme in her mind. If Sir Ivor was accustomed to the gaiety of the capital, then he might soon become bored with country living. She had never seen him except in London, and had no idea whether he liked rustic entertainment or not. But gallantly she set to work to disillusion him.

"Of course, even before we went into mourning we enjoyed such a charmingly quiet life," she said, "I suppose that we went to Scarborough to the assemblies not above once in two years. I believe, though, there are several very pretty little walks in the park. One day, when the weather is finer—and fortunately it stays hot no more than a sennight at a time—you might like to make an expedition to the river."

Ivor was not listening. Instead, while his attention was apparently focused on Mrs. Dalton, he could catch revealing glimpses of Jessamine from the corner of his eye. She sat clearly wrapped in her own thoughts —not pleasant ones, at that, judging from the flush in her cheeks.

Did she dislike him so much? For the first time he was visited by the realistic thought that his scheme to make her jealous of a fictitious Lady Dorine, although sounding invincible in the dead of a brandy-fueled night, could very easily fail.

The thought moved him to action. He had come to take charge, not so much of his estates, as of his own future happiness, a state which could not be expected without Jess. It was no time for a faint heart.

Gently moving into the stream of Mrs. Dalton's flowing conversation, he suggested, "I hope, Cousin Elizabeth, that it will not be inconvenient for you to provide me with lodging? I do not quite like the look of the inn in the village!"

"Oh, no! You must not consider the inn. Indeed we have the great bedroom made ready for you. You will not mind, of course, that my father died there?"

Refraining from observing that the bed must surely have been aired in recent weeks and not left as a shrine to the old man, he said only, "I suspect there is not a bed in the kingdom in which someone has not died."

Without knowing quite how it happened, Jess found herself proceeding through the ground floor of Oakminster, Ivor very attentive at her right hand.

"You will of course wish to gather an impression of the extent of your legacy," said Jess, firmly holding to a neutral tone.

"Actually," said Ivor calmly, "I did not know how else to get you alone, Jessamine. I enjoy your mother, but I did not come to see her."

"Of course you didn't," said Jess soothingly as though to a child. "You wished to see Oakminster. And that is what you are going to do."

He had begun on far too familiar a note. She had little enough control in the drawing room, where he and her mother had conversed for some time and Jess sat somewhat aloof. Now, with his hand gently on her arm, turning her to look at him, she trembled on the edge of tears, or failing them, strong hysterics. Anything to relieve the unbearable tension that held her in thrall.

"This is the state dining room," she said, entering a dark-paneled room of some size. The buffet at the side held a good many silver serving dishes, all polished to a high degree, and the long table was provided with a dozen chairs on either side. "It is said that the Regent himself stayed here overnight on his way to take the cure at Scarborough."

Ivor glanced thoughtfully at the old-fashioned furniture, the heavy Georgian silver, and murmured, "No doubt this is why he turned his attention to Brighton."

Jess exclaimed, "Do not tell me you admire that very odd Pavilion he has had constructed!"

"Since I do not, I shall not tell you so. But I cannot

think this . . . this very weighty style of furnishings would recommend itself to him."

A laugh caught in her throat. Recognizing that Ivor's sense of humor had more than once undone her, she sought protection against her own weakness.

"I think it best to show you the upper floors. You must inspect your quarters to see if they are to your liking. Doughty, pray come with us. Sir Ivor may have a question or two for you."

She started up the stairs. Ivor followed her almost at once, but she did not see the imperative wave of his hand that persuaded Doughty to stay below. The butler, lest Miss Jess turn around and again demand his presence, thought it expedient to disappear through the baize door to the kitchen.

Even considering the servant's absence, which she noted as soon as they had reached the top step, she need not have worried that Ivor would take advantage of her. He was courteous but impersonal as they stood together looking down the long expanse of the corridor on which the bedrooms opened.

It was a handsome corridor, clearly planned by someone other than the dining-room designer. The floor was covered by a long Aubusson runner. A number of doors, now closed, lined the hall, but the woodwork was painted white, giving a light and comfortable look to the entire floor.

The starkness of the light walls was relieved by a series of large, heavily framed portraits. "The Bellamys," announced Jess. "Your ancestors are already in place."

He examined the two nearest them. "Aunt Minerva, I believe. My parents cringed when she announced a forthcoming visit. I do not know this man, however." She enlightened him, and the conversation moved along easy lines until they stood before the double doors which obviously led to the great bedroom.

"How regal," murmured Ivor. "I can see footmen springing to open the doors at my approach."

"The chamber faces the front of the house and is considered to have a fine view."

"Let me see if I can conjecture what lies behind those very imposing doors. There are heavy maroon draperies obscuring your very fine view—"

"You no doubt noticed them as you drove up. There is nothing out of the ordinary in that."

"Ah, perhaps not. But I do believe there will be a heavy mahogany chair, before a hearth large enough to roast an ox, a great abundance of Turkey rugs, and a vast overpowering mahogany bed enclosed with maroon velvet curtains." Smiling, he turned to Jess. "Am I right?"

The air between them fairly crackled with tingling tension. What might have been hung heavily between them, and his vision of the bed, private behind the drawn bed curtains, he could swear was equally visible to her—the massive bed in which not only had Bellamys died, Sir Mumford merely the most recent, but many Bellamys had, in the most conventional way possible, been conceived. Was it her vision too?

Her flushed cheeks suggested as much, as did her remark. "Have you plans to wed soon?" Then, overwhelmed by embarrassment at her forwardness, she added quickly, "Not that it is of any interest to me, except that I cannot believe you will need Oakminster unless you have plans to enlarge your establishment!"

"How could it be of concern to you? I recall well you have told me as much, in the past," he agreed, watching her closely. He added in an altered voice, "It depends on the lady."

Impulsively Jess exclaimed, "I cannot believe anyone would refuse you!"

"Not everyone," he said, amused, "is as persuaded of my many virtues as you were once—that is, as you imagined!"

She could not meet his glance. But she said softly, anxious for information that seemed vital to her, "Then she has not accepted?"

"Alas, no," said Ivor, enjoying himself. He did not add: Since I have not offered. Instead, he continued, "Nor, to be honest with you—are we not always scathingly honest with each other, Jess?—she has not refused. However, even an acceptance is no guarantee of a marriage. As you know well."

Feeling driven into a corner, she stamped her foot. Hastily she changed the subject. "I imagine your valises are already unpacked, Sir Ivor."

"I imagine so."

"And down the corridor beyond the stairs are the rest of the family bedrooms. At least for the moment."

Detecting a faint note of resentment in her voice, he told her, "I'm sorry, Jessamine. I did not intend to take over your home in such a marked way."

"Did you not?" She had recovered her cool poise. "On the contrary, I suppose that was exactly what you meant to do. How else could one interpret your message?"

They still stood before the double doors. Suddenly the right-hand door opened, and Ivor's valet, Tyson, appeared, an inquiring expression on his undistinguished features.

"I beg your pardon, sir," he said after an assessing glance at his master, and realizing that the pair before him were on the verge of a spirited and no doubt acrimonious discussion. "I . . . I heard voices, and thought I might be wanted."

Without waiting to be dismissed, he backed into the room and closed the door. His interruption had reduced the temperature of the confrontation, and Jess turned away and started down the corridor.

"You will perhaps need to know that my mother's sitting room is here . . ." she informed him over her shoulder.

"I should not dream of disturbing her."

"That painting there is of Lady Lydia Bellamy. She is reported to have been a dear friend of Arbella Stuart, although the family believes her morals were more elevated than Arbella's, as I suppose you know."

Impatience seized her escort. "No, I don't know! Nor do I care. Jess—"

He did not know what he might have said, or even done, had his ardor not received a setback.

"Yes, Sir Ivor?" she responded in a sweet, calm, and cool voice.

Looking down at her, her enormous dark blue eyes fixed steadily—but, alas, impersonally—on his face, he was exasperated beyond belief. If the wall next to him had not been so solid, he might well have rammed his fist through it. Noticing that Jess's attentive gaze slid downward to take note of his clenched fingers, he drew a deep breath. She had always had this effect upon him, driving him past exasperation. He had, he thought, put his temper entirely behind him. However, it was not so.

He was in a towering passion, she saw with some satisfaction. Passion was passion, she thought suddenly, and perhaps the depth of his anger was also the measure of his love for her. Could it be?

His anger was gone almost as soon as it was recognized. But there was left a wish to take young Miss Jessamine down a peg. *Sir Ivor*, was it? He'd give her Sir Ivor!

"But of course your mother has sufficient knowledge of the world, even if you do not, that it is totally ineligible for you and your family to remain in the house while I am in residence. What would the busy tongues make of it if my former betrothed and I were to be living together? Under the same roof, I mean."

He was pleased to hear his voice as light and faintly amused as he could have hoped. Further, he noticed with satisfaction that she wore a tiny vexed frown. God, she was desirable! That heart-shaped face with the deepest blue eyes he had ever seen, her wealth of golden curls, in disorder as though she had run her fingers through them—or as though *he* had! He noted the slightest trembling of her slender frame, and believed that she might not be as indifferent to him as she pretended.

He was wrong. She shook with repressed anger. "Then there is a simple way to avoid such a scandal, Sir Ivor!"

He waited, hoping unreasonably to hear her suggest a renewal of their betrothal, but in vain.

"You might well return to your priory in Wiltshire, or your house in London, and leave my mother to enjoy the home she grew up in!"

"I think not," he said quietly, as though he had previously given thought to the issue. "Gossip might make too much of my indulgence to your family. I should not like to have it said of me that, were I to give in to your request, I did so because I feared whatever accusations you might spread abroad about me."

There you go, she thought bitterly, twisting my words again! But she said only, "I myself have no fear of the truth, but of course you know best where your reputation is most vulnerable."

The guided tour of Oakminster proceeded in silence, but with such tumultuous thoughts ringing peals through their minds that they were unaware that they did not speak, nor did they notice their surroundings. At last, to Jess's unspeakable relief, her companion pronounced himself satisfied.

"I confess the house is overcrowded for my taste," said Ivor.

"No doubt you can dispose of the surplus to advantage, or is the furniture entailed as well?"

"I believe not."

They returned to the drawing room. He felt a pang of guilt when he saw that his cousin Elizabeth looked up apprehensively, as though she saw the bailiffs at the door. Hesitantly, hoping that Ivor had taken a dislike to Oakminster and would forthwith depart, leaving them once more happily alone, she said, "Did you find the house not so fine as you believed? I know there are repairs needed this past year."

"I found all quite to my liking."

Jess drifted toward a window, looking out unseeing into the grounds. She hoped devoutly that Ivor had not read in her face the sentiments she was sure were there to read. He had always been sensitive to her thoughts, conning her features as though they were an open book upon whose pages were written her every mood.

Upstairs, he had seemed for the most part indifferent to her. Alas, she was learning that she was far from indifferent to him. Although she had managed to keep her poise, and not given way to her impulses, yet she was deeply distressed to recognize those impulses for what they were.

She longed for revenge on him, and she would have it! But there could be consequences to her scheme that she might find unwelcome.

On seeing Ivor step down from his carriage, she knew at once that all the months and years of separation, of believing she would never see him again—nor did she want to!—of truly believing she had recovered from the devastation he had wrought in her emotions: all those months and years were as though they had never happened. He was here, near enough to touch, and she could again be as desperately in love with him as ever.

It was the most lowering thought imaginable! And she did not know how in the world she was going to deal with it! Her only hope was to recognize her reaction for what it was—a simple physical attraction—and to remember that marriage and love do not usually go together. She must keep her head!

Bits from the conversation behind her caught her ear. "Not suitable," her mother was saying, "although of course your wishes must prevail."

"I shall wish to see you properly settled, Cousin Elizabeth," said Ivor.

"Jess, my dear, pray come and tell me what you think is best."

For Ivor to get back into his carriage and *go away* would be best! she thought, but did not say. "Best?"

she said, apparently coolly, returning to the others.

"We are talking of an appropriate residence. Dear Ivor has suggested the dower house for us," said her mother. "What do you think?"

"We may as well move to the gatehouse," she said. "The dower house is no larger than the porter's lodge, and we might well make ourselves useful to Sir Ivor by opening the gates and closing them as required."

Mrs. Dalton, shocked, exclaimed, "Jessamine!"

Ivor was greatly encouraged by his Jess's tart response. She was herself again, and not entirely indifferent to him. But all he said was, "I did not think the dower house to be suitable. I have studied the plans of the estate—quite a broad expanse, to my surprise—and I have given much thought to the best and most comfortable house for you, Cousin Elizabeth. There is a house on the plans that is quite removed from this one. I think you might find it better to be well removed from the comings and goings here at the manor."

"You will be entertaining a good deal?" Mrs. Dalton said brightly, at the thought of social doings quite close at hand, to which she might expect to be invited. "We are quite far from London and I do not think we —that is, you, of course, Ivor—can entertain above thirty guests at once."

"I shall, naturally," said Ivor, with deceptive languor but with a keen glance at Jess, "allow a certain lady of my acquaintance to arrange for the entertainments she may desire."

He might as well, he thought, take the plunge at this moment, set his scheme into motion.

"In fact," he said with literal truth, "I expect soon to entertain a very special guest from London."

Glancing blandly around him, he thought: I'll send for Giles even before the Daltons have left Oakminster!

8

The house Ivor had in mind as a new residence for his Cousin Elizabeth and her family was one at the far edge of the Bellamy estate, so far out of sight and out of mind that Jess remembered it only vaguely. Oaklane, while sharing the "Oak" part of the name of the residences of this branch of the Bellamy family, could be envisioned only by a mighty effort on Jess's part.

However, her mother had lapsed into a depressed state, which Jess took to be only a natural reluctance to experience a disruption of her settled life. Quietly Jess took more and more of the responsibility for the arrangements, in part to ease her mother's burden, but also to occupy her mind, which continued to bring to her attention far more questions than were answerable.

For one, who was the lady Ivor was clearly expecting to take over his life? He had mentioned that she—the unknown—would be arranging entertainments for Oakminster. Not only was Jess immediately jealous, but also the clearly unfeeling way in which Ivor had announced his plans was abominable.

Imagine flaunting a new love directly under the nose of the old love!

She was outraged, forgetting entirely her plan to revenge herself on Ivor by smiling sweetly and often on Henry Hartnell.

Jess could not ask Ivor directly the name of her successor. She had not been in society for four years, dreading the sympathy of her acquaintances more than the lack of their company. Many new faces would have appeared on the scene, and it would not in the least surprise her to find that Ivor had offered, or was about to offer, for a lady who was a stranger to Jess. A lady who, ran Jess's speculations, would be young, possessing great charm and beauty, as well as fortune.

While Ivor did not need any addition to his own fortune, newly augmented by the Oakminster estate, yet no one could overlook such an asset as a considerable dowry.

Very well, then, concluded Jess, she was lovely and young and wealthy. If she were young, then most likely she would be malleable to Ivor's wishes. As Jess had never been!

Never malleable, she thought with a laugh. And yet here I am, beside Ivor in his curricle, traveling the two miles from Oakminster to our place of exile, simply because he wishes us to live here.

"I wish you will be frank with me, Jess," he said, after a few moments, "and tell me precisely what you think of the house. I wish your mother to be completely comfortable."

"How can she be," retorted Jess, "when she is removed from the home she has always loved?"

"Do you think she would be happy at Oakminster knowing that she may be dispossessed at any moment? Better to face the move now rather than later."

"If she does not move now, why should she fear a later removal?" Jess's voice died away. The reason was clear. If—or when—Ivor married his malleable young miss, the new Lady Bellamy might well wish to live at Oakminster. Besides, unless she was a very secure young lady, she might not welcome the thought of a former betrothed enjoying the house that rightfully was hers.

"Precisely," said Ivor, answering her thoughts.

They did not speak again until the house came into view. Jess's spirits sank. It bore the look of a forgotten old woman, ragged skirts of ivy growing rampant up the walls, giant oaks darkening the house and the narrow uncut lawns surrounding it—a derelict!

"Famous!" said Jess under her breath. "*Castle*

Rackrent to the life! I must assume that Marie Edgeworth passed by at one time. I suppose there is a
ghost?"

Suppressing a smile, Ivor said, "No doubt you will
find out when you move in."

"You do take this very calmly!" she said, incensed.
"No doubt we shall be murdered in our beds!"

"If I thought so," countered Ivor, "I should of
course make other provisions for you." Since his plans
included taking Jess away to his own priory, and
removing Cousin Elizabeth back into Oakminster as
soon as Jess came to him, he could not be overly
alarmed about the appearance of the temporary
Dalton residence.

But he said only, "Surely you do not believe in
homicidal spirits? You will have the Crosses with you,
after all, and I expect several other servants, and I
assure you, you will have nothing to fear."

"Very reassuring. However, I do not want you to
think I am so fainthearted as to expect a ghost to throw
me down the stairs. But I am persuaded there are rats,
and doubtless the ceilings are apt to fall down, and one
can only hope that the pieces of plaster which shower
down upon one's head are small enough to be
harmless!"

With gravity, he said, "At the first rain of plaster, I
am sure you will inform me so that I may have repairs
made."

He helped her down from the vehicle, and they
went up to the door. Without warning she was seized
with the utmost reluctance to enter. Ivor had his hand
on the door latch when she cried softly, "Pray do not
open the door. I do not wish to go in."

"But how do you expect to inspect the house? From
the outside?"

"I know it sounds foolish, but please, Ivor, I cannot
go in. I have the most idiotic notion that someone is
inside the house."

An intent look into her distressed face, and he said, "Very well, you need not. But Simpson and I will go." He was about to call to the groom, when she clutched his arm.

"Let us go around the grounds," she suggested, "and then perhaps I will be ready to go in."

Mystified, he agreed. Calling Simpson to him, he said in a low voice, "Miss Dalton suspects someone may be in the house. Do you keep an eye out, but on no account try to seize anyone who may emerge."

Simpson assured his master that he had not the slightest intention of risking his limbs in battle with an unknown assailant. "Place do look haunted," he observed. "And if I was to be knocked out, who would look after the cattle?"

Ivor agreed with the sound reasoning presented to him, and hastened after Jess, who was making her way with some difficulty across knee-high grass toward the back of the house.

She could not explain even to herself the queer notion that had come over her. There was no possibility of anyone being in the house, Ivor explained as they inspected the side door to the garden —to a former garden, that is, since nothing but tangle could be seen—and the door into the kitchen wing. "You see, there is no sign of entry, and these cobwebs are not the work of a day or two." She had to agree.

But that day they did not go into the house. Instead, they walked around the stables, approving of the soundness of the timbers. From the stables a path ran between the belt of trees belonging to the park and a tilled field. They halted at the opening of the path, uncertain whether to continue.

The land before them slanted downward, but gently, so that one would not perceive the decline at once. "It goes down to the river," Ivor said, musing, "but did I not hear once that the river used to follow a different bed?"

"Yes," said Jess, calm now. "There was a flood, back in my grandfather's time I believe. The villagers consider it second only to Noah's. It was a damaging storm, though, and when it was over the river had altered its course to where it is now. The fields turned out to be on the other bank, and that is when the folly disappeared. You know about the folly? A collection of columns—"

"Capability Brown?" murmured Ivor.

"Grandpapa seemed to think so, but since it vanished overnight, it has taken on a kind of mythical existence, and now no one is really sure that it ever existed."

He felt her fingers tighten on his arm. "What is it?" he said softly.

"See, there at that rise at the far edge of the field. Is there someone there?"

The fear had come back into her voice. He looked intently at the spot she indicated, at what seemed to be a grass-covered outcropping of rock, but saw nothing. He shook his head.

"It was just a movement, really," she said with a huge sigh. "I must be seeing phantoms in every cloud shadow."

He was concerned for her more than he allowed her to see. His Jess was not a fearful woman. He suspected now that there were sleepless nights behind her, and a state of nerves that were the result of the impending departure from Oakminster. She had taken on the management of the removal, to ease her mother's distress, and he must see that she did not suffer overmuch. It did not occur to him to suspect his own part in the restlessness that kept her from sleep.

They turned and walked back the way they had come. "Someday soon we must find a boat and make an excursion on the river. Perhaps the collection of columns lies somewhere in the deeps."

"Making a temple for Neptune?" Jess was swiftly

recovering her whimsical cast of mind. "Perhaps you will find an oread, or is it Nereid? Neptune's court, at least."

"Oreads are mountain nymphs. But what would I do with a nymph?"

When he had a lady of his own! Jess bit her tongue in mortification, and they returned to Oakminster in silence.

The next time Jess saw Oaklane, she entered the front door with only a memory of that other occasion. The house was occupied this time, but with a small army of maids, hair tied up turban-style, from Oakminster, supplemented by a levy of girls from the village. A platoon of men was arriving at the back, even as Jess stepped through the front door. They were sent by Ivor from the farms, to do the heavier cleaning. And Jess, ready to work in her oldest gown and her fair ringlets tied back, stood looking around her in amazement.

A beginning had been made. The main part of the house was built four-square with many windows, in the style begun by Bess of Hardwick in Tudor times. An early Stuart addition now housed the kitchens, where she knew Mrs. Cross was seeing to putting her kitchen in order.

On Jess's left a door stood open to a drawing room of fair size, and on her right a similar door revealed what had once been a library, although the shelves were now empty. No doubt the books were at Oakminster, saved from mildew and rot.

The walls and wood were light in color, giving an airy look to the downstairs. At the back of the entry hall a wide stairway rose straight to the upper floor, from where at the moment a stray sunbeam fought its way through the great oak trees and spilled its light on the bannister.

Ivor had been right. The Daltons would be comfortable here.

Since Doughty was staying with Ivor, Mrs. Cross and her husband would be coming to Oaklane with them. "The new master, so it seems," Mrs. Cross had sniffed contemptuously, "being overparticular about what he puts in his mouth, must bring down his French cook, a monsewer of some kind, to make his fancy sauces for him. Well, I've never had any complaints about my cooking—good English fare as it is—and well rid of him, I'll say."

Sometime later, having had a restoring cup of tea with Mrs. Cross in the kitchen, Jess was suddenly aware of Acton's voice. The farm manager was his usual brooding self. He had been born and bred on the estate, and while Ivor might hold the deeds, Acton considered the estate entirely his own. He was now shouting outside the house, and since Jess had insisted on opening all the windows to the fresh spring breeze, he might as well have been in the room with her.

"Slater's coming by noon," he was informing an unknown listener. "See them slates is all ready by t' ladder there. And you, Samuel, get to work on those shutters. Not a one of 'em is square. Get old Harry to help—"

Suddenly the hopelessness of the entire situation swept over Jess. She was wiping down the walls of the dining room at the moment, with a cloth tied over the broom end to catch the dust, and she now simply leaned the broom in a corner and sank to the floor, her back against the wall.

How could she ever go on?

Removal from her home to this place. Her mother alternating between putting a brave face on adversity and sudden bouts of tears. Philip trying desperately to read all the books in the library before they were beyond his reach. Silvester taking out his frustrations by riding headlong over the countryside through lanes that were no longer theirs.

And Jess herself, knowing that a mysterious lady would soon probably be installed in the manor house, entertaining her little head off! Jess hoped that Doughty, partial to the Daltons, would spill Ivor's French chef's turtle soup down that lady's French decolletage! She heard herself sob.

Enough of that!

But she did not at once get up from the floor. The old-fashioned wainscot, curiously carved, caught her eye and she began to trace with her fingers the odd rosette, the curving line that represented a draping of heavy ribbon. There were signs of dry rot, she thought, exploring with a fingernail. No doubt Ivor would not mind if the whole house, and not just the plaster, fell down about their ears!

She was being unfair, she knew, but in an obscure way, to think the worst of the man seemed to ease the dull pain that had been with her since she first learned of Ivor's new lady.

A kind of dull, thudding pain—she could even hear it now. Then she knew it was not the pain that thrummed in her mind, but the sound of a horse being ridden fast, approaching up the drive. She rose briskly to her feet and went to see who it was.

If it were Silvester, she would put him to work at once, since there was at least one window stuck upstairs, and he could also see what should be done to the stables to make them habitable for horses. Lucky we don't have to move into them ourselves, she thought darkly, going to the front door.

The new arrival was not Silvester. The enormous gray stallion that snorted, impatient at the restraining rein, on the wide grass-infested graveled space before the door, was in the firm control of the man she wanted least to see.

So she told herself. But it was not in her power to prevent her heart leaping at the sight of the broad shoulders, the indefinable air of authority that invested

Ivor's every move, and the thought that was, above all else, wayward—that he would now take charge and she could thankfully turn all things over to him.

A deceptive, subversive, outrageous thought! Without being aware of it, she tightened her lips and gave her visitor a glare of defiance.

Ivor had had time over the few days since his arrival to recover his balance. The first sight of Jess had all but unmanned him. He had momentarily lost sight of his devious plot, and he knew he had almost lost the game by his devilish temper.

He had lost her once before from the same cause, and Giles Leighton had warned him only a fortnight ago.

He had already sent for Giles. He could well use a steadying influence, and Giles would keep him sweet-tempered until his dear Jess was won.

His dear sweet Jess was now standing on the broad steps of her new house, hands on hips, a becoming smudge on the tip of her adorable nose, and glaring at him in a temper.

"What do you want?"

Ivor swung down, handed the reins to a groom temporarily assigned to shutters, and began to peel off his driving gloves. He let a smile touch his lips. "I shall hope you do not contrive to drive all your friends away with such a warm welcome! Or perhaps all your spleen is mustered for my sole benefit?"

"I'm sorry, Sir Ivor," she said, clearly unrepentant, "I rather expected to see Silvester. I have a few chores for him."

"Indeed I should be surprised to learn that Silvester could accomplish the smallest practical function. His training leaves much to be desired."

Hotly Jess retorted, "My grandfather—"

Ivor interrupted her calmly. "Do not fly up into the boughs. It is not too late to bring him around. Although I do not as yet see him climbing up the ratlines in the Cape Horn storm."

Jess stared. "Did that . . . did he approach you? He was strictly forbidden to mention his hope that you would purchase a naval commission for him."

"Forbidden? Now you have me curious. Do you dislike me so much you would stand in your brother's way?"

"Ivor! You know I wouldn't!" Aha, he thought, back at last to "*Ivor*." "It was my mother's desire. She does not wish to become a nuisance to you."

With warmth, Ivor protested. "Your mother could not be anything but a delight. I fear you underestimate her. She has a great deal of sense. Do you know, the navy might be the making of the boy."

Jess said with a gurgling laugh, "My brother will be fortunate if our mother does not write to the Lord of the Admiralty urging the most tender care of him."

With an appreciative chuckle Ivor said, "I think we can circumvent such a development."

Warmed by the relief of Ivor's taking charge of Silvester's future, and by the good feeling of companionship, Jess melted.

"But perhaps I may serve as Silvester's proxy?" suggested Ivor. "What do you wish him to do here?"

Eyeing his impeccably tailored riding coat and his highly burnished boots, she said dryly, "I should not dream of risking damage to those fine feathers."

"But at least I should like to be invited in. Perhaps the house is not as commodious as I thought, and I should like to see for myself."

Unable to protest—after all, it was his house—she turned and went through the open door, and he followed.

The scene that met his eyes struck a pang to his heart. In no way had he ever seen a house in such a state of disorder. Even empty except for a few dusty furnishings, these rooms had looked better.

Always before, he had simply given instructions for refurbishing, and then gone to London or to one of his

eight other large establishments. Now he was faced
with bare walls, an oaken floor unevenly painted,
with large rectangular areas reminiscent of former
rugs. Cobwebs hung, gray with dust, in the corners of
rooms net yet touched.

"Good God! How long has it been since this house
was inhabited?"

"Truly I couldn't say," said Jess. "Not since I have
lived here certainly. Acton was to take Grandpapa to
inspect all the houses once a year, but that may not
have happened."

"You can't live here!"

Upon hearing Ivor echoing the same words she had
spoken more than once, most recently only a few
minutes before as she sat on the floor of the dining
room, she turned obstructive.

"Of course we can! It still needs much work, of
course. I must thank you for sending the farm men to
help. And the maids too. We are most grateful."

"Stuff!" he said under his breath. Aloud he said,
"Now, what would you ask Silvester to do?"

They went upstairs. There was a puzzling smell
reminiscent of a cellar, but neither spoke of it. The stubborn window at the far end of the hall, looking out over
the tangled memory of a garden, gave way under the
hands of Sir Ivor, armed with a chisel and a hammer.

"You really are useful," she congratulated him.
"Silvester could not have done so well."

Insensibly glowing under her kind words, Ivor
retrieved his coat, which she had held while he
attacked the window.

"Let us look over the rest of the house. There are
likely other repairs that need to be made at once.
Acton should have seen to these before they became so
bad."

Jess recalled a few questions she had raised during her
inspection of last quarter's statement. Acton's answers
had not pleased her, but her mother disliked her busi-

ness activity so much that she had dropped the subject.

Ivor glanced through the window. "I see a few idle fellows out there."

With Jess, Ivor examined the house in all its evocations of former glory. Large marks on the walls indicated where furniture had been moved or paintings taken down. The floors needed refinishing. The list was endless.

"Not only did Acton fail to maintain the building," said Ivor, frowning, "he did not give me a comprehensive report of what needs to be done. I wonder why. Did your grandfather consider him incompetent?"

"I don't know. But I have always disliked him, for no reason that I know. I did not like some things I noticed on his last report, which I dealt with because Grandpapa was too ill."

When Ivor was ready to leave, Jess accompanied him to the door. "I'll put all these repairs in train at once," he told her. "You should be able to move in by the end of the week."

"Thank you. But one thing puzzles me. You did not come here just to unstick our windows and look at the dirty walls?"

"No," he said, swinging up into the saddle. Since he could not say that his only reason for coming was to refresh himself by looking at her, he was forced to improvise. "I wanted to tell you that I am expecting soon to receive a guest at Oakminster who is important to me, and I hope you will make h—" He stopped short and reframed his words. "I hope you will be welcoming."

He cantered down the driveway, savoring the last sight he had of Jess's expression. He had almost lost an opportunity there, almost said "make *him* welcome." Now he was as sure as could be that Jess's thoughts were revolving rapidly, and if she did not think that the mysterious Lady Dorine was coming for a visit, instead of Giles, who had just accepted his invitation, then Ivor was far wide of the mark.

9

The Daltons at last were removed from the manor house to the newly refurbished residence called Oaklane. Mrs. Dalton, although she had at first felt as though she had been sentenced to exile in some outlandish place like Tibet, even though she was to be only two miles away from her former home, and that still on the home estate, began soon to settle in.

Pastilles were burned frequently in the downstairs rooms to rout the fresh smell of new paint, and the windows were sparkling clean for the first time in memory.

The breakfast room particularly warranted Elizabeth Dalton's approval. Presently shaded from the coming heat of summer by the centuries-old oak trees, the room would in the leafless days of winter receive the welcome morning sun. The builders had carefully sited the house at an angle, to take advantage of the prospect. The view from this window was across the narrow lawns to a border of shrubs—nothing to fret the mind early in the morning.

This particular morning, only a few days after their arrival, she said as much to her family, gathered around the table.

"This really is not too bad a domicile," she said. "A bit cramped of course, since it was not lately a principal house for the Bellamys, at least after they began to prosper."

"Who did live here then?" Jess wondered. "No one has ever told me about this place, except Henry. I don't understand how he would know more about one of our houses than we do."

"No one lived here," said Mrs. Dalton firmly but not truthfully.

Silvester pointed out kindly that no one would have

built a residence of this consequence for no one to live in.

"I didn't say that," said Mrs. Dalton. "No one for a hundred years or so. When Oakminster was built, then this place was abandoned."

"Come, Mama," coaxed Jess, "you know more than you are telling us. Someone did live here, didn't they? Even after the family moved to Oakminster?"

"Well . . ."

Mrs. Dalton could not resist the insistence of her children, not now or anytime. "No one I knew. In truth, how should I know her when she lived in the time of my great-aunt?"

"But you know who she was?"

"Someone you never heard of—the Italian countess."

Jess paused in the middle of spreading her toast with damson-plum preserves, and stared at her mother. Even Althea, her mouth full while her hand held a muffin at the ready, paid attention to her mother.

Jess had an odd insight into her mother's recent behavior. Mrs. Dalton had been oddly silent concerning the move to Oaklane, and took no part in the preparations for the transfer. Jess had thought her mother was consumed by sadness in leaving her old home, and believed too she did not wish to accept the necessity. She would answer none of Ivor's questions, or Jess's, about why Oaklane was left empty, and even allowed to deteriorate over the years.

But now it was as though Mrs. Dalton were forced by reasons Jess did not yet fathom to unburden herself.

Silvester's attention was fairly caught. "Never knew we had an Italian in the family!" he said, his mouth full.

Althea added in a muffled voice, "To say nothing of a countess, Mama! Then what am I if we had a countess? Am I Lady Althea?"

"Don't put on airs," her sister advised her. Turning

to her mother, she repeated, "An Italian countess? Why have I never heard of her?"

"She was not spoken of in the family."

"Then," mused Jess, diverted by the beckoning trail of genealogy, "I . . . that is, we all have Italian blood! Probably that accounts for—"

"No, no," interrupted her mother crisply. "Saxon and Norman, I will agree. I would even admit to Viking, for your golden hair must come from some-place, Jess. But Italian—never!"

Ivor must not have been made privy to this family offshoot either, or he would surely have flung her "Italian temperament" in her face whenever relevant.

"But if she were in the family . . . ?"

"She was not in the family. That is, not *of* the family. So to speak. She was not, in fact, Italian. She was . . . well, she . . ."

Jess turned thoughtful. Her mother's delicate morals were clearly offended by the countess. Suddenly it was clear that there must have been an enormous scandal swirling around the head of the Italian lady. Or no lady, as the case might have been! "Is that what Nanny meant, Mama? She used to say, 'Be good or you'll come to a bad end like . . .' And then she would never say any more."

"And this is where she lived, Mama?"

"I do not wish to say any more," said Mrs. Dalton.

But Jess detected an uneasiness in her mother's manner, and suspected there was more to the story than a simple scandal whose effect upon the Bellamys had over the years dissipated into the mists of time. "Mama, something troubles you. What is it?"

"I am very sorry I mentioned the woman. Even though we are related to her, she is better off for-gotten. You will please put all this out of your minds at once."

"You know we cannot pretend from now on that we

never heard of her. Shall you not feel better by telling us the whole of it?"

After much coaxing, Mrs. Dalton was moved to confide her worries to her children. She had been much concerned over moving to what she had been informed, as a child, was a haunted house. She did not think that even four children, a host of servants, and new coats of paint would be sufficient to ban the ghost, if there were one. Hesitantly she related her unformed fears. "I confess I cannot be entirely happy here, at least at first."

"But why would the countess's ghost come back?" said Silvester, intent upon the mechanics of the haunting and oblivious of his mother's nervousness.

"Would she have reason to haunt the house, Mama?" asked Jess.

"Well," said Mrs. Dalton, reassured by the support of her offspring—even Philip, who did not speak, yet listened intently, "I suppose if you think being an outcast is cause enough, then she might well still be angry. She married an Italian count, you see, or she thought he was, but it turned out he was only a dancing master for the Cavendish family at Chatsworth."

"A dancing master? Then she wasn't really a countess?" cried Althea, her visions of titled glory fading.

"When her brother," Mrs. Dalton continued, "my great-grandfather, you know, went to Italy to bring her home, she was living in the most squalid circumstances you might imagine. Of course she was ruined, poor thing."

"But didn't his family at least take her in?" demanded Jess, horrified at such inhumanity.

"It was not at all certain that they were ever married." Agitated, Mrs. Dalton tossed her napkin on the table. "I don't know why I am telling you all this.

My goodness, I haven't thought about her for *years* until lately." But her memory still had treasures to unfold. "They brought her here to live, you know, and of course no one would receive her, not even the family. You may say, Jess, that she was treated barbarously, but truly anyone so wayward today would suffer the same consequences."

"Then she lived here, in this house, like a hermit?"

"Not entirely. It was said she had a . . . a gentleman friend, from some distance away, who came occasionally to call on her. But nobody ever saw him."

Jess, nurtured on the more lurid of contemporary fiction, exclaimed in delight, "The demon lover! Coming and going in a burst of smoke!"

"Jess! I cannot think where you learned such ideas! If Miss Addison was responsible for your common ways, I should have let her go long before I did!"

"Not Miss Addison, Mama. Only the same lending library that sends us both the newest volumes. But I have never figured out how some of those villains could escape the notice of the servants. I am persuaded that our servants know the slightest particular of our lives. Surely our countess was not left here to fend for herself?"

"No." The answer was flat, final.

Jess realized she had gone too far in teasing her mother. A vagrant memory came to her: could it be true, as Ivor had said, that she underestimated her mother? With a lowering feeling, she had to admit that he could be right. The possibility did not put her more in charity with him.

But Silvester, immune to nuances, had been thinking. And while he scorned the lending-library horrors, believing them to be fit only for women's diversions, he was well-versed in bookish adventures of various other kinds, and now gave his relatives the benefit of his researches.

"The secret tunnel!" he said as a matter of course. "That's why no one saw him."

Mrs. Dalton gazed at him without favor. "How did you know?"

Now that the secret was out, Mrs. Dalton was induced to expand on her story. "There was supposed to be a tunnel, in fact, left over from when every family in the north of England had what they called a priest hole. Not that everyone was Catholic, you know, for we are not, but some of our neighbors were, and it was only humanity to protect them. What good could it have done to kill a poor priest who was only trying to do what he thought was right? But that was how he got in, so they said. That is, the gentleman caller. Through the tunnel."

"But where does it come out? How can we find it? Is it still there?"

"I just don't know. There was the folly, of course, but that was simply a platform with a few columns. There was certainly no door to it. And it was destroyed by the flood, so there is no use looking for it, Silvester."

"I'll wager I can find it," he said with adolescent confidence.

"You will do no such thing," ordered his mother firmly. "It is only an old wives' tale, as they say, although Great-Aunt Minerva, who told me the story when I was a child, was hardly an old wife. In truth, she was a hardened and spiteful spinster. It does not do to rail against marriage, as she did. No matter how wretched a match is, it does provide *experience*!" Hearing how her words sounded, she flushed, and returned to her first subject. "No, Silvester, you will forget this story at once!"

"All right, Mama," said Silvester. He excused himself from the table and left the room. Jess watched him with speculation in her eyes. He was unwontedly obedient, she thought. Too bad he was not able to take up a naval commission. Going to sea as a midshipman might well keep him too busy to think about scandals and tunnels.

Mrs. Dalton, now removed with Jess to the morning room, continued to speak her pleasure with her new house. Cleaned and painted, and put in excellent repair, there was little to disapprove.

"A bit small, but then, we shall not have so many servants underfoot. I am so pleased that Cross and Cook came along with us. She does wonders with small fowl."

"She wanted to come from the first," said Jess, having enjoyed Mrs. Cross's confidence from the time the Daltons had returned to Oakminster. "Cross was unwilling to come. He said there would be naught but trouble—his exact words, Mama—by stirring up old shades. Do you think the servants now are acquainted with the story of the countess?"

"I cannot see how they could be, when even the family does not know. Certainly we have never talked about the lady in their hearing. No, I rather think that Doughty simply wanted to be difficult. You know he is quite under her thumb."

"For a while I thought that Cook might come and leave him behind."

"I should not think so. Whoever heard of a butler and cook not going together to a new situation? If they were married to begin with, of course."

"I can quite understand that!" laughed Jess. "The husband gets fond of his wife's cooking, and cannot give it up."

Mrs. Dalton moved on in her mind, leaving her devoted servants behind. "But, my dear, I find this house very poorly furnished."

"Poorly? Mama, we have all your own furniture here, and surely it is of the finest quality? I myself went through the storage rooms in Oakminster and told them which pieces to bring. Did I miss some items?"

"No, dear, I do not think so. I have not said so before, but I was most grateful that you arranged everything for the move. I gave way to the vapors, and I am sorry that all fell on your shoulders."

Jess leaned forward to pat her mother's hand. "I wish you had told me your reluctance to move here. The countess will not trouble us in the least, I am sure. Why should she? We did no harm to her. From what you say, if she entertained a . . . friend, let us say, from time to time, she must have had a happy life, after all." Better than her own prospects, thought Jess.

"That is even worse, Jess," said her mother, "for a person, that is, the ghost of a person, often returns to a place where she has been happiest. Or *he*, of course." Catching Jess's startled expression, she added in confusion, "Of course, that is what I am told. Not that I have ever seen a . . . a troubled spirit, or even an untroubled one, as the countess must be if she was happy, but . . . well, Aunt Minerva was very specific as to details." In a burst, she confided, "I didn't sleep for months!"

"That was naughty of Aunt Minerva," said Jess with a smile.

"I told you she was spiteful."

"Perhaps the entire story, countess and all, was a fairy tale to frighten you?"

"No," said Mrs. Dalton, "for I went to the churchyard to see. I thought if she were truly buried in church grounds, she would not be walking abroad, so to speak."

"Did you find her stone?"

"You know that corner where the yew hedge ends? There is an odd corner there that looks empty. But her stone is there."

"Well, then," said Jess triumphantly. "We are not apt to entertain an unbidden guest, after all."

"Perhaps you are right. But may I tell you something? I keep wondering about the furniture."

"Mama . . ."

"I know. These are all my own things, and I have no complaints at all on that head. But what surprises me is that there were not more of the original furnishings here in the house."

Jess remembered having thought the same thing when she first came into the house. Many pieces had been removed, judging from the clean—or rather less dirty—areas on the walls and the marks on the floors. She had detected the outline of a long buffet, several paintings, and a side table in the drawing room. But also she knew that in the storage rooms, when she had been marking her mother's things for removal, there were several pieces that would match the areas in question.

Of course the most valuable furniture would have been removed for preservation, but even so, the amount stored would not have furnished this house in its heyday. But the house had been left to itself, with only an annual inspection by the farm manager, and it was likely that smaller pieces left here and deteriorated over the years and then been discarded.

Perhaps she should have been less obstinate when Ivor talked to her about furnishing Oaklane.

"You will want your mother to be comfortable," he had said. "Surely the house will need to be supplied with the first quality of chairs, settees, what you will. I shall send to London—"

"There is not the slightest need to send to London," Jess interrupted firmly. "We will have all we need. I do dislike cluttered rooms."

They were standing in the salon at Oakminster at that moment. Ivor looked around him and said, amused, "How you must be relieved, then, to remove from this house. I wonder that anyone can even move through some of the rooms."

Defensively Jess cried, "We brought all our furniture from our own house when we came to live with Grandpapa, after my father died. My mother did not wish to lose anything that reminded her of Papa, she said." Jess thought a moment, and added in an altered tone, "But I think all our things are stored in the attic."

Ivor looked around and said in mock dismay, "Then this is all mine?"

"I wish you joy of it," said Jess crisply, adding silently: You and your new lady!

"Well," said Ivor pacifically, unaware of her thoughts, "your mother must have her choice of all the furniture here. God knows there is enough for three houses." He rubbed his hand over the gleaming surface of a hunt table. "Or four."

Some demon prompted her. "What is my mother's we will take with us. Nothing else."

Ivor's temper shot to the surface before he was even aware of it. "You will take what I send you."

"We do not wish to impose on your goodness." She hoped he heard the edge on her voice. "Certainly we do not need to live with borrowed furniture. Or donated items."

"So," he said with a dangerous glint in his eye, "you are determined to make me out a wicked tyrant. I have no doubt you will go back to your desk—I assume you will allow me to send your own desk to you?—and write to all your friends saying how you have bested the evil villain by your own wits."

"Believe me," said Jess, in full spate, "that would be naught but a trifling victory, hardly worth the notice!"

She saw with some satisfaction the flare of anger in his eyes. His gray eyes could be cold as a wind from Scotland, but she saw them now as hot. Why was it that she got such satisfaction from tormenting him when she had not the slightest feeling for him?

She could believe that he was aware of her, at least not indifferent. Anger, frustration, exasperation—any of these was more to be desired than indifference! So omens were favorable for her getting her revenge, refusing him once again, and this time with a better choice of words than had risen to her tongue the last time, and then she would be done with him. Out of mind, at last!

But not yet. He had reached the stage in his exasperation where the only relief to be gained was by raising his voice. "You will have the furniture I choose to send you!" he shouted.

"Take care," she retorted swiftly, "not to send your best, for I will not vouch for its not being used for firewood!"

With a strenuous and visible effort, Ivor slowly mastered his features and gained some control over his emotions. His plan was not going well, predicated as it was on what was proving to be an impossibility. How could he hold his temper when this golden-haired witch could glare at him with those enormous dark-blue eyes, and by some alchemy turn his being inside out?

He really needed Giles! He could safely give vent to his frustration, his annoyance, his misery of mind with his old friend, who knew him well and loved him in spite of all.

In the meantime, he must mend a fence or two with Jess. "Very well," he said quietly. There were the remains of a tremor in his voice, evidence of imperfect control of his temper. "You will make whatever arrangements you wish for the furniture you need."

Pleasantly aware of victory—not the trifling matter she had told him moments before—she pressed her advantage.

"There is one thing I should like to ask. Oh, not for me, Ivor. I should not wish to rely upon your favor for myself. Philip will miss your library most dreadfully. Indeed, he is trying to read all the volumes he can

before the library is out of his reach. Could you let him
have the use of whatever books he wants? I assure you
he is most careful . . ."

Ivor's memory took him, as it did far too often for
comfort, back to the momentous quarrel. Jess had
spoken words then that had scored him deeply. He
could not know that she had at this moment long forgotten them. Words flung out in heat bypass the
memory, but words heard in emotion take on a life of
their own, and wound, boring into the heart and
remaining constantly at hand, ready to wound again.

"Why should he want to read?" he snarled, driven
by savage memory. "Why do you not tell *him* that to
be overly educated is a crime that leads to unattractive
condescension and inhuman feelings?"

Jess, at sea over the reasons behind his sudden
fierceness, gasped. Then, in a sympathetic manner,
she said, "You must have felt the want of those
qualities for all your life!"

Quickly she left the room, feeling as she turned her
back on him that she might well see that enormous
flowered vase crash beside her on the wall.

She had had her way in the end. Now, looking
around the rooms at Oaklane, which were comfortably if not elaborately furnished, she wondered why
she always seemed to strike sparks from Ivor. Flint and
steel, that's what they were—opposites. She refused to
carry the thought to its logical conclusion, that each
without the other was of little use.

At any rate, she did not have to face him every
morning at breakfast, as she had since his arrival at
Oakminster, and her emotions were therefore not
constantly abraded.

Instead, let him growl across the table at his houseguest. Even though the guest had not arrived—the
guest Ivor had hoped she would welcome—nonetheless Jess had not forgotten her.

Who was she?

10

Jess, who considered herself a reasonable and calm person, found that there was an anger in her that would not go away. And of course that anger was the sole fault of Ivor Bellamy, who had come to Oakminster for the prime reason of distressing her.

Summoning up her good supply of common sense, she examined Ivor's presence with the goal of putting her finger on the exact location of the thorn he provided, so that she could pluck it out and be rid of Ivor once and for all.

Was it because he had shunted her family off to the farthest reaches of the Bellamy estate, sort of an out-of-sight, out-of-mind project? She could not believe she was angry over that, since Ivor had treated her mother with the utmost consideration any man could do. The house had been totally improved, refurbished, cleaned, made sound and whole. Her mother had no complaints, so why should Jess?

Probing a bit deeper, she turned over in her mind the thought that she might well be upset because he had obviously not leapt to claim his inheritance, and taken the opportunity to rush posthaste to Oakminster to renew his courtship of her.

But she had told him, once, that she would sooner consider eloping with the Prince Regent than marrying him.

Neither of these reasons was sufficiently weighty to cause her deep-seated anger with him. Right at bottom, she knew that it was because she had so clearly indicated that he was on the verge of offering for someone else. Jealousy, pure and simple!

Possibly, if Ivor thought she herself had also found a new love, he might come around. But could she marry the man who had found her so unattractive that he had, four years ago, accepted her dismissal of him without protest?

The idea was, she reminded herself, not to *marry* Ivor, but only to disturb him—in fact, to bring him to his knees. He would offer again for her, she saw in her scheming mind, and she would spurn him, not this time in hot anger, but in coldly planned, excessively wounding phrases. She looked forward to the event with grim satisfaction.

It was that very morning that Ivor made a formal call on his kinswoman Mrs. Dalton in her new home. He gave the reins of his mount to the groom, and entered the foyer. Dressed in unobtrusive but extremely well-fitting country clothes, he gave his hat to Cross.

"Miss Jess," said the butler, following instructions quickly given to him only moments before, when Ivor was first glimpsed coming up the drive, "is not receiving this morning. She feels somewhat unwell."

"Indeed?" answered Ivor, lifting an eyebrow. "My best wishes for her recovery."

The golden-haried young lady listening, concealed, from the railing at the top of the stairs was hardly gratified to receive by proxy Ivor's goodwill. Moreover, she noticed a distinct lack of warmth in his expression of concern. So might he have received word that an upstairs maid in one of his well-appointed houses was suffering from the toothache. To add insult, the caller added smoothly, "My purpose is with Mrs. Dalton, if she will receive me."

If the caller in the center of the entrance lobby was unaware of motion at the top of the stairs, if he noticed a small fist pounding savagely on the balustrade, he gave no sign.

Cousin Elizabeth was eager to receive Ivor. She had grown quite to like him in the weeks he had stayed at Oakminster before this residence was made ready, and she considered that Jess was behaving in quite a *farouche* manner, particularly since she knew that Jess had been perfectly well only a quarter of an hour since. Alas, sighed Mrs. Dalton, for all the gold spent on governesses with the highest qualifications, and her own kindly strictures on Jess's behavior—and all for naught. The girl was not acting with the slightest civility, not even the most elementary common courtesy. How could Jess expect Ivor to renew his attentions if she behaved in such a repellent fashion?

But Mrs. Dalton had noticed that Jess's incivility was directed only at Ivor, and that might prove something? Love, after all, was only the reverse side of hate, and perhaps she could dream a little . . .

She greeted her guest in the foyer. "My dear Ivor," she exclaimed, her hand outstretched in welcome, "have you come to see us settled in? We are quite comfortable, you know."

Ivor bowed over her hand, and cut short her further expressions of gratitude. He glanced around him. Outside the door Elizabeth had just come through, he could see the clear attractiveness of the arrangements in the drawing room, not so crowded as to feel stifling, and yet affording every comfort. Even the foyer, containing two side chairs and a small table, seemed empty compared to the overwhelming number of objects that had found their way into the hall at Oakminster.

Even as his glance swept the hall, he caught sight of a fold of green skirt moving at the top of the stairs. If Jess were ill, he thought with silent amusement, at least she was not bedfast!

Considerately, he raised his voice so that she would not have to strain to hear him. Mischievously, he told Mrs. Dalton, "You may lay your comfort entirely to Jessamine's account. She is totally responsible for furnishing this house. Your own furniture, I believe she told me. I did urge her to take anything she wished from Oakminster, but of course her scruples were too fine to allow the gift of any other furniture from the manor."

"Indeed?" said Mrs. Dalton with a wisp of regret.

"I must apologize for my purpose in coming this morning," Ivor continued smoothly, "for I was unable to give you any notice of my intent. But I find I have a day of liberty, and I wonder whether you would be kind enough this afternoon to drive with me to call on our nearest neighbors, and perhaps the vicar as well? I believe the living is in my gift, and of course I should like to meet him."

"Yes, certainly you should. I should not like to say anything against him, but I do find he is a bit too scholarly for my taste, and I often wonder what the villagers make of him."

"Perhaps," said Ivor kindly, "I can persuade him to come down to earth, at least on Sundays." Still with a mind on the eavesdropper, he added deliberately, "We—that is, I—do not wish to be lectured to."

Jess, believing herself unseen, was struck by Ivor's misstep. *We?* Then he is planning to wed? She was so distraught by the thought that she failed to hear Ivor's next words. When she again listened to the conversation below her, her mother was saying, "That would be old Lord Hartnell, and his son, Henry. Lord Hartnell has been an invalid this long time, but Henry is quite devoted to us, particularly . . . Jess."

Mrs. Dalton recognized too late the pit she was falling into. She did not want Ivor to think that Jess was attached to Henry, for that would spoil everything. But perhaps a little rivalry might be helpful. "Henry is an unexceptionable young man, and they have known each other since childhood." In answer to a question Jess had not heard, her mother answered, "I am sorry that Althea is not here. She got underfoot so tediously while we were planning this removal that I grew quite out of charity with her. A cousin of her father's took pity on us, and sent a carriage, as well as a governess and a maid, to fetch her away."

Upstairs, Jess clenched her fists. That wretch Ivor! Using her mother to establish his position in the neighborhood! After the shabby way he had treated them. . .

Reason returned. He had not in truth treated them in the least way shabby, and it was a lowering thought that her mother's comfort in her new house was less important to her than the chance to come to verbal blows with Ivor. She had intended to fence lightly, with blunted weapon, riposte for riposte every time they conversed—to partake of an exhilarating exchange. But it had come to savage, blunt blows of a kind she could only regret. How similar they seemed to be in temperament! Must they strike sparks every time they met? What had happened to the great poise and serenity that she had rehearsed before her looking glass for a week before Ivor arrived at Oakminster?

So wrapped up had she been in assigning blame to herself that she had failed to catch what was going on below. Ivor had left. She could hear the diminishing sound of hoofbeats down the driveway. Now she heard her mother's footstep on the stairs, and not wishing to be caught eavesdropping she skittered down the hall to her own bedroom. Here her mother found her, reading, in an elaborately casual pose in an armchair.

Her mother eyed her without approval. "I understand you told Cross to deny yourself to our visitor because you felt not quite the thing. You must be very ill indeed to forget the simplest courtesy, Jessamine. This *malaise* must have come upon you very suddenly. You alarm me. I shall send Cross at once for Mr. Robbins. It does not do to take the slightest chance with a summer illness."

"I do not need a doctor, Mama. You know how I detest being physicked. I simply did not want—"

Mrs. Dalton interrupted. "I do not care to hear your reasons, or, more accurately, I should say your mere excuses. I must decide what to wear this afternoon to go with Ivor to the Hartnells'. Had you been feeling well, you might have enjoyed the outing, my dear."

"But, Mama, do you think—?"

"What I think, Jess, is that you are being foolish. Perhaps 'childish' is more to the point. I must assume you do not wish to fix your interest again with Ivor, for you are certainly going about it the right way to give him a strong revulsion of you. But then, you must know best how you feel." At the door she paused. "Truly," she added with a twinkle, "you would be much more convincing if your book were not upside down."

The house was echoingly empty that afternoon after the carriage bore Mrs. Dalton and Ivor away down the graveled drive. Cross and Mrs. Cross had been given the afternoon off, and Meggie, the parlormaid, was no doubt snoozing in her narrow bed on the top floor.

Silvester was away somewhere, and Philip had disappeared, probably to Ivor's library. All the other servants were out of sight too, for without Cross's minatory glance, they dispersed to their own advantage.

Jess took downstairs the book that had betrayed her to her mother. She had no idea why she had picked up a volume entitled *Sermons on Little-Known Scandals in the North of England*. Indeed, she had no idea how it came to be in the house, unless Philip had borrowed it from Oakminster. It seemed to have been written by some excitable clergyman whose need for attention outweighed the decency to let old scandals bury themselves.

Much like that of the Italian countess. That had certainly buried itself. Jess had thought she knew the family history backward, from the Bellamy who received a land grant from Tudor hands, to the Bellamy who reportedly buried the family plate and jewels as Oliver Cromwell rode up the driveway of Oaklane, to the Bellamy who (also reportedly) dug them up once the danger was past and built Oakminster with the proceeds.

There had been no Italian countess on the family tree as taught to Jess, not even on one of the widest branches. The scandal had been buried deep. But now it had climbed into the daylight. But the lady had been a Bellamy, after all, and for that reason had been rescued from an Italian gutter, and given shelter, a rather nice shelter at that. But what would she have done all day, alone, disgraced, and therefore denied the companionship of her family and friends? Of course, it went without saying that she had no hope of a conventional match!

Jess suddenly felt a spiritual kinship with the countess, at least this afternoon. She too was forsaken by friend and family. She too was lonely and prey to tedium. And she too was not blessed by a desirable match. At the moment, even a scandal-born isolation might be preferred to marriage with, for example, Henry! Depressing, and not to be thought of!

At least the countess had loved once, even though unworthily, and most likely twice, assuming that rumor was correct in giving her a "gentleman caller." Even a Demon Lover!

Whereas Jess had—

She rose quickly from her chair. Melancholia was a condition she scorned. Walking briskly to the kitchen, she found a basket of early fruit on the table, clearly sent by Ivor from the manor's greenhosues. Choosing a peach, she ate it as messily as a child might, letting the juice run down her chin. Cleaning up afterward, she wondered that Mrs. Cross had not tidied away the table linens from luncheon. The cloth was badly folded and placed on the end of the long worktable, just as though it had been dropped when Meggie cleared away in the dining room.

Well, she would mention this untidiness to her mother, and if she chose to speak to Mrs. Cross, that was her mother's right. Jess did not run the household —except, she thought, when it came to hard work like supervising cleaning and arranging furniture!

Returning to the drawing room, she considered the possibilities for amusing herself the rest of the long afternoon. The house seemed curiously full of noises, as though it twitched in its noontime nap. Jess became aware that there were now sounds she had never heard before. One sounded like a shutter at the back of the house, perhaps in the scullery, banging in the wind. She glanced through a window. The leaves hung unmoving on the oak trees. A breeze moving shutters and yet not touching leaves? Perhaps Meggie had let a cat in.

Swallowing hard, Jess advanced on the scullery. She called, "Kitty, kitty!" but no one answered. The window was closed—as it should be, Mrs. Cross fearing even the daytime air as being full of unseen dangers to the unwary, to say nothing of the deadly miasma of the atmosphere after the sun set.

She called again, but no cat stirred. There was a stillness in the scullery, and the kitchen, that she found oppressive. The door, when she looked, to the back stairs was firmly closed, and the shutters seemed fixed in their proper places.

There was nothing more. Old houses made noises; she knew that. Her old nurse had told her the house was settling. But surely this house should have settled long since?

This house, of course, was much older than Oakminster, but likely, having been left empty for so long, it now was adjusting to the invasion of people, and possibly to changes in temperature, for it was growing warmer outdoors.

How could Jess know the house had not made these same noises over the years when there was no one to hear? She couldn't.

Still not satisfied, however, she moved back into the entrance hall in time to hear an undefined but sharp sound, this time from upstairs. She grabbed at a chair, pulling it away from the wall, with a vague idea of using it for protection.

Against a noise? Suddenly the absurdity of the entire afternoon came over her, and instead of wielding the chair, she sat down in it and laughed aloud. Imagine making up noises and frightening herself to death, simply out of pique at being left alone. Alone by her own choice, too, in a house that was perfectly safe from any kind of intruder, with servants within call. At least Meggie might be roused, although with difficulty, since she usually slept like the dead.

She wished she had not used that word.

Besides, common sense told her that the noise upstairs could have been Silvester, returning from one of his wide rides down Bellamy lanes and even into Hartnell lands. Silvester had absented himself from the household removal process, to Jess's disgust, and had formed the habit of going out in the morning and coming back late in the afternoon. She had no idea where he went, and she knew better than to ask him.

Or even Philip might have returned from his secluded haunts in the Oakminster library. Jess paused to wonder whether Ivor was aware that Philip was usually to be found in his library. Any house of good size, even those smaller than Oakminster, would have ways of egress that were not obvious. Perhaps a convenient window projection or a sturdy ivy provided means for wayward young men wishing to follow their own pursuits without parental censorship. And a way out must also provide a way in. Philip's presence in Oakminster would not necessarily be known.

She wished she hadn't thought of secret passages. No house was invulnerable to intruders . . .

But the sound a few moments ago upstairs was likely one of her brothers. If Silvester were upstairs, then he

THE LOST LEGACY 93

was home earlier than custom. A feeling of unease struck her. He might have fallen from his horse—not fallen, for he was an excellent horseman, but anyone but a centaur could be thrown—been hurt, dragged himself home and upstairs . . .

She hurried.

At the top of the stairs she turned left, toward Silvester's room. The corridor itself was empty. But surprisingly it had a feeling, almost as though someone had just departed. There was no one in sight. She knocked at Silvester's door. When there was no answer, she opened it and went in. The room was empty.

She crossed the hall to Philip's room and entered it. Again she stood in an empty room. There had to be an explanation, a book fallen to the floor, an open door slammed shut.

She paused on her way out of Philip's room. Looking behind her, she noticed that the bookshelves seemed unusually full, but then, she had not been in Philip's room for some time.

She stepped into the corridor. Something caught her eye. Something moved. Something, without question, moved!

She would have called, but her mouth seemed full of cotton and she could not utter a sound. But what could she have called to? A shadow?

She did not kow how long she stood there, a cold trembling overtaking her limbs, and a mist arising before her eyes. She could not faint, she *dared* not, for who knew what could happen to her when she was unconscious?

Not without difficulty, she managed to release one slippered foot from the roots it seemed to have grown into the carpet, and take a step. With some anxiety, she turned to the window at the end of the corridor. This was where she had seen the movement, the apparent solidity of a fold as of a garment, perhaps a coat. It was there, and then it wasn't there.

There had to be an explanation. The boys, Meggie, even one of the grooms from the stable. While a groom had no business to be upstairs in the house, yet that was preferable to a more unpleasant alternative.

A reasonable explanation—that was what she searched for. And she found it. An intruder was impossible. No one in his right mind—and she wished she had not thought of *that*, for an unsound mind she did not wish to contemplate—would enter a house where there were servants, even though they might be away at the moment.

No, it was all her nerves. The first time she had been alone in this house, and of course the noises were all new to her. She had not noticed any sounds when the family was present. That was all there was to it!

Thankful at finding the answer, she laughed, a little shakily, at herself. What a peahen she was! She turned to go back downstairs, where it would be easier to escape. What a thought! She would never flee from her own house!

A few steps away from the window, she stopped and sniffed. A strange odor, one she did not recognize, but probably merely the scent of soap. The maids would have cleaned the corridor this morning. They should then have waxed the floors, but the telltale household smell of wax was not present. A clean smell, though, but somewhat unpleasant . . .

Not until she reached the ground floor did the thought come to her: that soap, if it were indeed soap, that she had caught a whiff of upstairs was no ordinary household cleaner. Her mother would never have allowed the use of anything but pure lye soap.

And this whiff smelled strongly of musk!

11

Jessamine lifted her skirts in both hands and fled down the hall, nearly overshooting the head of the stairs. She sped down the stairs as though the Furies were after her. *For all I know,* she thought wildly, *they are!*

She stopped to catch her breath at the foot of the broad stairs. She did not want to look behind her, but nothing on earth could have prevented her from turning to look up the stairs. There was nothing that she could see.

What did I expect? she thought as her blood pounded more slowly and her breath came less raggedly. *There is nothing in this house except Meggie sleeping as if she were . . . that is, sleeping soundly. And, of course, Jess herself.*

She walked, making herself move deliberately, into the drawing room. It was the measure of her recent fright that she stood in the doorway for some moments, scanning the room with her eyes to make sure that whoever had banged the shutter, or dropped a large article upstairs, had not in some way passed her and taken refuge in this room.

There was not space enough for anyone to hide behind the bergere chair, the settee, the long side table. Reassuringly the draperies lay flat against the walls, not bulging out from some obstruction behind them, no irregularity at the bottom of the damask.

Nonetheless, before she sat down, she took the fireplace poker out of its stand, brandished it a few times —as though she thought someone were watching her!— and sat with it awkwardly in her hands.

She set herself, while waiting for Ivor to come—that is, for her mother to return—to reasonable thought. What in fact had she seen? Nothing but a dark fold of cloth. What kind of cloth? She found herself thinking of the tail of a coat—the kind of coat a gentleman might wear. Did ghosts appear in the apparel of their time, or did they find more fashionable wear? She suppressed a hysterical giggle.

She could not describe the garment. Only a triangular dark shadow, reminiscent of a coattail. It had come and gone so quickly she could not even be sure she had seen anything.

A fold of cloth, and a strong smell of musky soap.

And that was all. Nothing to terrify any healthy young woman!

But she had unquestionably had that very definite feeling that there was someone—or had been someone —lurking in the upstairs hall. Someone watching her, without friendly intent.

She shivered. What an imagination! She must find reading material more to the point than Maria Edgeworth! Perhaps a book of sermons? But certainly not the *Sermons on Scandals* she had picked up this morning.

Imagination it might have been, but she found she was still looking around her from the corners of her eyes, alert to catch the slightest movement. She considered available armament. The poker in her hand was certainly formidable. However, to wield it she must be closer to the enemy than she considered desirable. From where she sat, the only alternative that she could see was a Chinese vase that some ancestor had brought home from Canton. It was too large for her to handle, and she dismissed the possibility of using that.

But from the chair she had chosen, she could see both the front door and most of the entrance hall, including the bottom section of the broad staircase. At least she would not be caught unawares.

Unless—the thought came to her, not for the first

time—the intruder was not of a nature to require conventional means of entry.

It was then that she lost her grip on herself. The Demon Lover moved from a witticism to a dark possibility. The haunted countess had reason to resent the intrusion of an entire family, especially since they were of the same blood as those who had tucked her away in disgrace. If the—the whatever it was— upstairs had indeed been the gentleman's ghost, then it followed that the countess was here also.

Jess told herself that broadmindedness, especially in this instance, was a virtue. If the lady were happy, even under such drastically altered circumstances, then Jess wished her well. But she did wish the lady and her lover would choose another setting for their *amours*.

She shifted in her chair, and the poker fell to the floor with a clatter that chilled the blood and emptied the mind.

After some moments, she picked up the weapon again, and resigned herself to the slow passage of time. The only conclusion she came to, before the enormously welcome sound of carriage wheels on the drive came to her ears, was that if the intruders were indeed spirits, what did they need with musk-scented soap?

Through the open door Jess could hear the sounds of a fashionable party arriving. The horses' hoofbeats, the harness jingling. The thud of footmen leaping to the ground, running footsteps of the groom going to the heads of the horses, the opening of a carriage door, the careful positioning of the steps to permit Mrs. Dalton's descent from the coach.

And the approaching steps of her mother and Ivor.

"I can't think why the door stands open," said her mother. "I do not permit it as a rule, you know, even in the finest weather, for there is always the possibility of small creatures coming into the house. I do not think Cross would allow a cat, but I do not care to go constantly in the apprehension of some animal creeping furtively into the room."

They had come into the foyer, and Ivor looked around him with some irritation for a servant, Cross or a maid, into whose hands he could confide Mrs. Dalton's person. Besides, although he was very sure that Jess's ailment of the morning had been perfectly imaginary, he held a hope that he might see her before he left.

His hope was fulfilled. He glanced through the door into the drawing room and saw Jess, in a posture he had never seen before. She sat bolt upright in a narrow chair, facing the hall, very oddly holding what looked like a poker in her lap.

He moved toward her. "I am delighted to see you recovered . . . Good God, Jess, what's amiss?"

She found her voice. "N-nothing . . ."

"Nothing? Don't try to fool me, miss!" said Ivor, angry because he was frightened for her. Her dark blue eyes were almost black, and wide open as though she stared at something behind him.

"Now that . . . you're here."

Ivor was taken out of himself by the spectacle of Jess rigid and terrified. He abandoned Mrs. Dalton and strode across the room to kneel beside Jess. He removed, with some difficulty, the poker from her stiff fingers, and laid it beside him on the green floral carpet.

"All right," he said as gently as though to a child, "I am here now. What could I have done for you earlier?"

Gradually, under the warming pressure of his hands on hers, she began to thaw. Finally, haltingly at first, but then with rising confidence, she told Ivor, as well as her mother, who had come in from the foyer, of her experience that afternoon.

At length, seeing disbelief in the two pairs of eyes

fixed on her, she stopped. "You don't believe me, I know that. I cannot help it. That is what happened."

"The noises, Jess," suggested Ivor, "could they not have been a limb tapping on the windowpane?"

"If a limb tapped hard enough to make that kind of sound, the window would have been broken. Do you think I don't know a limb against the window when I hear one?"

"But you were not well this morning," Ivor continued, whether baiting her or not, she could not tell, "and perhaps your shadow was simply a trick of your headache."

She glared at him. If she had still held the poker in her hands, she would not have gone bail for the likelihood of his leaving Oaklane uninjured. As it was, her fingers clenched underneath his hands, which still held hers lightly.

So he didn't believe her! Very well. "As a matter of fact," she said with an earnest air, "it was most likely a symptom of the megrim. One often sees spots before one's eyes, and you have shrewdly touched upon the right of it. Although I do not recall before having seen a small brown creature with four legs standing with his front paws on the windowsill, looking out into the garden." Invention did not desert her. "And crying. Probably it was because his silver antlers banged against the window and hurt him."

She was gratified to see a leaping fire of anger in Ivor's eyes. Make little of her terrible fears, would he? Regard her as a fool, ready to fly up in the boughs over a simple headache, especially when she had not had one? Very well, she could return the favor.

"At any rate," she continued, "the front door was open, so I must suppose he has gone off into the wood."

Ivor released her hands and stood up. Looking down at her with cold gray eyes—an expression in them that she had seen to her regret some years ago—

he said, "You must suppose? You did not see him, or it, as the case may be, depart?"

Chastened, Jess murmured, "No, I did not. But if it were a consequence of my headache, then . . ."

Mrs. Dalton had sunk into a nearby chair and listened without saying a word. There were many thoughts crowding into her mind, but it would require some time before they could become clear. All she knew now was that Jess had been frightened—even Ivor could not have mistaken that first sight of Jess, clearly terrified. And Mrs. Dalton had not been here to protect her, or at least share . . . whatever there was to share.

It was the moment to intervene. "Jess, you are talking nonsense. How can you expect Ivor to help if you don't explain to him?"

"Mama, I did explain—" began Jess, but Ivor interrupted.

"Of course, this is all nonsense, Cousin Elizabeth. And if there were an intruder," he continued grimly, "then I must say that Jess invited such a one, since the door stood open when she was alone in the house. I suppose you were alone? What about the servants? Cross? Your brothers?"

"I gave the servants the afternoon," faltered Mrs. Dalton, "for I thought I might persuade Jess to accompany us to the Hartnells'."

"Silvester?" persisted Ivor. Upon being assured that the servants were away, some with leave and some without, and that Jess had indeed been alone, he tilted his head, his expression altered, listening. Soon the others heard it—the leisurely cantering hoofbeats of a lone rider coming up the drive.

It was Silvester.

When Jess's story was told again for her brother's benefit, Silvester's reaction was all that Jess had feared. "And I was not here! Jess, you let him get away? How could you, when you know I would want to give him a lesson! I'd make sure he never came in again!"

"How would you do that?" inquired Jess testily. "You would not lay a finger on him."

After a moment, Silvester's features expressed the utmost delight as the truth of the matter disclosed itself to him. "A ghost! The real Bellamy ghost! And I missed it. Well, ghosts always come back, don't they? I'll make sure I'm here next time."

"Silvester, ghosts do not leave aromas behind them," said Jess in a damping fashion.

"Aromas?" said Ivor quickly.

"Surely they do," argued Silvester. "Clanking chains, and a smell out of the cellar. That's what Acton told me when I asked him."

A faint cry from Mrs. Dalton recalled them all from their spirited discussion. "All right," said Jess, attempting to allay her mother's distress, "I imagined the whole thing. Mama, how did you find the Hartnells?" Turning with the ease of rigorous social training, she added to Ivor, "Such a pleasantly situated manor, I always thought."

Mrs. Dalton added, valiantly rising to the occasion, "So I have pointed out to you, Jessamine, very often."

"Not as nice as ours," said Silvester to Ivor, adding in confusion, "I mean, as *yours*."

Mrs. Dalton had subsided into a troubled silence. At length she said to Jess, "My dear, I think I shall go upstairs and lie down. When Mrs. Cross returns, send her up with a cup of that restoring tonic she makes."

Ivor interjected, "Pray, Cousin Elizabeth, wait. I think it might be well for me to make sure that nothing has been removed before you go upstairs." Ignoring Jess's murmured "Removed by a headache?" he beckoned to Silvester. "We shall be back in only a few moments."

Jess pressed her mother's hand and said, "I'd better go with them. I should not trust a pair of blundering men to deal in any way with delicacy."

She followed them up the stairs. "You will not know, will you, Ivor, whether anything is missing?"

"I was sure you would join us," said Ivor, unabashed. "You mentioned an aroma? You did not tell me that."

Unreasonably, she retorted, "You did not ask. But it was something like soap, but it had a tincture of musk in it. I have not before met a combination like that."

Ivor thought a moment. "Nor have I."

The three of them moved through the bedroom, looking for signs of a hasty intruder, of jewel boxes ransacked, wardrobes emptied. There were none. Even the rugs were flat and undisturbed.

The only thing amiss, to Jess, was nothing she knew. A wisp of uncertainty, the faint hint that something was not as she had left it—there was nothing to point to. She stood in the middle of her bedroom, Ivor at the door. There was the wardrobe—the door slightly ajar, but perhaps she had left it so. The clothing inside seemed to hang in undisturbed folds. The dresser surface was untouched, and no hand had invaded the privacy of her intimate garments.

But yet there was something . . .

"Anything amiss?" asked Ivor.

"Not that I can see," she answered honestly, and joined him to search the rest of the floor.

Back in the drawing room, they saw that Cross had returned, and had brought in a tray of hastily made tea. Meggie was assisting him in passing the cups with shaking hands. Jess looked curiously at her pale face.

"Meggie," she said in an undertone when the maid brought her cup to her, "did anything . . . did you see anyone in the house this afternoon?"

Meggie's only answer was a negative shake of the head. Jess knew she was not being truthful, but her questioning would have to wait until they were alone.

If Cross possessed any guilty knowledge, he had it carefully hidden behind impassive features. He and his wife had gone away for the afternoon to visit her sister in the village, and the only information of value that had come to his attention there was that the mill-workers were getting near to boiling point, and young Mr. Henry Hartnell—one of the owners—was all that kept them from taking care of the spinning machinery to their own specifications. He had dismissed that gossip as being greatly out-of-date, since the talk had gone on for a couple of years without any action. Put up or shut up, was his motto. And the millworkers did neither.

In the drawing room, Jess reported that nothing appeared to be missing in the way of valuables. Silvester had lingered upstairs at the window in question, sniffing like a foxhound on a warm trail, and trying to open the window.

When he came downstairs, he went directly to Jess and told her, "There is nothing wrong with that window."

"I never said there was. I only said that I couldn't open it. What I saw was in the hall. Inside the house."

Mrs. Dalton said mournfully, "To think, Jess, that I exposed you to all this."

Ivor agreed. "It might have been better had we not gone visiting this afternoon. But I judge that nothing would have happened had we been here."

"They, whoever *they* are, would simply have waited till another day?" asked Jess.

Silvester was following his own thoughts. "I didn't smell anything upstairs, Jess. You imagined the whole thing!"

Lightly Jess agreed. "Of course I did. The afternoon was tedious!" She stopped short, realizing that she was revealing more than she wished to. Her excuse had been the headache. Tedium had nothing to do with her refusal of Ivor's invitation—at least so she said!

She bit her lip to keep from setting Silvester entirely straight, even though the words sprang at once to her tongue. It would do no good to bicker, particularly in Ivor's hearing. She knew what she had smelled. She was not quite so sure about what she had seen.

She was impatient for Ivor to leave so she could retreat upstairs again, to try once more to puzzle out the mystery of what might be amiss in her own bedroom. But Ivor, comfortably settled in a large chair, seemed reluctant to take his departure. Instead, he said to Silvester, "You suggested that a ghost—I believe you said *the* ghost—might be responsible for Jess's fright. I confess I have never given much credence to the possibility of hauntings, but certainly I shall not allow Cousin Elizabeth to continue to occupy a dwelling that is in the least uncomfortable."

"It's haunted!" said Silvester with enthusiasm. "It has to be!"

Ivor's expression said clearly, and skeptically: You can prove this? But his words were less blunt. "I should imagine you have a story to go with this haunting? I should like to hear it, if you have the time."

Silvester would have found time in the middle of a sea battle to oblige Ivor. Since he could not sail with Captain Cook, long dead in glory at the hands of feathered savages with bones through their nostrils—although Silvester would very much prefer to remain alive in order to come home in triumph with the treasures of the Indies in the hold, like Lord Anson—he would, as next best, plunge into the supernatural.

"I only heard the story myself a fortnight or so ago. Just after you wrote that you were coming down to stay. We were all in a turmoil, you know," Silvester chatted, oblivious of the glances of dismay sent his way by his mother, and the quelling glare of his sister.

"At any rate," he continued, "Mama broke open the cupboard where the family skeletons are kept—not precisely a cupboard, you know . . . ?" he ended on a note of inquiry. Upon Ivor's understanding nod, he continued. "A countess we never heard of—Italian at that, except I guess she herself was a Bellamy, but she married an Italian, although he wasn't a count either." Silvester came to the point in his story where his mother had expressed doubts about the marriage itself, and stopped short, like a man who had just realized he was about to say something offensive when ladies were present.

Ivor was amused. "I suppose I may conjecture certain elements of the story," he said dryly. "But is it this . . . this lady who is reported to haunt Oaklane?"

Silvester agreed. "Who else? Surely not the gentleman!"

Ivor objected. "How could he? Was he not in Italy? Or did he come back? Most foolhardy, if he did."

Jess thought it time to take a hand in this discussion. "Not the Italian. There was another man—supposed to be a gentleman from no great distance . . ." She reddened in confusion. This was certainly not an edifying tale to narrate in company. Still, she retreated in embarrassment. "Only a rumor, a foolish story."

"At least she lived here," said Silvester, feeling snubbed, but anxious to be accurate. "And I suppose she was unhappy. Aren't all ghosts unhappy?"

"Assuming she is the ghost," said Ivor severely, "one most also assume she is unhappy. But suppose she is not the ghost? Jess saw something she believed was more fitting to a gentleman."

Jess could contain herself no longer. "Ivor, for goodness' sake, don't tell me you believe in ghosts, for I will not credit it." Grandly dismissing her own strong conviction that she had only an hour ago firmly believed that she herself had seen a specter, she turned on her brother. "And you, Silvester, don't you see that Mama is distressed enough, without all this doing about the ghost? I tell you, unless ghosts are in the habit of using strong musk-scented soap, then we have no wraith inhabiting this house with us."

Ivor said, "For myself, I believe the aroma you detected must be one left by the cleaning crew." With a warning glance, he added in an undertone to Jess, "A burglar might distress your mother even more severely than the thought of a ghost."

Quickly adopting Ivor's thought, Jess said, "Mama, should you not like to rest now? We found nothing amiss upstairs, and Mrs. Cross is here now to make your restorative tonic."

"And lie down in my bedroom all alone?" demanded Mrs. Dalton, ignoring that only half an hour ago that had been her dearest wish. "I think not. Not that I fear ghosts, precisely. But I am rested now."

Jess was not deceived by her mother. She said only, "But I must have seen no more than a shadow. All the rest is mere idle conversation—to amuse Silvester!"

Silvester was far from acquiescing in such a tame explanation as Jess offered. "The house is old enough to have more than one ghost. Why, it was likely from here that our ancestor scurried out to bury the family treasure!"

"Through a priest hole?" Ivor was clearly dubious. "I should think not."

"Don't you think there might still be buried treasure around somewhere?" The expression on Silvester's face reminded Ivor strongly of a puppy longing for his master to throw the stick again.

"Pray confine your efforts to seeking a secret-tunnel entrance in the house," advised Ivor dryly. "I should not like to see my fields dug up in order to find a non-existent cache of plate. Besides, the Bellamy treasure, whatever it consisted of, was dug up after the Restoration. My father told me so."

Jess objected. "Of course it was, and if you are looking for a priest hole, it will not be a tunnel."

Mrs. Dalton said faintly, "There was the folly."

"Of course," crowed Silvester, "the folly! But it's gone."

Noticing that Mrs. Dalton seemed unusually nervous, her eyes frequently gazing into the corners of the room, Ivor said firmly, "Silvester, you are not thinking. The folly would be the first place Cromwell would look. Priest holes are hidden within the house as a rule."

"And there is none in this house!" Silvester's disappointment was obvious.

Jess too realized that her mother's distress was growing. "Silvester," she said quickly, "can't you see you are boring Ivor? And it is the greatest ingratitude to find flaws in the house he is lending Mama."

Ivor eyed Jess keenly, and was struck by the shadows beneath her eyes. She had indeed been frightened, and therefore there had truly been something amiss more than her imagination. Jess was not one to fly up in the boughs without reason.

Soon he made his excuses and left. He had things to do, and certainly a thing or two to think about.

12

After Ivor left, Jess had gone upstairs and searched for the source of her uneasy feeling that something was amiss there, although she could not put her finger on it.

Alone, she searched her room thoroughly. Instead of being reassured by its normal appearance, she found more questions raised than settled. For one, the garments hanging in her wardrobe, which had during their previous search seemed somewhat jumbled, now were neatly arranged.

The rug on the floor in front of the hearth still lay flat, but she gazed at it thoughtfully. Had it been quite so close to the chair drawn up to the fireplace? She could not be sure, but it seemed to her that the room had been neatened since she and Ivor had searched this floor for signs of an intruder. That intangible alteration was, again, only an impression, no more certain than that fold of cloth she had seen before!

But at last, in a corner, obscured by the chest of drawers that stood out from the wall—and she was sure she had not left it so—she found it. It was an elegant little piece of furniture, a table with delicately turned legs, and of all things, a small drawer, so shallow that only by noticing the unusual thickness of the top of the table could one suspect the drawer. Even the drawer pull was made of wood to blend, so that it was nearly a secret drawer.

Jess was sure she would have noticed it had it been there earlier. But again, could she be sure that one of the maids, or even Cross himself, had not moved the table in? But when could he have done so?

The table had not been there in the morning, she was sure. But it must have been there when she and Ivor visited the room, for it had given rise to her mystification. Anytime in the morning would have given opportunity.

Almost without thinking, she pulled open the drawer. It was empty. She pulled it all the way out and peered into the opening. Something light-colored caught her eye, and she reached in after it. It came loose with a little tug, and she looked down at the small three-cornered piece of paper she held in her fingers.

A bit of paper, not foxed, as one might expect if it had been in the drawer since the Italian countess's time. She turned it over thoughtfully. Then she peered intently at it. There was writing on it.

Only a part of a word—or parts of two words. She carried it to the window to get a better light on it. There was an L. Surely it was an L? The last letter in a word, of course. On the line directly below, there was a full word: "ton." A ton of what? But puzzle as she might, she could make no sense of it. With an odd feeling that in some way this scrap of paper might be valuable, she looked around for a place to secrete it. The small drawer was the best place, but she dared not put the paper back where she had found it, for someone else might also look for it precisely in that place. There was nothing else for it. She thrust it into her pocket, to keep it with her until she thought of a better hiding place for it.

But still, the mystery of the table itself was not solved. She started out of the room with the express intention of confronting Cross with the question, but she stopped short on the threshold. Suppose Cross denied bringing in the table? And suppose, upon questioning, none of the servants confessed? What then?

Jess had not the slightest doubt of events likely to follow. The maids would decide the house was haunted—and no maidservant alive would stay in a house where there were "queer goings-on." And then what would they do?

Jess decided to say nothing. Her mother did not need the additional worry of having her servants depart *en masse*, as was the certain outcome if Jess strove to get to the bottom of the matter. Jess kept her doubts to herself.

After a night's sleep, the deep sleep of weariness, she reviewed her decision and found it good. However, Mrs. Dalton had had an uneasy night. At breakfast she informed her children that she had not slept a wink.

"I blame myself entirely," she said, "for your great fright, Jessamine."

"How can you, Mama? Certainly you were not upstairs—"

"And that is the entire point, my dear. Had I not gone and left you alone, although heaven knows what might have happened in our absence if you had gone with us, this . . . this invasion, I suppose we must call it, would not have happened. I am sure of it. I was away—enjoying myself with Ivor and Henry, although I admit I do not *truly* enjoy myself with Henry, for he is much too intelligent to be interested in anything I say, and he talks in such a strange way."

"He is not intelligent, Mama. He is, to put it plainly, merely tedious. He is forever talking about the men in his factories, how rebellious they are, and how the government must get the army to fire upon them."

"I confess I did not quite like the way he spoke of his men. And it seems to me that until recently he has been almost secretive about his factories. I hope I can overlook his grandfather being in trade, but constantly to boast of it I find very daunting."

Jess stared into her coffee cup. She had had such elaborate plans for flirting with Henry, for giving Ivor reason to believe her heart had been captured by Henry Hartnell, making Ivor jealous. But if Ivor had experienced the same conversation as her mother now related, as of course he had, he would never believe that Jess would find Henry anything other than a consummate bore.

Mrs. Dalton had put her finger on a development that Jess had noticed without noticing, so to speak. Until recently, Henry had scrupulously avoided any mention of his industrial grandfather, but now it was as though he were obsessed by the factories he had inherited. Heedless of revealing, apparently even to Ivor, that his lineage was not entirely that of a gentleman, he allowed his mind and tongue to run upon subjects that would never have seen the light of day in London society.

Jess added, "I find him heartless as well, at least in regard to his workers. Henry is simply not good enough for you to find virtue in him, and particularly of all things for you to believe him intelligent."

"Well, dear, you do make me more comfortable in my mind. I confess I had hopes that you might make a match of it with him, because I would dearly like to see you settled into a happy marriage, but truly . . . Jess, do you really think so little of Henry?"

"He is not anything more to me than a neighbor whom it will not do to snub." She did not feel it necessary to add that she had looked upon Henry with some charity before Ivor had come back into her sphere.

"Too bad, for I have engaged us to go to dinner with the Hartnells in three days."

"Mama!"

"Well, it did not seem that I could help it. Ivor mentioned that his friend Giles Something was coming down . . ." She stopped short, dismayed. "I was not to tell you that. Ivor wanted his guest to be a surprise for you, and now I have spoiled it!"

A spark of glee appeared in Jess's eyes. "So that was it!"

"I don't understand. Pray, Jess, can you not forget I told you?"

With a smile bearing a tinge of malice, Jess agreed. "I haven't heard a word. And he thought he could annoy me . . ."

That man! He had indicated in every way he knew without resorting to outright falsehood—and Ivor was too proud to lie in any circumstance—that his coming houseguest would be the Lady Dorine. The same lady he had mentioned in such terms as to make Jess believe he was all but betrothed to her. And, fool that she was, Jess had believed him.

If did not occur to her then to wonder why, if he were as indifferent to her as he appeared, he would take the trouble to mislead her. As it was, she acknowledged the existence in her of a flame of revenge to be visited upon the villain, and cast about for fuel to feed it.

She had thought that she would be very nice to Henry as soon as Ivor arrived at Oakminster, but it was an ill-defined notion at best, and now that Ivor had been exposed to the full scope of Henry's ability to bore, she could see that plan was not practicable. Besides, there had been so much to do in packing and removing the household to Oaklane, and, though she did not wish to admit it even to herself, it seemed that Ivor had taken possession of all her thoughts. It would look queer beyond measure if she suddenly, at this point, took an obvious interest in Henry.

Well! Now she had two counts against Ivor. First, he did not believe her experience of yesterday. Soap left by the cleaning crew—ridiculous! And now, his attempt to deceive her into believing he planned to marry Lady Dorine, whoever she was.

The making of a plan, for Jess, was immediately followed by putting it into action. "Such a good idea, Mama," she said artlessly, "to welcome Ivor's friend to the neighborhood. Perhaps he will find the Hartnells dull, but I think we can manage to entertain him."

Mrs. Dalton eyed her suspiciously. Her daughter

THE LOST LEGACY 113

was prone to sudden impulses and wayward thoughts. "Shall you not have the headache again? Since you dislike Henry, and I must say I do not blame you, perhaps you would not like to make one of the party."

"Henry? Well, I have been forced to make do with Henry until now, but I confess to being greatly pleased to hear that Giles Leighton is coming down. I took quite a liking to him when I met him in London."

Mrs. Dalton gave passing consideration to the thought that a quarrel over Giles Leighton might have been the crucial event in breaking off Jess's marriage plans with Ivor. Then she dismissed that idea. Ivor would not still be friendly with a man who might yet have a *tendre* for his former fiancee.

She said, "Now, Jess, you are not planning anything foolish? I do not quite like the expression I discern in your eyes."

"Mama, nothing in the least foolish. But Ivor has had his own way long enough!"

She excused herself and left the room, leaving her mother filled with unwelcome anticipation of future events, and not a little dread.

Ivor had severely blotted his copybook, thought Jess grimly. She could forgive his dragging the red herring called Lady Dorine across her path. While there might well be a Lady Dorine in England, and without doubt if she were unattached she would be delighted to entertain Ivor Bellamy's suit, yet the immediate advent of the lady as forecast by Ivor was proven false.

However, the item of Ivor's dereliction that stabbed Jess to the quick was his clear indication, yesterday afternoon, that he did not believe her narrative. There was no ghost, he suggested, and therefore there could be no real fright on her part. The only conclusion, even though unspoken, she could draw was that he cared not a whit for her. If he had found her weltering in her own blood in the hall—though whose blood she

would welter in, if not her own, she could not tell—
likely enough he would not even have stooped to pick
her up.

Silvester had been slow to leave the house that
morning. Usually he was gone early, in his restless
need for motion, saddling his horse and cantering
away down the driveway right after breakfast. This
morning, however, he had something on his mind.
That much was evident to Jess at breakfast, but since
he did not confide in her, she had no idea what
troubled him.

However, she was to receive a hint. She was going
through the corridor that led to the door at the back of
the house, opening on the garden, when she heard her
brother's voice. Automatically she hesitated, as the
words came clearly to her.

"But you must know something, Cross," he was
persisting. "You've been with us all your life, and your
father too. Surely you've heard something about the
ghost?"

Cross's voice came slowly and sullenly. "No, Mr.
Silvester, I know naught."

"But you must know about a tunnel. Isn't there one?
Does it go from the house? Where would it come to?"
Cross's reply was an indistinct rumble, but Silvester
was hot on the trail. "What about the pavilion, the
folly?"

Goaded, Cross spat the words out. "All I know, Mr.
Silvester, is what my grandfather told me. They was a
pavilion once, and when the floods came it fell in the
river. And that's all I know about it."

Jess could not possibly have moved away. Eavesdropping was *common*, but she stood as though rooted
to the ground.

"But where was the pavilion? And when did it fall
into the river? How long ago were the floods?"

"It was just what the gentry call a summerhouse,

that's what I was told. And you know right well, Mr.
Silvester, when the floods came. They were in your
great-grandfather's time, rest his soul, and I'll tell ye
this and it's my last word. You got better things to do
than ram around the countryside looking for
something that floated away in the flood."

So must Noah have sounded, thought Jess, obsessed
by the floods. Clearly, at least in old Gaffer Cross's
time, there had been two eras—before flood and after
flood. And the pavilion, the summerhouse where the
Italian countess must have taken the air of a summer
afternoon, was antediluvian. She heard Silvester's
protests dying away, and she was released from her
immobility. She had reached the garden before
Silvester burst through the door behind her.

"They was a pavilion, Jess! Cross said so! Imagine!"

"I imagine one thing—you had better watch your
language. 'They was,' indeed! If Mama hears you,
you'll be set to writing your lessons again."

Silvester reddened. "I was listening to Cross."

"Obviously."

On a chastened note, he continued. "A pavilion.
Must be what Mama called the folly, don't you think?
Before the flood. It was swept away downstream, so
Cross said."

"So we may forget the countess," said Jess briskly.
"If you think she would constantly walk between this
house and the folly, I feel you are mistaken. Perhaps
she haunts the folly, but not Oaklane."

"Why not?"

"In her worst days, I would judge that the countess
would not make use of a musky soap."

Not following well, Silvester said, "So?"

"So whatever, or whoever, was upstairs yesterday
was no ghost. Now, for goodness' sake, Silvester, stop
this nonsense. Mama is so distracted she cannot sleep.
It's bad enough for her to have had to give up Oakminster, but to move to a house where there are

reported to be tunnels and priest holes, and all that—really, Silvester, it's too much!"

Silvester suddenly donned a new air of maturity. "No ghost? Then, Jess, you made up that tale of coattails and all that just to annoy Ivor? And that smell. I didn't smell anything—"

Jess thrust angrily, "You can't smell anything but the stables, anyway!"

"Because you don't fool me, Jess. You've still got sheep's eyes for him, and just because he doesn't pay you all the deference you want—if you did this dying-away act yesterday just to get his attention, then you're the one to blame if Mama can't sleep!"

Stunned by the force of her brother's tirade, Jess restrained a strong desire to slap his face—to begin with! Instead, she merely stamped her foot childishly. "I did not make it up! Especially did I not make it up for Ivor! Why should I? He is nothing to me."

Silvester glanced at her out of the corner of his eye, and, surprisingly, chuckled. Even though she demanded that he tell her his thought, he refused. She might eventually have won out, she thought, but they were interrupted by a rumbling sound that seemed to come from behind the stables, on the farm road.

Spellbound, the two watched as a team of Belgians appeared, drawing the biggest farm wagon on the Bellamy estate. Riding on the wagon were half a dozen men belonging to the estate. They had been laughing and shouting to each other, but they fell silent when they caught sight of Jess and Silvester.

Silvester strode over to them as the wagon halted before the stables, and the men began to jump down to the ground, one after another. One, clearly the leader, detached himself from the group and came to meet Silvester.

"What are you doing, Yancey?"

"I don't rightly know," said the foreman, giving a careless salute, "but my instructions are to check the house over. Seems like rats been getting in? Perhaps you could show me, Mr. Silvester, where you saw them?"

"Nobody saw any rats!" protested Silvester.

Jess had joined him, and tugged at his sleeve. "Mama will be relieved to be assured that there is no way vermin can get into the house. After yesterday—"

"But that was not rats!" Her stern gaze compelled discretion, and he lapsed into silence.

"I'll show you," she told Yancey.

Jess watched through the morning, Silvester darting here and there to see what the carpenters were doing. He heard much to give him thought, and eventually he returned to Jess's side. In a low voice he told her, "Looks like Ivor believed you after all. He sent the men to close up ratholes."

Coolly she replied, "He is simply maintaining his property, as any good landowner would do."

"Come now Jess, don't be mean-spirited. It's not at all like you."

She glanced curiously at him. He was growing up fast, she realized with a surprising feeling of sadness. He was her little brother, the one who had come to her with his problems and at times his wild schemes, in many of which she had joined him. Philip was so much younger, and besides that, he was so lost in his books, that there had never developed the companionship that had grown up between Jess and Silvester.

"No, I think I am wrong," she said at last, "I think he must have believed me. At least he must have thought I saw *something*, and so he wishes to set Mama's mind at ease."

Jess noticed, however, even though she did not confide her thoughts to Silvester, that the men were checking and sealing windows. Rats, coming through windows? She had a fleeting vision of rats supporting other rodents on their backs, and the leader, at the top of the heap, working busily to raise the sash.

Obviously ridiculous!

But equally obvious was the notion that the house was being made burglarproof as well as sealed against vermin.

Clearly, and most satisfactorily, Ivor believed her!

Before the carpenters packed up their tools and swung aboard the wagon to return whence they came, Yancey came to report to Mrs. Dalton.

"Couldn't find much, ma'am," he told her. "Any road, we calked it all up tighter than a drumhead, and they won't be any vermin—or two-legged vermin *as* you might say—getting into this house!"

He grinned then, remembering the talk he'd heard in the kitchens at Oakminster. "Can't guarantee as much about ghosts, ma'am, nosiree!"

He backed out of the room, appalled by the reaction his simple jest had caused. For Mrs. Dalton had paled to the color of ashes and crumpled to the floor in a dead swoon!

13

Looking from her bedroom window, Jess saw the workmen, finished with their hammering and sawing, climbing into the big wagon. Her mother's fears should by now be allayed. Not the smallest field mouse could find a way into the house now.

At the bottom of the stairs, she paused. The foyer was empty, for even Oakminster had not been run on a grand scale, demanding the constant attendance of a footman in the hall to open and close doors.

Hearing a slight sound from the drawing room, Jess hurried to the door, expecting her mother to be within. Instead, a sight met her eyes that caused her to stop abruptly in the doorway and stare, a shriek trembling on her lips.

Yancey's back was toward Jess, and whatever he was doing was hidden from her. He appeared to be holding something—someone—in his arms.

Jess took a step into the room. He was holding, in what seemed to be an embrace . . . her mother!

How dared he! She crossed the room in a few strides and grabbed the man by the shoulder. The look of heartfelt relief on his features when he recognized Jess gave her pause.

"I'm glad to see you, Miss Jess. I dunno what I said, but all of a once your ma, that is I should say Mrs. Dalton here, keeled over like a shot pig." Hearing his own rude words hanging in the air, Yancey turned red. "I should'n said . . . But it struck me all of a heap, don't you see." His apology would have been more believable, thought Jess, if he were not still holding her mother in his arms.

However, Jess could see her mother was in a faint, and no doubt Yancey had done his best to help her. The outrageous suspicion that had come first to her was gone, and indeed the whole encounter had taken only moments.

"Put her down here, Yancey," said Jess, moving to the sofa and helping him to lay her mother gently on it, pulling the rumpled skirt decorously over her ankles and lifting her head gently to insert a pillow.

"Now then, you had better explain," suggested Jess.

"Well, now, I'm that glad to see you, Miss Jess. I didn't know what to do. But you don't want to hear that. I just told her," he said with a bewildered air, lifting his cap to scratch his head as though to stimulate thought, "I just said she didn't need to worry about vermin coming in."

Yancey, while not a notably quick thinker, decided that it was not necessary to mention his remark to Mrs. Dalton about ghosts. If Mrs. Dalton had fainted, Miss Jess might do the same were he to repeat it, or even worse, fall into a rage. Neither eventuality appealed to him.

But Jess had already fallen to her knees beside the sofa, and was looking anxiously at her mother's ashen face. Yancey, seeing that nothing further was required of him for the moment, made a hasty retreat, stopping in the kitchen long enough to tell Cross that he might just look in on the drawing room to see what was amiss.

Some moments later, Mrs. Dalton reluctantly opened her eyes. Truly, it had been so peaceful in that moment when she first came to herself, hearing voices she knew speaking at a muted distance, as she floated in space without conscious thought.

Now, having thoroughly awakened, she longed to return to oblivion. But the anxious looks of her children, even of Philip, who had come downstairs from his room, one finger still marking his place in his book, commanded her to consciousness.

To repeated demands to be told what was amiss,

what dire development had occurred in their absence, she answered only, "It's all my fault!"

She was assisted to sit up. Persistently urged to further explanation, she moaned, "I am so guilty. I should never have mentioned that foolish countess, if that's what she was, but of course she wasn't because *he* wasn't, if you understand me."

"Barely," said Jess, repressing impatience.

"But if I had not spoken of her to you, then she might well have rested quietly, and we would never have thought of her again."

"Mama! Surely you cannot believe you . . . brought her up, is I think the way they speak of it in the Bible?"

"Why not? If Saul could command the witch to bring up Samuel, then I see no reason why I, that is, other people, might not bring up others, of less eminence, of course. But after all, the principle is the same.

"What's the Bible got to do with your fainting?" asked Silvester, abruptly, because he had been very worried.

Jess, gratified to see that her mother was fast recovering her color, did not wait for an answer to Silvester. "But why would the countess come back to haunt us? We have done her no harm, and certainly wish her no ill."

"I don't know, Jess," said her mother crossly, "and I wish you will not continue to press me. I am guilty, if not of bringing the countess back to haunt her house, at least of leaving you alone in it. I shall never let all the servants go at once again, but I had promised them before I knew you had the headache."

To her rescue, unwittingly, rode Ivor Bellamy. The sound of hoofbeats on the drive brought the questioners up sharply, and Mrs. Dalton not for the first time breathed gratitude to her cousin.

"Henry is with him," announced Silvester without enthusiasm.

"What does he want?" snapped Jess. Her feelings toward Henry, once tolerant and even somewhat affectionate, had suffered greatly in the last weeks. She had claimed only this morning that he was an enormous bore, with his constant talk of his workmen and his factories. But on clearer assessment, she realized that this obsession of Henry's was of recent date. Before this topic had come to claim Henry's entire attention, he had been, if not exciting, at least companionable.

Jess regretted the change in him. She did not connect her present aversion to the reappearance of Ivor, and to the inevitable comparison between the two. Jess, if one believed what she said, was totally indifferent to Ivor.

Such indifference would not have been obvious to an observer as she greeted the two men now in the foyer.

"I am so glad to see you both," she said cheerfully, her eyes meeting Ivor's. "My mother is feeling not quite the thing, and she needs a diversion." And if anyone mentions the countess, she added silently, I shall simply pick up the poker and hit him.

Philip, noting with approval the arrival of a distraction, had escaped upstairs to his room, his finger still marking his place in his book. Silvester, covered with embarrassment at the tears that had sprung to his eyes when he saw his mother unconscious, had incontinently fled.

After the first expressions of civility from the visitors to Mrs. Dalton, Jess found herself seated next to Ivor on a small settee somewhat removed from the others. Under cover of their conversation, Jess said in the most innocent fashion she could manage, "Then you are not at home waiting to welcome your houseguest?"

Avidly she watched, through her eyelashes, for the least change of expression on his features. He did not know that she believed she had learned the whole of his secret, and she was anxious to see whether he would continue on his deceitful way with her.

He did. "I do not expect that he . . . that is, the expected party . . . will travel fast. I should be greatly surprised to see my . . . guest before quite late this afternoon." He allowed himself a gentle smile, as though thinking with delight of a lovely lady who would soon be with him.

Believing that his deliberate slip of the tongue had succeeded in misleading Jess on the gender of his approaching visitor, he eased away from the subject. "In any event, I could not refrain from inquiring about your mother's health. I hope she did not take any harm from our outing yesterday?"

"No, not at all," Jess told him. "But she has only a few moments ago recovered from a swoon. We were quite anxious, but she seems to be nearly herself again."

"Should you not have the doctor for her?"

"She does not wish to be physicked, and that is the first remedy Mr. Robbins thinks of. No, it was a reaction, I fear, from our disturbance yesterday." In case he did not remember, she added helpfully, "The incident of the stranger upstairs."

He frowned. "But surely she must be at ease now that the carpenters have seen to it there is no possible access for rats."

"Why don't you believe me?" she demanded. "I did see something upstairs."

"Did I not send workmen to correct the problem?"

"Indeed you did. And I am sure no rodent will dare to chew his way into the house. But I did think it queer that the men checked the windows. And," she added firmly, "the windows were already sealed."

"So I understand."

"But you thought it was only a . . . a creature."

"You have never," he said, an odd note in his voice, "been able to discern my thoughts, Jess."

If she could read his mind at this moment, he mused, she might spurn him forever, even if she were still of the same mind as formerly. He dared not move too swiftly. He was so far not seized with an impression that she would leap into his arms and declare her love for him if he gave her half a chance.

No, she was still to be won again.

Jess, more to conceal her thoughts than to tell the truth, murmured, "You are very kind to take such care of my mother. I truly am sure she will rest more easily now."

This seemed not to be the occasion on which to confide her mother's strong conviction that the countess had returned.

Ivor said, "I find it difficult to understand why you were entirely alone in the house yesterday. Silvester?"

"Out riding, as is his habit. He often goes out for the entire day."

"He should have his commission. In another year, perhaps, I will see to it. I consider him still a bit young."

"He has not spoken to you about the navy? Oh, I give up on him! I did not believe he could be so . . . so . . ."

"So forward? If he did not speak to me about his wishes, then whom would he ask? I am surely his nearest relation."

"My mother would grieve so."

After a few moments, in which Jess watched Henry speaking earnestly to her mother, Ivor returned to his original subject. "But no servants at hand, even though you felt ill?"

"One of the maids was in her room, but I vow she would sleep undisturbed if the roof fell in on her!" She did not wish to talk about her pretended headache.

Soon the conversation between Mrs. Dalton and Henry spread out to include Jess and Ivor, and after some time the gentlemen rose to take their leave.

Henry left first, and managed to speak to Jess in the hall. "My dear Jess, I wish you will not be anxious about Sir Ivor. He cannot force himself on you, you know."

"That is the last thing he would do!" exclaimed Jess. If there were bitterness in her voice, Henry did not notice.

"Nothing will harm you, Jess," he vowed. "I shall see to that."

He did not wait to answer her surprised questions. How could he see that no harm came to her? What kind of harm? Was he jealous of Ivor?

The only answer that came to her was that he was nerving himself to make an offer of marriage to her. She was appalled at the prospect. She could never marry him, but she could not hurt his feelings either. The only thing she could do was to avoid him, seeing him only in company.

Then she laughed at herself. Was she a ninny-hammer who thought that every man was eager to throw self and fortune at her feet?

She turned back, laughing, to find Ivor emerging from the drawing room. How long had he been standing there?

He gave no sign that he had overheard Henry's earnest reassurances. "I fear I must leave. My guest may already have arrived," he told her as she stepped with him to the door. "I really should not keep such an important guest waiting." His lips twitched, hiding his secret amusement. He could not resist toying with his Jess. "I shall introduce you at the first opportunity."

Jess smiled gravely. Introduce her to Giles Leighton, a man she had already met in London, would he? And watch her face fall in surprise, having expected to meet Ivor's intended bride? I think not!

She said simply, "I shall look forward to that," and watched, her features perfectly composed, as he mounted his stallion and cantered away down the drive.

14

Even before Ivor was out of sight down the avenue between the rows of tall oaks, Mrs. Dalton was in the hall.

"Have they gone? Good. Jess, I do hope you thanked Ivor for his promptness in sending his workmen to close up the wainscoting. He is so thoughtful. You know he does not allow a single day's delay before attending to our comforts. He is kind, Jess, and beyond reason accommodating. One does not find a gentleman of such address as considerate as he is, as a rule."

Unreasonably, Jess thought her mother's advocacy of their cousin was very much like treating with the enemy. Her mother should have realized that Jess could never be friends with the man who had once loved her, and now did no more.

Surely her mother understood her feelings? Mrs. Dalton was possessed at times of a shrewdness that bordered on the supernatural—a word that Jess wished she had not thought of, with the Italian countess perhaps watching them all from a vantage point. It was not in character at all for her mother to ignore Jess's bristling whenever Ivor came into view.

And even if Jess were at times very kind-spoken to him—it was only to lull him into unsuspicion, the better to bring him to his knees when the time came. Her plans were vague in the extreme. At first she thought to bring Ivor to a jealous seething, so that he would offer again and she could spurn him with well-chosen and acid words. However, Ivor had—perhaps —a love of his own to take her place.

There was no alternative in view. She could not use Henry. But suddenly her mother's slip of the tongue brought a new plan, full-fledged and without visible flaw. If Giles Leighton were coming down, as he certainly was, then a mild flirtation with him might serve.

"I wonder, Jess," her mother was saying, "whether he is being a good landlord, or whether he has another reason for visiting us so frequently?"

Her suggestion was accompanied by an arch look, so obvious that Jess had to laugh. "Mama, you cannot fool me for a moment. You are a born matchmaker, but I warn you your scheme will not work with me. I have seen Ivor, remember, when he was far from accommodating, and I promise you I did not have the same exalted opinion of him that you have." Her voice turned brittle. "He is not for me, Mama. We decided long ago we should not suit!"

Surprisingly, her mother agreed. "Of course not, my dear," she said comfortably. "I should never expect Ivor to offer for you again. His pride is too great."

What about my own pride? demanded Jess of herself. There was no answer.

"No," continued Mrs. Dalton, "I may be a matchmaker, but I have had much more experience than you, and it is perfectly clear that you and dear Ivor would not make a success of marriage. Gentlemen do not like a quarrelsome household."

"And you find me quarrelsome?" said Jess forlornly.

Mrs. Dalton turned and went into the drawing room again. Jess, as though drawn by a strong cord, followed her. Would the lady of Ivor's choice be restful? Of course she must be. Another word for "restful," at least in Jess's new lexicon, was "namby-pamby." Or "timid." Or "overly submissive." Or perhaps she was only concealing her true nature in order to trap Ivor!

Would Ivor be happy with someone so pliable? To Jess's sorrow, she must answer "probably," since he had already rejected her own spirited stand.

"How comfortable we will all be," said Mrs.

Dalton, picking up her embroidery, "with Ivor close by and *also* settled in a good marriage."

Jess was at a loss to understand her mother, until her memory presented her with a picture, from only a few minutes ago, of Henry speaking with earnest intent, and in a private voice, to her mother.

She dropped, appalled, into a chair opposite her mother. "I hope you do not mean what I think you mean."

"Now, where did I put my scissors?" demanded Mrs. Dalton, apparently addressing her embroidery. "Oh, there they are. Well, Jess, I have the greatest reluctance to see you unhappy. You well know I cannot take you again to London, certainly not before next year, since we will not be out of mourning until then. And if by then Ivor has made a match of it with someone else, then pray consider your position. It would be so clear to the *ton* that, having failed once, you were somewhat desperate in trying to find another husband."

"But, Mama—"

"No, no, Jess. I am quite sure that the match was broken off by your choice. However misguided you were. I am simply telling you what would be said in London."

"Mama!" cried Jess. "You shock me! I am *not* desperate! I have no need to put myself up for the highest bidder—or the only bidder. Just because Ivor and I did not suit . . ." Her voice died away, stifled by the strength of her indignation.

"Of course not, my dear. I daresay you would not think so far ahead, but you must agree that one can never underestimate the malice of a desperate dowager, warning against any rival of her own daughter's. Now, I myself will be perfectly content to have you live here with me. I shall be grateful for your help in launchng Althea, of course."

Mrs. Dalton snipped off a thread end with a satisfied air. Fully aware of the opinion of her family that she was not overburdened with intellect, she had found it more comfortable to accept their assessment rather than try to prove her own quality. If she were often resentful, or more frequently amused, none of her family knew it.

"But then, I do not wish to plan your life for you, my dear. Be assured I shall be glad of your company as long as you choose to live at home."

Stunned into expressing more of her true feelings than she had ever done before, Jess cried, "But what shall I ever do?"

With a practical air, Mrs. Dalton said, "There is always Henry. He will probably have a title before too long, for he told me his grandfather's health is failing daily. Can you not consider him?" Suddenly in earnest, she added, "Believe me, my child, to be satisfactorily settled in life is by far the happiest state possible. Marriage is a gamble, and one does not always win. But a good marriage settlement is far better than none."

After a bit, Jess recovered much of her good humor. "Was that what Henry was talking so privately to you about?"

"Suppose he was? Jess, you could do worse."

"But suppose Henry has doubts?"

"My dear, everyone in the house expects Henry to offer for you."

In this, Mrs. Dalton was mistaken. Her information was sadly out-of-date. Henry had been in the front running in the wagering in the servants' hall, not because Miss Jess gave any sign of a softer emotion than simple civility, but because Mr. Henry was the only eligible suitor at hand.

But there were those with a keen eye who noticed that Miss Jess had come to life as soon as Sir Ivor came upon the scene. And now the wagering was spirited and divided. At this moment, Sir Ivor was somewhat ahead in the odds.

Mrs. Dalton, deciding that she had said sufficient for the moment, diverted the conversation into other channels, leaving Jess to ruminate on her mother's words.

Indeed, Jess had much to think about. If she could only decide how to deal with revenging herself on Ivor, she might look upon Henry with a less jaundiced eye. On the other hand, she considered Henry much as one might look upon a rowboat tossing in heavy seas, while one's own ship was still well afloat.

Her dilemma stayed with her the rest of the day, and in the end kept her from sleep. Long after the rest of the household was wrapped in night-silence, she stared wide-eyed at the ceiling over her bed.

The night was windless, and she fancied she could hear the sound of the river streaming down toward its meeting with the Trent, somewhere above Hoveringham. She imagined the smooth glide of the water, since the river was too far away for her to hear, and in addition her bedroom was on the east, away from the river.

Once in a while a vagrant breeze stirred the leaves of the great oaks that girded the house, and, once or twice, a premature acorn dropped onto the roof with a soft thud.

She went over every word her mother had spoken that day, testing each one. Ivor was so kind, so thoughtful . . .

Jess was willing to accept her mother's opinion of him, since she herself had seen that Ivor took great pains to see to Mrs. Dalton's comfort. But the one phrase that came and stayed was: Ivor settled at Oakminster, and Jess herself married, doubtless to Henry.

Ivor "settled" meant Ivor wed. How could Jess, even

without Henry, live contentedly at Oakland knowing that Ivor was happy with his lady no more than two miles away?

And while Jess could chuckle over Ivor's idea of teasing her with the supposed advent of his intended bride, when his guest was only Giles Leighton, still it was inevitable that at some time Ivor would take a bride.

Jess threw off the covers. Suddenly she was hot, even feverish. The truth was that Ivor, happy with anyone but Jess, was unpalatable. That was a truth she did not wish to consider, particularly in the small hours of the night when reason is distorted and optimism has fled.

She would simply shut down her rambling thoughts, the thoughts that were so loud in her mind as to make her think she could hear them. She would wait until morning, and then take them out and dispose of them. She had had her chance, and—as her mother had also said—no gentleman asked twice.

Even as she commanded her thoughts to silence, she found they were still making small scrabbling sounds in her mind.

Nonsense! she thought, and raised herself on one elbow, the better to listen. The lengthening silence told her that her imagination was running rampant, and she was about to compose herself for sleep when she heard the scratching again.

It was the smallest of sounds, furtive, cautious. A mouse? The scratching turned suddenly into a muffled thump—a thump very close at hand. No mouse! A chill started at the nape of her neck and moved swiftly down, to paralyze her.

The sound had been almost in her room, she thought, straining her eyes into the darkness to see what she dreaded to see—a shadow darker against the night, a movement. There was nothing. For a moment, even the trees outside were quiet. In the obscurity there came, then, a tiny noise of movement. Later, when she had to put words to it, she recalled it as a kind of wood-sliding-on-wood noise.

But at that moment the sound was formless, and because of its vagueness was so alarming that she cried out, "Who's there?"

There was no response. The silence grew, and seemed so tangible until in her fancy she thought she might be able to reach her hand out and touch it.

She was in no mind to reach out and touch anything. Suddenly chilled, she clutched the eiderdown with rigid fingers for a time that could be measured in aeons rather than moments. At last, when she thought her heartbeat must be vibrating the very walls of Oaklane, she became aware of an alteration in the air. It was the unmistakable feeling of emptiness, and she knew she was now alone.

But if she had not been alone before, as she had had every right to expect, then . . . who had been in her room for that brief time?

Later she was to think how odd it was that, telling herself she heard only a mouse, she was moved to cry "Who's there?" instead of "What's that?"

Even knowing she was alone, she was unable to fall asleep until the twittering of birds reached her, and she knew the dark night was over.

15

In the sanity restored by the morning light, Jess was inclined to brush off her night's adventure as being the product of an overwrought mind. She had been feverish, and had thrown off the comforter. Her chill, only moments afterward, had of course been a simple reaction to the cold air.

However, it would do no harm to change bedrooms for the next few nights. She would say nothing about her fright, but simply claim that the morning sun woke her too early. She sent Meggie in to make up the bed, while she began to move her clothing from the wardrobe to a large chest in her new room.

When she came to help Meggie, she was astounded to find the girl in tears.

"What in the world, Meggie? Surely you don't mind helping me remove into this room?" Then, recalling Cook's disposition, she added, "Trouble in the kitchen? You know Cook, she'll get over her temper in no time."

"Not Cook, Miss Jess." Meggie wiped her eyes with her sleeve. "It's just that . . . well, now look at that. Mr. Cross will be sure I did it, and Miss Jess, I never!"

Meggie pointed to the chest. It stood against the wall, and appeared not to have been moved. Jess pushed it, and the marks of the legs on the carpet were sharp and of long standing.

"Done what, Meggie? This chest looks all right."

Meggie gulped down a sob. "Not the chest, Miss Jess. See the top? They's wax all over it. Candle wax. And Mr. Cross will say I didn't clean it good when we redded up before we moved in. And I did!"

It was clear that a candlestick had stood upon this chest. Jess could see the round shape as outlined by gouts of tallow. Thoughtfully she scored the wax with a fingernail. Soft—this wax had not defaced the surface of the chest for long.

"Never mind, Meggie. This happened after you cleaned it. I shall tell Cross if the subject comes up."

She eyed the girl with speculation. Could she ask the questions that were springing to her mind without sending her into hysterical panic? Meggie was prone to emotional upheavals, and Mrs. Cross would not thank Jess if she frightened her into flight.

"You did clean all the furniture in the bedrooms?" she began. By delicate steps, she learned more than she had wanted to. There was the small table in Jess's bedroom—that had not been in the house when Meggie had first come. A rocking chair had suddenly come to rest in Miss Althea's room. And from somewhere had appeared a candlestick and two lanterns in the kitchen. Mrs. Cross had scolded her husband for bringing in such dirty articles for her to clean, although of course it was Meggie who actually set brush to work.

After the room was made ready, and Jess's belongings had been transferred, Jess had leisure to think. And her thoughts were not at all pleasant.

Furniture had come unheralded into the house. And since Ivor had seen to it that the house was vermin-proof and burglarproof, some other explanation must be found. She dismissed the noises in the night, and the impression she had had that someone was in the room with her. An overwrought emotional state—that was it, as manifested by the feverish feeling followed by chill.

Her thoughts roamed over the possibilities that would explain the odd increase in the furnishings of Oaklane, and pounced at last upon the solution. She recalled well the argument she had had with Ivor on the subject of the items to be brought to Oaklane from the manor.

Only a day or two ago Ivor had mentioned the

uncluttered rooms, saying that Jess herself had chosen what he called the Spartan look. And Ivor—without a doubt—had chosen to alter the situation!

Jess had experienced by now a great sufficiency of the domineering attitude of her onetime love. He had always been arrogant, which must have been expected of a young man who had wealth far beyond his needs and a coterie of servants and relatives who had believed, in spite of substantial evidence to the contrary, that the sun rose in him.

The trouble that had flared up four years ago between Jess and Ivor was quite simply that she had refused to join the adoring throng around him. So she told herself now, marching along the country lane that led from Oaklane to the manor, fuming with every step she took. However much he had taken on himself with regard to the future of Mrs. Dalton, seeing that she was well-housed, and even making her an allowance in his capacity as head of the Bellamy family, he had not recommended himself in any way to Jess herself.

Through discreet questioning of her mother this morning, she had learned that the table which had appeared upstairs in her own bedroom had not done so with her mother's knowledge. Therefore, and there was no other answer, Ivor had simply, and in a characteristically high-handed manner, sent it from Oakminster to fill up empty spaces in Oaklane, without so much as a word to her mother or to Jess herself.

Well, such outrageous disregard of her wishes must stop!

Jess had told Ivor they had furniture enough. With the cleaning of the walls before the Daltons moved in, nearly all traces of the existence of former articles of furniture were erased. She liked the more austere look of their new house, as did her mother, and felt no lack because the rooms were not crammed with the accumulations of some bygone generations.

And she had told Ivor so. Now, as it seemed, he did not take her opinions at all seriously. He thought the Daltons should have more furniture, ergo, it was provided!

Jess possessed, even though she would not admit it even to herself, an underlying need to make some kind of impression on Ivor. Even a small dent—preferably on the crown of his head!—would give satisfaction. How totally degrading it was to speak and believe you were attended to, only to learn that either he had not bothered to listen or that he thought her opinions so worthless as not to be worth arguing over! Either way, he was impossible!

She walked faster and faster, trying to keep time with her thoughts. She turned into the drive at Oakminster, past the gate lodge. She noticed that the shrubbery, which had grown up unattended for some years around the building itself, had been trimmed, and a beginning made in improving the environs—the gravel drive weeded and raked.

The lodge itself was taking on an air of comfort. Doubtless Ivor was planning to install a gatekeeper, whose sole purpose in life was to watch for the comings and goings of Sir Ivor Bellamy. How useless!

She had reached the sweeping curve that would in a few yards bend once more and debouch on the drive before the entrance of Oakminster before she saw where her speculations had taken her. She stopped short in the middle of the drive, appalled.

Her imagination displayed for her edification a long series of weeks and months, even years, of Ivor's comings and goings, here at Oakminster. Ivor, and in due course Lady Dorine, whoever she might be . . . and children. . . .

And all right here, under Jess's very nose, flaunting his love and his growing family and his contentment in front of her. She could not bear it, she really could not! To see every day the evidence of what she was missing —to know that Ivor had never loved her, or he would have come after her when she retired to the country four years ago . . .

No! She would not bear it!

She stood in the middle of the drive, heedless of her surroundings, and let the tears come, hot on her cheeks, blurring her vision, and changing her anger into a far more desolate sense of utter loneliness.

How had it happened that she had reached such a state? How could she ever have believed that happiness might be hers without Ivor at her side? Or, she thought wryly, across the table blazing with anger, as he had been in that quarrel that had destroyed their betrothal.

Arrested now by memory, she was aware that that last quarrel was as vivid in her mind at this moment as though it had occurred an hour ago. Deliberately she plucked the details out of her memory and examined them.

She had thought she had buried all the unhappiness, during all the years in between. But no—it was right here, plain as could be. She had objected to the Cyprian in Ivor's life. She had just discovered, by an unfortunate and accidental eavesdropping, that a female of the demimonde enjoyed Ivor's favors. Not only in the past, she had learned, but to that very day!

And so, rejoicing in her position as the affianced bride of Sir Ivor Bellamy, and secure in the influence on him that she believed herself to wield, she had objected, even demanded—such was her innocence then!—that he give the woman her *conge* at once.

Ivor, at first amused, became grave. He taunted her with the stinging accusation that she was naive to a degree. In truth, he had countered her demands with a pointed suggestion that she had in some way fallen far short of his expectations, since no young lady as well-bred as she claimed to be would have any knowledge of that other world in which gentlemen moved, to say nothing of speaking of it in what was, after all, mixed company!

Besides—and this was the final cruel blow that had sent her reeling—he informed her that he had been going to rid himself of the Cyprian upon his marriage, but since Jessamine had made such an issue of it, he would keep the woman on as long as he wished. It was of no use for Jessamine to nag at him, for he would not be dictated to by a female, even though she might be his affianced bride.

"Very well," Jess had said waspishly, and the words echoed sharply in memory even now as she stood under the sheltering trees along the Oakminster drive, "then you will have no further concern along that line, for our betrothal is at an end!"

To give him his due, he had called several times at the Dalton house in Portland Square, but she would not see him, and at length he called no more. She could not eat or sleep, and fell into a fever. Her mother had brought her back to Grandfather's at Oakminster to recover. Jess had not seen Ivor since, until this horrid development of his inheriting the Bellamy estates had occurred.

Eventually, there on the drive, she came to herself. Her wish to challenge Ivor on the subject of the mysteriously appearing furniture had vanished. Her sense of humor, never far away, returned, although in a bleak fashion. There were two ways to deal with Ivor and his approaching marriage and his probable continuing proximity. One was quite simply to seize the closest blunt weapon and use it with purpose. The other was to convince her mother to remove to Bath, or Scarborough, or London, or . . .

Unbidden, a third solution leapt into her mind. She could quite easily follow her mother's suggestion and marry Henry. It was in the nature of things that his grandfather would soon leave his mortal remains behind, including substantial wealth and an ancient and respected title. If the family were tainted by a long-ago marriage into trade, the flaw had long since been forgotten by most persons, and the money which poured into the Hartnell coffers was accepted without question as to its provenance.

Marriage to Henry was of course a good solution, even the best possible solution if Ivor were to marry soon. Jess would be very comfortably off, and as a titled lady would have much consequence in the district. Also, of course, the price to be exacted from Jess by this marriage was impossibly high!

She was so engrossed in her own thoughts that she failed to hear footsteps approaching on the gravel from the direction of the house.

"Good morning," spoken in a pleasant voice, was her first intimation that she was not alone. "Good heavens, it's . . . it's Miss Dalton, surely? I have been looking forward to seeing you again."

She stared at him without recognition for a few moments. She saw a well-proportioned man of middle height, not so tall as Ivor, and as fair of complexion as Ivor was dark. His eyes were of a pleasant blue, and his light-brown hair was dressed simply.

Smiling at her, he added, "Of course you will not remember me. I am Giles Leighton, and we have met before. In London."

"Of course," she said, instantly offering her hand. "I remember you perfectly well." Remembering her mother's slip of the tongue, she continued, inaccurately, "I had not expected to see you here, Mr. Leighton, or I would have known you at once."

"I arrived only yesterday, quite late. I was delayed by an accident—no, no, not to me. I came upon a stagecoach, overturned at the bottom of a hill, some- where south of here. The fool driver thought he could descend the slope with a full complement of baggage without putting on the drag-shoes at the top. Of course the coach ran out of control and there was naught but wreckage left at the bottom."

"The passengers?"

"They had left the coach at the top of the hill. It seems that the driver is well known for his headlong descents of that very hill, and none of them chose to ride down with him."

"I wonder someone has not prevented him from driving, if he is so careless."

Dryly Gies told her, "I think that the sight of their coach as so much painted kindling may succeed in awakening his employers to their duty. But I should not have spoken of such an unpleasant episode to a young lady. My apologies, ma'am."

With a wave of her hand, his excuses were accepted and dismissed from mind. Even as she had listened to his narrative, her thoughts, following their own line of country, had tumbled madly, but to some purpose. Ivor had led her to believe that his expected guest was the Lady Dorine, although he had told her mother that Giles Leighton was arriving.

That Ivor was devious was not news to her. But she could not at once divine his purpose in this ploy. But perhaps she could find out—and, armed with such knowledge, might turn the tables on him. How satisfying that would be!

"Did you come alone, Mr. Leighton?" she asked innocently.

Somewhat mystified, he answered, "Yes, except of course for my man and a groom."

Daringly Jess inquired, "Then Lady Dorine will be following soon?"

Now greatly bewildered, Giles nearly betrayed his friend. "Lady Dor . . . ?" he began, before he recalled that whimsical and brandy-sodden conversation he and Ivor had held just before Ivor departed for Oakminster. The fool! thought Giles, exasperated. He surely didn't go through with that idiotic scheme! And without putting me on my guard, either!

But of course, Ivor had done just that. The proof was standing here before him in the attractive form of a golden-haired girl with deep blue eyes.

"Oh, yes, Lady Dorine," he said manfully, trying to retrieve his *gaffe*. "She will, I believe, be coming soon. I do not know precisely what her plans are."

Jess was no fool. While she might be young enough to toss away a grand *parti* on a missish whim—as she had later decided—she was quick of mind. Giles's hesitation and awkward recovery had given her something to think about. It seemed exceedingly clear that Giles Leighton had not an intimate acquaintance with Lady Dorine—supposedly his great friend's chosen bride.

It might have been that Giles did not expect Jess to be aware of the lady's existence, but Jess thought she could not be mistaken. Giles's mystification was genuine. And now Jess, in the grip of sudden enlightenment, would have bet a groat that Lady Dorine was of no moment in Ivor's life, no matter how strongly he might have hinted about her importance to him. In fact, it was within possibility that she did not even exist.

Ivor had done it again! And this time it was worse. When they quarreled before, on the subject of Ivor's *petite amie*, only Jess and Ivor knew the details. But now he had made her out a fool in the eyes of Giles Leighton. Giles would realize that she was concerned about a possible rival, and he would return to the manor and relate his amusing tale to Ivor, and they would enjoy a hearty laugh at her expense.

At that moment, if a suitable weapon and the victim had both been at hand, she would have enjoyed carrying out the first of the alternatives she had considered less than an hour before.

Giles was speaking when she again paid heed to

him. "Are you coming up to the house? If I may walk with you . . ."

"Thank you. I think I shall do better to write a note to Ivor. He will have time then to consider his answer," she improvised.

Giles turned with her and walked as far as the gates. There he glanced toward the refurbished lodge. "I suppose you will be moving back to the manor house when Ivor returns to London?"

"Oh, no," said Jess, her eyes deep blue with anger, "I am sure Ivor expects to make Oakminster his primary country seat. We are all quite looking forward to it, I assure you."

She left him there, turning into the country road that led back to Oaklane. She did not turn around, but she fancied she could feel his eyes boring into her back, in speculation, or, a horrid possibility, in compassion.

She would never forgive Ivor—never!

16

While Jess was stepping smartly down the road, working off her irritation with Ivor by physical exertion, still out of sight but approaching swiftly, came a coach and entourage sufficiently elegant to stop an onlooker in stupefaction.

Cleo, Lady Chicester, traveled lightly. Only the barest necessities were brought with her on her journey north from London. She scoffed at the elaborate preparations always made by her mother-in-law, whose ideas of what was due to her elevated status resulted in a procession remarkably like a Tudor royal progress. The dowager had required her own bed linen, since inns no matter how well kept were apt to harbor dampness in the beds. Her favorite chair, her own plate and serving dishes, even her own steward accompanied her on even the shortest journey.

The coach now on the road, having traveled the few miles from the Flying Horse Inn in Nottingham this morning, was, in comparison with the dowager's, almost inconsequential, having only four outriders (armed and well-mounted), two footmen, a coachman, and a groom. Within the comfortable coach sat Lady Chichester and her husband's pensioned cousin, Beatrice Berwick, to serve as companion. Cleo's maid, Stokes, was consigned to the backward-facing seat, sitting bolt upright with an air of martyrdom in every muscle.

Not for the first time, Beatrice gave voice to her worries. "I shall be pleased when we arrive at Scarborough," she said. "I dread the thought of Sir Ivor's dislike of guests coming unexpectedly upon him. Will our arrival not overcrowd the household?"

"I think not. As I recall, Oakminster is quite spacious."

"But I must suppose that since we will stay only overnight before resuming our journey, Sir Ivor will not be discommoded."

Cleo smiled at her. She had a kind of affection for her husband's cousin, to whom they had given a home and an allowance when she was left without resources, and in the main tolerated her fussy anxieties. Indeed, Cleo was more often amused than irritated, as she was now.

"Dear Beatrice, do you really think we are going on to Scarborough? I have no need to suffer those ill-tasting waters, nor do I find the assemblies in the least entertaining."

Beatrice gasped. "Not Scarborough? But—"

"No, my dear, we shall claim my brother's hospitality for a time. No, no, don't ask me, for I do not know how long we shall stay."

Beatrice squeaked. "Sir Ivor will take such a dislike to me, I am sure of it. After all, I am no kin of his, and you have told me that he is not overfond of Charles. Dear Cleo, are you sure this visit is wise?"

Cleo gave her companion a shrewd glance. "Did Charles talk to you before we left? I suspect he gave you instructions to keep me from meddling, did he not? Well, I hope I may visit my brother anytime I wish?"

Beatrice, not wishing to distress Cleo, and wishing even less to confess that Charles had said nothing to her on the subject of trying to guide Cleo in the way he thought she should go, fell silent. It had been her own observation that Cleo had a well-developed tendency to meddle, but she had received nothing but kindness from her cousin and his wife, and to criticize would be most unbecoming—as well as giving her benefactors cause to wish her elsewhere than in their household.

Unfortunately, thought Cleo, her companion's

silence gave her occasion to consider her current situation. Her thoughts turned back to the moment, only four days ago, when she had informed Charles of her intention to journey north.

"So soon?" Charles had said in surprise. Then, with concern, he demanded, "You are not feeling well?" She was prepared for this question, but surprisingly her answer did not seem to be convincing. "I thought so. I know I have been engrossed in this sitting at Westminster, but I think I should have noticed any fading away on your part."

"Fading away! Charles, I never fade away when I am ill."

"Only when you are *feigning* illness, my dear." He leaned back in his chair and eyed her thoughtfully. "You are clearly healthy. Therefore there is another reason for your plans. Let me think. . . . No one could possibly have insulted you so that you wish to drop out of society for the moment."

"How do you know that, Charles?"

"I have never seen a lady you could not instantly put in her place. And if you wish to take the waters for some unknown reason, why not Bath?" He fell silent for a moment. "Is it," he said at last, "more than a coincidence that your brother's new inheritance lies not far from the road to Scarborough? Aha! I have you, my dear wife!"

"I should have known," said Cleo as sadly as though she had not led him to this knowledge, "I could not deceive you for a moment." She went around the desk and bent to kiss him. "Can you not go with me? I shall miss you."

He returned her kiss with enthusiasm. "I shall hardly know how to go on without you, my dear, but this wretched government is doing some reprehensible things—setting spies on Englishmen—and I cannot approve. I really must stay here."

"Spies? Oh, I know—those workers in the north.

But how can you stop the government, Charles?"

He merely smiled, clearly keeping his own counsel. "Ivor won't like your meddling, you know. And I confess I should like to know myself just what you intend to do. Get him married? I wish you joy of that!"

Thus challenged, Cleo admitted that she did not know what she planned. Ivor was unhappy, she knew that. And he was now in close proximity to the lady he had once asked to marry him. There would be fireworks again, or she did not know her brother. She recalled that last conversation with him. An idea had struck him then, even as she watched, and she did not trust that wicked gleam in his eye.

Curiosity as much as distress now led her north.

"I suppose," said Charles, "I shall be able to reach you at Oakminster, in case of need? You will likely arrive in two days, I imagine."

"My dear, you must not worry. I shall simply stop at Oakminster overnight."

Charles laughed outright. "If you need me," he said, "I will come! Ivor might be a handful for you."

While Charles had not been able to come with her, he had insisted on the armed escort, and, although she did not know it, the footmen and the groom both had loaded weapons within reach as they trundled through the insecure roads of what was becoming a mill-dominated region.

But the discontented millworkers were far from Cleo's mind as she considered her reasons for coming north to Oakminster. She had no clear idea of what could be done to ease Ivor's unhappiness, nor did she really think it her duty to arrange the conduct of his life for him. Even if that were possible!

One thing she did know: No matter what Charles's instructions were, if interference in Ivor's affairs were called for, then interference would take place.

*   *   *

At that moment, the coach rounded a bend, and Jess caught sight of it. It did not take a practiced eye to note that the team pulling the equipage were prime cattle, and the number of outriders seemed excessive. Two mounted men preceded the carriage, and Jess stepped to the verge out of their way. As they slowed, she could see they were armed, heavily.

The vehicle could be going nowhere else on this road but to Oakminster. Jess, for all her prior skepticism, leapt at once to the conclusion that here, in enormous style, arrived Ivor's intended bride—come, no doubt, to examine Oakminster to see whether it were fit to live in!

Lady Dorine did exist, then—and here she was!

The coach slowed, and lumbered to a stop, the coach door exactly opposite. Jess felt a constriction in her chest that would doubtless impede any word she might say.

The lovely face looking out of the window was in a way familiar. When the lady spoke, Jess's doubts were dissolved.

"My dear Jessamine! How fortunate to have come upon you in just this way. William, why do you not have the steps ready for me? Jessamine, do not leave, for I must speak to you. William!"

The steps were provided with alacrity, and the door opened. The lady stepped down, and Jess knew her at once. "Lady Chichester! How . . . how unexpected!"

"Yes," said that lady with bubbling good cheer, even after having traveled for two days and slept, not well, in commercial inns. "But you were used to call me Cleo, you know?"

"Y-yes, of course."

"But . . . shall we walk a ways? I cannot take you up in my coach, for you must know Beatrice Berwick—do you remember her? . . . Charles's cousin—is within and, I think, asleep."

Jess, overwhelmed by the flood of good cheer that

Ivor's sister poured out, could find only the barest words. "Yes, I do recall her. I hope she is well? And you, of course?"

Brushing off Jess's inquiries, since Cleo always enjoyed rude good health, and Beatrice, as a matter of course, entertained various ailments, Cleo slipped her hand through Jess's arm, and they moved out of earshot of the carriage. The coachman gestured to one of the armed men, and the rear guard, so to speak, moved to keep the ladies within sight.

• "You go for walks often?" asked Cleo, looking around her with some distaste. "On dusty roads? I should have thought Oakminster had many attractive walks."

"It does," said Jess crisply. "However, I am on my way home."

"Home?" Cleo was bewildered. "But, do I have my directions wrong? I was under the impression that Oakminster lay just ahead. Surely we did not pass any house of consequence!"

"But we do not live at Oakminster," said Jess. She was unhappy over Cleo's arrival, although she did not kow precisely why. She had been much relieved to see that the arriving guest was not Lady Dorine, but only Ivor's sister. She was still angry with Ivor, and even with Giles. She would have walked off her ill temper, but she was still in the throes of strong irritation, and she was puzzled. Why was Cleo here?

Unless—the unwelcome thought occurred to her—Cleo was here to chaperon Ivor and his intended bride? Involuntarily her lips tightened, and she frowned.

"Good heavens!" cried Cleo, noting Jess's displeasure. "He did not throw you out into the road?"

"No, of course not," said Jess. "We are living in one of the estate houses, down that road." She pointed to the mouth of the Oakland drive. "We are . . . very comfortable."

"I wish you will not try to bam me, Jess. You are not in the least comfortable. Oh, well, perhaps the roof does not leak, and your mother may like the prospect, if there is one—and how is your mother? I remember cousin Elizabeth with affection." Upon being reassured that Mrs. Dalton was indeed well, Cleo went on. "Although you and I have not known each other as well as I would like, that is a misfortune we may remedy at once. I fancy I can discern an angry lady when I see one. What has Ivor done now?"

Jess had had no one her own age and quality in whom to confide for longer than she remembered. Cleo's bright eyes, so different from Ivor's, fixed on her in affection and lively curiosity, moved Jess strangely. Suddenly she was impelled to trust Cleo.

Thankfully, she unburdened herself. "I just now came from the manor. I told him I did not want any more furniture, that we were fine with my mother's things, but no—he won't believe me, nor does he even listen! Even though it was Giles, and I am going back to write a note that will singe his ears! His eyes, rather, reading it."

Cleo, usually adept at the kind of comprehension that leaps from peak to peak without puzzling out the valleys, was baffled. Jess's words were recognizable, but they were put together in a totally unfamiliar way. "Jess," she said gently, "perhaps if you started at the beginning, I might understand you." She glanced back at the carriage. The coachman was walking the horses, and she knew he would be furious at the delay. However, first things first.

"We are living at Oaklane," Jess said slowly.

"Why not at Oakminster? That was your home, was it not?"

"Yes, but Ivor said it would not be proper for a formerly betrothed couple to abide under the same roof."

"Good heavens, your mother was there!"

"I pointed that out. Also, I mentioned—merely in passing, you know, for I would not presume to disagree with him!—that if he found living in Oakminster with my family a scandalous notion, he needed only to return to London or to the priory or wherever, to avoid any malicious rumors."

Cleo was not oblivious of the bitterness in Jess's voice, nor of another quality she could not quite be sure of. But Cleo's talents, much appreciated by her husband, lay in her acute perceptions of people and their inner thoughts.

Now she was certain of a few things about her brother. Judging from Jess's complaints, Ivor had every intention of staying at Oakminster. Since he had an excessively comfortable house in London, and his favorite country house was the priory, large, well-run, and pleasantly situated, he must have a reason for staying on here. And that purpose might well be getting Jess back.

Cleo, looking with affection at the girl beside her, thought Ivor would be fortunate indeed to marry Jess. Cleo had liked her from the beginning and had looked forward to a closer connection with her. Noting Jess's wide, dark blue eyes, and the unhappy vulnerability that lay in their depths, Cleo instantly scrapped her allegiance to her brother and came down firmly on Jess's side.

Something must be done, and if she had had any doubts previously about descending upon her brother, they had flown. Cleo saw clearly she must take a hand. Men were difficult, of course, but there were ways of dealing, and Jess must learn them—at Cleo's hand, of course.

Turning back, and murmuring that the cattle must not be left to stand, she took her farewell of Jess. "I shall be over to call on Cousin Elizabeth at my earliest opportunity," she told Jess. "Please give her my compliments."

"Then you are staying at Oakminster?"

"Wild animals could not prevent me," Cleo reassured her honestly.

"Of course, you must chaperon Lady Dorine," murmured Jess.

Cleo's answer was direct. "Whom?"

Jess resumed her tedious walk home to Oaklane. Cleo's questions had stirred up a tumult in her mind, as if someone with a long pole had dug into silt at the bottom of a pond and turned the water murky.

Ivor's sister had come on a prolonged visit. Clearly she must be here as a chaperon for the intended guest, Lady Dorine. But Cleo had not recognized the name.

With a huge sigh, Jess consigned Ivor and Dorine and everyone else whose very existence plagued her to perdition, at least temporarily, and turned her thoughts deliberately to her thwarted errand at Oakminster.

Furniture appeared at Oaklane, stealthily, without prior notice. This had to be Ivor's doing, for no one else in the house admitted knowledge of the phenomenon.

There was candle wax on surfaces that had no contact with candles—at least that she knew. And Ivor must be to blame here also, even though she did not quite see how.

She had told Giles that she would write a note to Ivor. She began to plan what she would say. "Dear Sir Ivor," she would begin. She walked steadily on, her pace quickening at times as she thought of particularly telling phrases. "Soon you will have sufficient interests at hand . . ." Would he know she referred to his marriage to Dorine? ". . . to keep you occupied, but in the meantime, I should appreciate it were you to refrain from exercising your idle thoughts by way of harassing me!" Or would "interfering" be better?

The missive worded at last as she wished, she wrote

it at once upon returning to Oaklane, lest she forget the fine turns of phrase she had concocted, and sent a groom off to the manor with it.

She found her mother in the drawing room. Mrs. Dalton's thoughts were not on the handiwork in her lap. Instead, she gazed at some distant prospect not visible to Jess.

Jess bent to kiss her mother's cheek before sitting down. "You will not guess whom I met on the road," she said.

Her mother returned from whatever she had been, and said with an accusing air, "I miss Althea. I shall write to send for her."

Jess was dismayed. However prosaic might be the explanations for some of the odd occurrences in Oaklane, still she was uneasy, and did not know why. But she was reluctant to bring Althea home until it was settled—even though she did not know what "it" was.

"Remember the countess . . ." murmured Jess.

Her mother paled. "Yes, of course. I had forgotten. But I do miss her—Althea, I mean, not the countess."

"And so do I," agreed Jess.

17

Ivor's delight at the arrival of his sister and her entourage was so muted as to be invisible. The confusion that followed upon the unheralded arrival of a team of prime cattle as well as mounts for the armed guards, eight male servants, and an elegant carriage soon settled into disciplined bestowal of man and beast.

Lady Chichester stood on the top step of the Oakminster entry and tilted her head charmingly. "La, Ivor, now tell me you are glad to see me, after I have come all this way."

"I should have known," said her brother cryptically. "Does Charles know where you are?"

"Of course. I am on my way to take the waters at Scarborough. Will you not invite me in?"

She recognized the man who had come to stand behind Ivor. "Mr. Leighton!" She offered him her hand. "Do you have any influence with Ivor? I vow I have never seen anyone so rude."

"If I know you," said Ivor, overriding Giles's civilities, "you have come to take a hand in what is in no conceivable way your business."

"All I want," said Cleo, laughing, "is a cup of tea. And here is Beatrice Berwick, Ivor. You cannot believe *she* is about to interfere in your bachelor life."

Ivor crossed the drive and offered his arm to Beatrice. "I am delighted to see you," he told her. "Pray come in and I shall send at once for refreshments."

Once in the salon, refreshed by two cups of tea each and an assortment of frivolous confections conjured up by Ivor's French chef, Cleo smiled. She had been in truth quite taken aback by Ivor's savage hint that she was not at all welcome.

What was Ivor up to? She knew as well as she knew her name that he was troubled. If winning Jess were all that lay heavily on his mind, the solution was clear. For Jess, Cleo believed, was as ready to capitulate, to fall headlong into his arms, as ever lady was.

Later, when Beatrice had already been shown to her room, and Stokes, having already unpacked Lady Chicester's clothes, stood ready to lead the way for Cleo, Ivor stopped his sister just inside the salon door.

"Now, Cleo, forgive me for my boorishness when you arrived. I am truly pleased to see you, even if only for overnight."

"Overnight? Whatever gave you that impression?"

"You said," said Ivor as though dealing with a child, "that you were going to Scarborough to take the waters."

"It must be seeing you again, Ivor, for I am feeling much better now. I do not think the waters will do me as much good as simply relaxing here in the quiet of the country. Charles is so occupied, you know, with this foolish matter of the millworkers, wherever they are, and I do not like to stay home alone."

"And of course you have been going from one entertainment to another," said Ivor. "I wonder Charles allows it."

Cleo laughed merrily. "Do you think that Charles would try to govern me? I think not."

Surprisingly, Ivor joined her in laughter. "I should have known better. Charles, after all, does have some common sense. I know you think I do not like him, but I do respect his acumen."

"How kind," murmured Cleo, taken aback.

Suddenly serious, Ivor took her arm. "Believe me, Cleo, you are above all others the most welcome guest I could have. You are to stay as long as you wish. But let me give you a word of warning."

"Warning?" echoed Cleo.

"Do not meddle."

"But what is there to meddle in?" she asked innocently.

He did not answer directly. "Believe me, I know what I am doing."

"I hope so," said Cleo doubtfully, pulling her arm away.

She had reached the bottom of the stairway, following Stokes upstairs, when she turned and said, with an air of great reasonableness, and a glint of mischief in her eyes, "I wonder you did not send for me, Ivor. I am certainly willing to stay and chaperon Lady Dorine."

She thoroughly enjoyed the look of utter stupefaction on Ivor's face.

"When is she coming, Ivor? I cannot wait to meet her!"

Ivor's plan to win Jessamine back, a scheme in which he had not previously detected any flaw, was rapidly falling to pieces around him.

Even Cleo, to whom he had not given the slightest hint of his dreams, was astoundingly well-informed. How had she heard of the mythical Lady Dorine? Ivor started up the stairs after her, determined to elicit an explanation from her, but halted midway.

"Wait, Ivor!" said Giles Leighton, looking up at his friend. Giles had been forgotten as Ivor and Cleo sparred, Ivor seeking to deflect Cleo's overweening interest in his affairs, and Cleo determined to take Jess's part if the slightest need arose.

Ivor paused, frowing at Giles. "That sister of mine!"

Giles gave a short laugh. "Ivor, do you think your sister will tell you anything she does not intend you to know? Come into the study. I've something to tell you."

Reluctantly abandoning his intention to choke the truth out of Cleo, a method that had served him well when they were toddlers, Ivor came slowly down the stairs and preceded Giles into his study. Giles closed the door behind them.

"No need for your servants to hear, although I suspect they are better informed than you are."

Ivor stood at the window, half turned away from his friend. How everyone seemed to know just what he ought to do next! As though he could not manage his own affairs! He had his hands full, trying to drive Jess into exhibiting some kind of jealousy, an emotion that implied a more serious emotion behind it.

"Well, Giles, what is it I should know?"

"I saw your expression when Lady Chichester mentioned Lady Dorine."

"So?"

"So I had not thought you had adopted that mad scheme! It is time for plain speaking, Ivor, and as your friend—at least for the moment, although I imagine you will like to shoot the messenger!—I must tell you that if you think you can deceive Miss Dalton with this havey-cavey plot, you are much mistaken!"

Stung, Ivor rasped, "Nonsense! She is daily expecting me to announce my betrothal to Lady Dorine!"

"Is she truly? Then why is it when I met her on the drive only an hour ago, she bore not the slightest resemblance to a jealous woman?"

"What? On the drive? Was she coming here? What was her errand?"

"I do not know. She decided against it, however. I suppose she changed her mind after she had asked me about the Lady Dorine."

"She asked you? And you foolishly think she is not interested?"

"I did not say that, Ivor. I said I did not think she appeared *jealous*. In fact, she had a very satisfied look when she turned back toward home."

"What did you say about the Lady Dorine? I hope you mentioned that she was brunette. Jess was always envious of raven-black hair, she told me once."

"I told her no such thing!" retorted Giles righteously. "How could I, when no such woman exists? Ivor, I despair of you!"

"And so you might," agreed Ivor. "I imagine your ignorance of the lady appeared on your honest face? I should have warned you."

Giles was rightly angry. "I imagine you did not, for you know I should not have gone along with your scheme!"

"But how did Cleo know about Dorine?" mused Ivor. A thought struck him. "When did you say you met Jess?"

"Hardly an hour since."

"Then . . . Aha, that must be it! Cleo met Jess on the road! If I know my sister, she has ruined all!"

"And a good thing, too," said Giles with some heat.

After Giles had left him alone—with a spirited injunction to mend his ways—Ivor slumped into the chair behind the desk and closed his eyes.

To his surprise, he was more than a little grateful for the sudden demolishing of his scheme to make Jess jealous. He truly had a higher opinion of her perception than to believe he might deceive her for more than a day.

That his scheme had succeeded even this far was due to her recent bereavement and the move to Oaklane that Ivor had required. Looking back, he could see that his enthusiasm for his play to bring Jess to her senses through jealousy was misplaced. He suspected darkly that is intent had been to bring Jess to her knees in penitence for spurning his attempts to make up their quarrel—to make her pay for his years of misery.

Forearms on the desk, hands clasped, he leaned forward. His eyes stared at nothing, except in his mind's eye, where the landscape was dreary and barren.

He had told himself that Jess's pallor, the signs of sleepless nights, her exceptional thinness, were the result of watchful care of her grandfather and grief at his death. Now he recognized in her the same wretchedness that he had thought visited him alone.

Was it possible that Jess too regretted, as deeply as he himself did, their separation?

Jess had mentioned the fictitious lady to Cleo, and Cleo, clearly, was more than suspicious of his deviousness. Did that not mean that Jess was jealous?

Suddenly Ivor was swept by a wave of self-disgust. How dared he tamper with Jess's feelings? How could he be so selfish as to toy with her emotions like a performer on a pianoforte, pressing keys that elicited jealousy, or rage, or—he still had hopes!—the softer passions?

There could be nothing but honesty between them, if he expected any lasting marriage. And he would this very hour go to her . . .

In the event, he did not go to Oaklane until the next morning. Late that afternoon the letter which Jess had written with high emotion was delivered to him. He read it quickly, and then again. He almost expected steam to rise up from the words on the paper, written in quick stabbing letters with a pen driven obviously by anger.

"I should appreciate it were you to refrain from exercising your idle thoughts . . ." Idle thoughts! They were all of Jess, and far from idle! ". . . by way of harassing me."

He could not go to her at once. He must have more than an hour before dinner in which to probe the soreness that moved Jess to write a letter obviously composed in angry heat.

Cleo and Giles gave him no clue as to what her errand to him had been. Giles reported that Jess had decided to write, so that he could have leisure to consider his answer.

But how could he, when he did not know her question?

It came to him that there was much he wished to know about Jess's experience a few days before. The house was all but sealed against vermin, burglars, but not against ghosts. Ivor did not believe in spirits wandering the earth to make mischief. Surely the departed had other occupations of more value. But the countess had lived at Oaklane, not scandal-free, and perhaps there were traces of her occupation still to be discovered. He could not imagine what they were. However—he smiled to himself—the subject would serve his own purpose.

The next day, at a decent hour in the morning, he set out in his curricle, leaving his groom behind, for Oaklane.

He was not surprised when Jess greeted him, eyes blazing, lips tight. "I am pleased that you have come, Sir Ivor," she began. "At last you take me seriously."

Gravely he said, "I have always taken you seriously, Jess. In fact, I have come to beg you to ride with me around the farms. I have sent Acton to busy himself elsewhere."

She lifted her eyebrows in inquiry. "Surely Acton has made himself obliging toward you?"

"Obliging, yes," said Ivor, "but totally open? I think not. Come, will you guide me?"

She glanced at the curricle standing at the door, the chestnut's head held by a Dalton groom. "I'll get . . ." She was about to send for her maid, because Ivor had obviously left his groom behind.

Greatly daring, she realized that, of all things in this world, she desired most to go away someplace, anywhere, alone with Ivor. She chided herself for her wanton thoughts, and finished her remark. "I'll get my shawl."

An engaged couple might travel alone, in daylight, on short journeys. Ivor and Jess set out from Oaklane without groom or abigail, but certainly without the ease of mind that might be expected of a betrothed pair.

"Where are we going?" she inquired after a few minutes.

"Where we can talk," he said quietly, thinking of Cleo, "without some well-meaning family interrupting."

Instantly she took umbrage. "You mean my mother, I assume?"

"Good God, no! I meant that sister of mine. I suppose you met her yesterday in the road?"

Wondering what Cleo had said to her brother, and rightly assuming he had been disturbed by it, Jess said simply, "Yes."

They rode in silence for some time. Ivor handled the reins expertly but absentmindedly, turning apparently without plan. When at last he slowed, she was surprised to see they had reached the bank of the river.

The stream was not wide, but surprisingly swift. The waters were muddy, carrying as they did the good farmland from leagues higher up the current. Ivor dropped to the ground and tethered the chestnut to a low-growing willow leaning over the water, the only hint of a tree to be seen, before reaching up to clasp Jess's waist and help her to the ground. If his hands lingered longer than proper on her slender waist, neither made mention of the fact.

Taking her arm, he guided her along the bank toward a low outcrop of rock, where they found a flat ledge to serve as seat.

She was acutely conscious of the air rising from the river and brushing her cheeks. The slight breeze was damp and redolent of wet grasses and the ripe smell of tilled fields. Insensibly her anger dissolved, and for the first time in months, even years, she felt at peace. No small part of her contentment, she realized, was the presence of Ivor sitting beside her.

Finally Ivor spoke quietly, so as not to rupture the silence. "Now then, Jess, what was that note all about?"

"The note?" echoed Jess, returning from pleasant

vistas. "Oh, yes." The spell of her surroundings kept her from reviving her irritation with him. In a reasonable manner, she told him, "Ivor, we do not need more furniture."

Bewildered, he agreed, "I daresay. I was not aware we needed to discuss furniture."

"Oh, yes, we do. You may think Oaklane is sparsely furnished, and perhaps, if you admire Oakminster, then you are right. But you must realize that a more austere style suits us very well indeed. We do not need the small table upstairs."

Since Ivor had expected to hear from his darling Jess's lips an insistent inquiry about Lady Dorine, he was mildly surprised. It took a few moments for him to realize that Jess was in earnest, and that she had a real grievance to lay before him.

"Table?" he repeated at last. "What table?"

Impatiently she said, "The table that your men took upstairs and placed in the bedroom I have been sleeping in. I do not quite see how you managed it without Mrs. Cross knowing about it. But then, I do recall your devious ways from . . . from before."

"Believe me, I had nothing to do with that table. You could not really have thought I did?"

"It does seem unlikely," she confessed. "It is only that . . . I did not know what to think!"

Watching her, he said gravely, "I think you must tell me about this."

In a few words she told him. The rocking chair and the appearance of the table, after she had seen the shadow, if that was what it was, of the intruder in the hall upstairs . . . the noises in her bedroom, and her decision to sleep elsewhere.

"In truth, I heard nothing last night. So I suppose it was all my fancy. So you said when I saw the coat and smelled the soap."

"It would not have served your mother well had I joined you in your distress, would it?" He watched her from the corner of his eyes. "There's more, isn't there?"

"There's the wax. When I moved across the hall to another bedroom, Meggie—one of the maids—helped me. She was wildly upset when she saw wax drippings on the dresser. She said she had scrubbed that dresser well, and Cross would likely not believe her. She lives in great fear of Cross, though I cannot see why she should."

Ivor, who had previously noted Cross's bullying ways—not unusual in a henpecked husband—did not see any need to enlighten Jess. "Perhaps one of the servants, or Silvester—"

"I don't think Silvester would even go into that bedroom," she interrupted. "Why should he?" After a moment she added slowly, "But he has been making a nuisance of himself asking about the ghost. Perhaps he was searching for . . . But what could he be searching for? Ivor, I just do not like what is happening!"

He thoroughly agreed with her, but it would not be useful to alarm her further. Instead, he believed he knew the next step to take. However, for the moment, he had Jess with him, safe, and he meant to enjoy the occasion.

"The time to worry," he said, "is when articles begin to disappear."

She glanced quellingly at him, but his smile disarmed her. At any rate, she thought with relief, she had placed the burden on his shoulders, with the certainty that he would take care of her—that is, take care of *it*.

He rose and pulled her to her feet beside him. "Worried now?" he said softly.

"Not now," she assured him, not quite truthfully. If he were to kiss her, as he appeared about to do, she believed she could resist him, at least momentarily. For the moment, she greatly regretted coming away without her maid.

The moment passed, and she was not required to resist

any advances. She was more piqued than relieved.

Ivor moved a few steps away and regarded the river. "Is this the great stream that was in flood and ravaged the countryside, I think old Lord Hartnell said?"

"Yes, although you see it now when the water is low. In the spring, especially if there have been heavy snows, the thaw can bring the river up six feet or more."

"Really? Then it is not beyond belief that it swept away a small building made of marble?"

"Apparently not. Farm buildings and livestock were carried off." She looked around her. "Do you know, I don't think I have ever been here before."

"No? I thought you were more adventurous than to ignore the ruins of the family folly!"

"You're teasing," she said calmly. "But you must remember that I never heard of the countess or the folly until recently, when we learned we were to move to Oaklane. And when we first came here to live, Grandpapa had very strict notions on what young ladies were to do. And then we went to London, and . . ."

And what happened then lay heavily in the air between them, separating them, but in an odd way binding them together in a shared past.

With an effort, Ivor looked away. His glance fell on the jumble of gray rocks, and he saw something that caught his eye. He bent to examine it. The rought-cut rock seemed to have been shaped into a kind of slab suitable for a foundation—likely one of the supports for the pavilion. The rocks had been lying just so for so long that they were covered with dirt blown by the winds, and small weeds and moss that had found a footing here.

But Ivor could not be mistaken. On one of the rocks, the moss had been scraped away—by a foot slipping? He studied the other rocks. He found three more signs of disturbance. Backing off and looking at the sequence, he fancied he could see a pattern as of someone clmbing up from the river and crawling with difficulty over these jumbled rock ledges.

But why on earth would someone climb over the rocks, when on either side for some distance the bank was clear of any barrier?

He turned back to Jess, a diversionary remark on his lips. She was watching him, her dark blue eyes wide, wondering, speculating. She had obviously seen what he had seen. Whatever conclusions he might come to had best be drawn in private. Just now his Jess was frightened enough.

They walked together to the curricle. Finally, in a small voice, Jess asked, "What do you think, Ivor? Could it not be a cow strayed into this field?"

"Any cows missing?" said Ivor crisply. "If an animal had made those tracks, it would have fallen into the river and gone downstream in that swift current."

The sunshine had gone out of the day. Something vaguely threatening loomed just out of sight, like a bank of sea smoke gathering itself together over the wintry ocean. She could not see well for the tears that filled her eyes, and she stumbled over a tussock of grass, and her hands went out to catch herself.

He caught her. She felt his iron muscles holding her safely, holding her against his chest—the most welcome support in the world. She tried to pull away, but his arms tightened, keeping her fast. Hesitantly she looked up at him, and the look she saw in his gray eyes was familiar, and yet warmer and more tender than she had seen in the earliest days of their long-ago betrothal.

Long-ago, and yet that sweetness that had bound them together then could have been strong and vibrant only yesterday.

He kissed her, gently at first, and then with commanding intensity. A part of her mind knew that such behavior, in a fallow field out of sight of any buildings, without a servant closer than a mile away—it was wanton, that's what it was!

And, shaken to her very shoes, she enjoyed every minute of it.

When, sometime later, he released her and steadied her on her feet—she was sure her knees would hold her no better than a column of water—she clutched at his sleeves and said, in such a low voice that he had to bend down to hear her, "I'm sorry . . ."

"I'm not!" he said with authority, "nor are you. Jess, are you?"

She shook her head. Indeed, she was not sorry. She was happier than she had ever been! If only they could linger here, forever, or at least another hour. But there were the alarming manifestations at Oaklane—the noises, the wax drippings, the unexpected appearances of oddments of furnishings. And now, the mysterious traces of . . . What? Something that scraped moss from rocks without apparent purpose.

"We had better go back," she said.

He lifted her into the seat, his hands lingering long on her this time. Without knowing she was going to do so, she leaned down and kissed him gently, sweetly, on the lips.

It was at that moment that all their schemes took to their heels and vanished unnoticed, sailing down the wind.

The Lady Dorine might linger like a thorn in Jess's mind, prickly and unwelcome, but Ivor, when he thought about it much later, could not in the clear light of conscience think how he could have planned such a despicable deception. He must win Jess—indeed he thought he was more than halfway to getting her back—but he must win her honestly, frankly, and forever.

As for Jess, Henry was, at least as a possible suitor, a nonexistent man!

18

In spite of his elation over his conviction that Jess returned, at least in little, his love, Ivor had passed a sleepless night, an unusual occurrence. Jess's response had been his ultimate goal, the beginning of a happiness that would wrap them forever.

But it did not serve. There was a good deal amiss at Oaklane, and he could not determine exactly the cause. Small things at best—a table, a bit of candle wax. And the telltale signs of someone scrambling over rocks at the edge of a river.

While he ate his excellent omelete, a unique concoction of Louis, the chef, he remembered that before he had helped Jess down from the curricle at the door of Oaklane, she had recalled a small scrap of paper in her pocket.

"I found it in the drawer of the table. It looks as though someone pulled out a paper in a hurry, and did not notice this corner was torn off. But a 'ton' of what, I can't imagine."

Now he brought it out and laid it on the table before him: "ton," it read. The word was at the righthand side, and therefore probably was not a "ton" of anything, for there was no room for further writing. It had to be "something-ton."

There was writing on the line below, caught in a crease of the paper. Writing? It was only one letter! A small letter L. A part of a word, obviously. "Will?" Or if it connected the line above, "a ton of gravel?" His mind played over possibilities without lighting on any that made sense to him.

When Giles entered the room, heading directly toward the laden buffet, Ivor waited until he had filled his plate and sat down before he laid the scrap of paper in front of him.

"There, Giles, is something to exercise your faculties on," he said.

Giles looked at the object, his lips drawn down in distaste. "That filthy thing? What is it?"

Ivor told him where it had been found. Instead of concentrating on the paper, however, Giles exclaimed, "A table where there was none before?" Thinking back to his encounter with Jess on the drive, he added thoughtfully, "And Miss Dalton is worried, as of course she should be."

"But what do you make of that clue?" demanded Ivor. "I know she is distressed, even afraid. I think I see my way clear to dealing with the situation, but there are one or two facets of the situation that I should like to understand first."

Giles continued to eat while he studied the writing. At length, he confessed failure. "You'll never find out what this means, Ivor, until you find the rest of the sheet."

At that moment, Cleo stood in the doorway. "I wish to have a cup of coffee . . . very, very hot . . . and immediately!"

"Since we dispense with Bruton at breakfast, dear sister, I suggest you pour it yourself. The silver pot at the end of the sideboard should do. The smaller pot, of course, has chocolate."

She poured the coffee and found it scalding, too hot to drink. "Just right," she pronounced. Picking up a breakfast muffin, she brought her breakfast to the table and beamed on her brother and his friend.

"I vow I do not know why I do not spend more time in the country," she told them cheerfully. "The fresh air makes me sleep excessively well, and I feel so restored this morning."

Against hope, Ivor suggested, "Well enough to continue your journey to Scarborough?"

"I find Oakminster so full of diversion, you know. Besides, dear Beatrice does not sustain travel very

well. She is still abed this morning, and I have sent
Stokes in to her to help her with all the medicine she
feels necessary to survive!"

"You never intended to go to Scarborough, confess
it, Cleo."

"I intend to confess nothing to you. La, I do not
even confess to Charles!"

"Poor man! If you are seeking diversion, Cleo, I
suggest you tell us the entire story of this scrap of
paper. A puzzle, I have no doubt, you can solve
easily."

Ivor, with a malicious glint in his eye, handed her
the mysterious scrap and watched, expecting her to
glance at it and then hand it back. Instead she said, "I
do not know precisely what you want of me. But I can
tell you that this is most likely a list of some kind. You
need a wife, Ivor, for you will never be domesticated.
How your household runs, I cannot fathom."

"My household runs very well indeed," said Ivor
sharply. "But how we could ever have discerned this
was a list, from a total of four letters, I cannot
surmise."

"Nonsense, Ivor. You are merely teasing me. This
paper is narrow, of a very rough texture. Used by
servants, at least in my household. Butlers or house-
keepers keep a supply on hand, in order to make lists of
needed supplies." Unaware of the stunned surprise on
the faces of her brother and Giles, she said, "I cannot
think of any household staple that ends in 'ton,'
though. Is that an L I wonder? Perhaps it might be a
list of names. Staff of some kind, perhaps. You are
right, Ivor. I can make neither head nor tail of it!"

Dryly Ivor said, "Don't be modest. Of course you
know you have gone almost to the solution of this little
puzzle!"

"Truly? Then perhaps you will tell me where this
came from."

Giles said softly, "A list of names! That has to be it!"

"What's on your mind, Giles?"

"I don't know," Giles said slowly. "There is something at the back of my mind, but I cannot understand what it is." With an effort he added, "You know, my own names ends with 'ton.' But why I should be on anyone's list, I cannot tell."

Cleo smiled at him. "On my list of charming gentlemen, you will find your name near the top."

He bowed in acknowledgment of her compliment. "You do not keep that list in a table drawer?"

Cleo became aware that the two men were under a strain. "Something's amiss here," she said abruptly. "Best tell me what it is. I should not like to blunder into a situation because of ignorance!"

"Well, if you plan to extend your visit here . . ." he began.

Amused, Cleo told him, "There is no way you can remove me save by force. And you will remember I arrived with a full complement of armed guards!"

Ivor laughed heartily. "Trust you to go to the heart of the matter! Very well, then, I agree you shall be made privy to the whole."

He told her all he knew: about the presence of an intruder the day he and Cousin Elizabeth had gone to visit Lord Hartnell, the appearance of the small table in Jess's room—"in the drawer of that table is where this scrap of paper was found"—and Jess's fears that someone had been in her room one night.

"Don't forget the candle drippings," urged Giles.

"I do not see what that has to do with anything," protested Ivor. "A careless maid, no doubt."

"Or an intruder who set down his candlestick in order to do something that took two hands."

Cleo's blood chilled. She had come to Oakminster for several reasons, primary among which was her distrust of the wicked gleam she had seen in Ivor's eyes. He had a scheme in mind, she was convinced, and from long experience of her brother's notions, she felt it incumbent upon her to be at hand, even if she need not intervene.

But surely he had not planned such an *outre* series of events!

She did not speak for some time after Ivor had finished his narration. Finally she said, "You came up here with a scheme, Ivor. Lady Dorine, indeed! Believe me, you malign Jess if you think she would not see through that device at once. Indeed, I am persuaded that she gives Lady Dorine her rightful due!"

"I did not ask you to interfere," said Ivor angrily.

"Someone needed to. But I must ask you, Ivor, to tell me the truth. Is this japery with the ambulating furniture a creation of yours?"

"No, Cleo, I swear not."

"In fact," said Giles, "I think there is a question of a ghost!"

Cleo fell back in her chair. "Good God! Can it be the countess?"

The effect on her hearers was stunning. The first coherent remark that came to her was her brother's. "Countess! The Italian countess? Was she real? I thought Cousin Elizabeth had concocted the whole tale! How do you come to know about her?"

"Nanny didn't like you!" said Cleo with a wry smile. "You played too many tricks on her. She told me all about the Bellamy lady who thought she would marry the Italian count. Unfortunately, he was neither count nor husband in the end, and she was brought back and stowed away in a family house . . . It could have been Oaklane. Ivor, was it Oaklane?"

"So they say. And they say it is haunted by the countess."

"But why? She was not unhappy, I should think. Of course she cannot have been ecstatic, for I should not like to be carried home in disgrace for the rest of my life. Equally, she could not have been wretched, for she did have a lover."

"Cleo! If our mother had known Nanny was stuffing your head full of crazy nonsense, Nanny would have been gone before nightfall."

"Perhaps so, but is it not fortunate that I do know the tale? Don't you see, the countess would not walk the corridors, as I am told unhappy spirits do. Why would she?"

"Did she leave any legacy?" wondered Giles. "Some kind of treasure, or jewels?"

"Not that I ever knew. There was, of course, the Cavalier treasure—buried when Oliver Cromwell rode up the drive, you remember, Ivor—but that was recovered long ago."

"You are sitting in the house built by that treasure."

Cleo looked around her. "Better than moldering in the ground. But I never heard of another treasure. Do you suppose the lover festooned the countess with ropes of pearls?"

"Cleo, your lurid imagination—"

"Well, our side of the . . . alliance, I suppose you would call it . . . inherited nothing from the countess."

Jess spoke from the doorway. "Except for a ghost!"

One look at her ashen face brought them to their feet. "Fresh coffee," Ivor demanded of the footman who had admitted Jess, "and brandy."

"Here, Miss Dalton, sit here," said Giles.

Cleo simply went to Jess and put her arm around the shaking shoulders. "Did you walk? A foolish thing to do," murmured Cleo in a soothing voice.

At length Jess was somewhat restored. "You were speaking of the countess? I heard a few words as I came in."

Cleo cast back into her childhood memory. "But the ghost would not haunt the house, Jess. Nanny said there was a folly, she said the word was exactly the right term. Folly there was, she said, and folly it was called!"

"The folly! But it's gone," cried Jess. "The flood

took it away! I wish the ghost had gone with it!"

"Something else has happened?" Ivor watched her with serious eyes.

"Yes. I apologize for my arrival, uninvited. But I had to see you." Although she pressed Cleo's hand as she spoke, her eyes were for Ivor. A part of Cleo's thoughts registered satisfaction—Jess certainly cherished her former betrothed, and with a bit of help, all would end well for Ivor.

Another cup of coffee for Jess, more lightly laced with brandy this time, and the color began to come back to her cheeks. "I didn't sleep well," she explained. "At least, at first I did, but something woke me up. I don't know what it was. You know I have moved to the room across the corridor from . . . well, from the room where the table turned up, and where I thought someone had entered in the night."

"Where you found the wax drippings," prompted Ivor.

"Yes. But last night no one came in. At least, I don't think so. But the room was light. I sat up in bed. The door to the corridor was ajar. You know, it is a strap latch, and it does not stay closed very well. But the light was coming from the hall, and I got out of bed to peer through the opening. The corridor was not dark, either. The light was coming . . ." She gulped, and Cleo held her more tightly, before she went on, "The light was coming from across the hall. In the room where I used to sleep. I called out, but not very loudly, I guess. Suddenly the light was gone and the hall was dark. Like someone blew out a candle. Or maybe shut the door. I don't know what I did then. I think I got back into bed, for I woke up there this morning."

She turned to Cleo and said urgently, "It was not a dream! At first I thought it might be. But I went across the hall this morning—the door was open then—and there were two chairs standing in the middle of the room."

"Chairs!"

Clearly on the verge of weeping, Jess said, "Chairs that match the set that is in the attic here at Oakminster."

Guessing her first thought, Ivor disclaimed responsibility. "Believe me, Jess, I did not take any furniture from this house to Oaklane!"

"No, of course not. But someone did. Or Some*thing*."

"You're not staying there another night," said Ivor in a calm but very authoritative voice. It was a measure of Jess's desperation that she did not at once challenge his assuming that he knew best. Indeed, she thought, I have put the load on his shoulders, and it feels wonderful!

Ivor turned to Giles. "How was a folly built, Giles? Do you know?"

"My grandfather had one at Landers' Reach. All the rage then, about the time Horace Walpole drew the plans for Strawberry Hill. They were simply a place for ladies to take the air on summer days. A floor, surrounded by pillars in the Greek style, and a domed roof. I believe most were made on that same pattern."

"No underground room? No heavy foundations?" Ivor was thinking about the jumble of rocks that had caught his eye. The scraped moss, he had decided, had been damaged under the foot of a dog or other animal. Now, he was not so sure.

Like Giles, he had the germ of an idea lurking at the back of his mind. But first, he must secure Jess's safety, and that of her family, of course.

"What are you fussing about the folly for?" demanded Cleo. "The trouble is in that house! I wish Charles were here! He would know what to do."

"I've been meaning to ask you why Charles did not accompany you," said her brother.

"Some idiotic thing about the millworkers, the stockingers, I think he called them—"

"That's it!" cried Giles, "that's what has been niggling at me."

"You are less than clear, Giles. What is it you have at last discovered?"

Not answering directly, Giles said only, "I must go to London at once. It should take me only a couple of days."

"*What* should?" demanded Ivor.

"I don't know yet."

With that vague disclaimer, Giles leapt to his feet and left the room. They could hear the diminishing sound of his footsteps as he bounded up the stairs to pack for his journey.

"You do have odd friends, Ivor," murmured Cleo.

"He's at the top of your list, you recall," retorted Ivor.

Jess, overcome by fatigue and worry, slumped in her chair. Giles's unaccountable spurt of energy had gone unnoticed. Her eyelids drooped and she longed to crawl under an eiderdown and sleep and sleep. Ivor would take care of everything, and she felt as though a two-ton stone had been taken from her shoulders.

"Come, Jess," said Ivor gently. "I'll take you home. I want your family back here at Oakminster."

Jess looked at him, bewildered. "I don't understand. You are not going to leave too, to abandon . . . my mother?"

"Not for a moment," he assured her. "You will not spend another night in that house. Cleo, do you come too. Perhaps Cousin Elizabeth will be more easily convinced if you add your arguments to mine."

"My mother does not know about last night," offered Jess in a small voice. "Must she?"

Ivor answered, "Her house, her daughter—of course she must."

He left the room to order the carriage, and Cleo turned impulsively to Jess and hugged her thoroughly. "How good it will be to have you here? We'll live in each other's pockets, and Beatrice can keep your mother company."

Soon Cleo's thoughts strayed. "What on earth could stockingers—is that the word?—have done to Giles to make him streak off like a fox before the hounds?"

"What are stockingers?" asked Jess.

"I don't precisely know, but they work in mills and they often are rebels. Charles has told me, but I cannot remember now why they rebel, or against whom."

"They rebel because they do not know their place in the world, and do not realize how fortunate they are to have employment instead of starving in the hedges, and the government is lacking in its duty to protect the mill owners, who are subject to the most dastardly forms of violence."

Cleo stared at her. Jess laughed a little. "Dear Henry Hartnell. I did not think I listened to him, but you see I have absorbed much of his tirade."

"He owns mills? He cannot be Lord Hartnell's son?"

"His mother's side of the family. He inherited his grandfather's mills. He has always felt the shame of owning the mills, but now, since he feels his income is at stake, he is most vocal."

Ivor returned. "The coach is ready. Jess, do you feel more the thing now?"

"Oh, yes, Ivor, I do."

Jess went into the hall, where Burton stood waiting to see his master and his guests into the carriage. Cleo tugged at Ivor's sleeve and pulled him back to stand with her.

"Don't worry, Ivor. Between us, Cousin Elizabeth and I will safeguard Jess's virtue!"

Ivor retorted, "Her virtue is *my* responsibility, not yours!" Cleo's giggle did not improve his temper.

In truth, with the memory of yesterday's kiss shining brightly in his memory, he was not at all sure that Jess, even if she were surrounded by Cleo's army, would be safe from him!

19

In three days, Elizabeth Dalton had settled into her old rooms at Oakminster, and felt as though she had never left home. To her delight, Ivor had sent for Althea, and she was returned, somewhat reluctantly, to the bosom of her family.

Nor was she the only Dalton who regretted the return to the manor. Jess, remembering with pleasure and a good deal of hope that interlude on the riverbank, had been anxious lest the renewed proximity to Ivor might strain her powers of resistance beyond their limits. She had fancied secret assignations in the corridors, or stolen moments in the study or the herb gardens, and while she was nothing loath to receive Ivor's attentions, yet there must be a few questions settled between them before she could give herself wholeheartedly to dalliance, however pleasant.

He had not renewed his former offer of marriage. He had not even given her hand a significant pressure, nor had he whispered any word about the future— their future. She was not at all sure how she would withstand his renewed attentions, or even endure his constant company.

She need not have worried. Ivor's companionship was very like that he would bestow on a spaniel—and not even a favorite pet, at that. He was never alone with her. In truth, Cleo was as close as a sister: "we'll live in each other's pockets!"

Indeed they did. Jess had no suspicion that Ivor had accepted Cleo's offer of guarding Jess's virtue. Since Beatrice Berwick found a compatible companion in Elizabeth Dalton, and Philip was back in the manor library, Cleo and Jess had much time to themselves.

"Since Mr. Leighton has gone to London, on some

THE LOST LEGACY 177

errand he did not tell us, my poor brother feels out-
numbered in a house full of women!" said Cleo
blithely. "Mr. Leighton should return very soon, but I
wonder what we shall do until then to amuse ourselves? I have had sufficient discussion of handiwork to
last me until next Season!"

Jess smiled. "My mother enjoys Miss Berwick's
company. And I am so pleased to see her spirits
returning. I had not sensed that she was—"

"Frightened," Cleo finished for her. "But of what?
Does she really believe in the countess's ghost?"

"I think not," said Jess. They were strolling across
the east lawn, and insensibly going in the direction of
Jess's herb garden. Arriving at the marble bench, they
sat down to rest. "But there is something in that house,
Cleo. If not a ghost, then what? There can be no
tunnel, for Ivor sent Yancey to make the house tight,
and he found no means of entry."

Musingly Cleo said, "But I never heard of chairs
moving by themselves around the house. Charles
would raise a storm if I moved, even by human hands,
one bit of furniture. He likes things the way they are,
he says."

"Well," remarked Jess, "the furniture can dance
quadrilles all night as far as I am concerned, as long as
we are safe here."

Cleo turned impulsively to her companion. "Jess! I
should like above all things to watch such a cotillion,
wouldn't you?"

"Nonsense! The furniture does not whirl around—
imagine that green brocade settee waltzing with the
Queen Anne chair! Cleo, what fustian!"

They fell silent for a time. Then Jess said
tentatively, "But I wonder what does go on in that
house? I am convinced that something does."

Cleo responded in her usual straightforward way.
"Then let's find out!"

Since their quickly made plans required lack of daylight, they moved, in a somewhat preoccupied way, through the rest of the day.

Henry Hartnell came to call, complimenting Jess on her wisdom in forsaking Oaklane. Drawing her aside, he added, "For some houses carry with them an inheritance of unpleasantness, one cannot deny that. How long will you be staying here at Oakminster, Jess?"

"I cannot say, Henry. I am too tired to care, I think. At least I have not inquired of Ivor what his plans are for us."

"It distresses me, dear Jess," said Henry earnestly, "to see you so entirely at the mercy of that man. Surely you must find his constant presence irritating?"

"Truly, Henry, I do not see much of him, you know."

Henry took her hand in both of his. "Jess, you know I have spoken to your mother. This is not the time for me to seek a private interview with you, nor is it the place. I could not speak freely in the house of the man who jilted you."

"Henry, he did not jilt me."

Ignoring her protest, he assured her, "Do not allow him to overcome your maidenly modesty, Jess. As soon as I finish a few matters I have in mind, I shall come to you, and settle your future."

She stood bemused while he lifted her hand to his lips. She would have been gratified had she been able to see the expression on Ivor's face as, his attention unexpectedly caught by the sight of movement on the terrace directly below his window, he watched the tender scene below. He stood in the great bedroom—the chamber allocated to the head of the family—at the front of the house. Jess had told him, that first day, that this room was reported to have the best view of any room in the house. It certainly had the most surprising vista!

THE LOST LEGACY 179

After Henry had gone, Cleo joined Jess on the terrace. "You cannot like that man!" said Cleo robustly. "Can you?"

Evasively Jess told her, "He has been a neighbor for a long time." There was something about him this time, she thought, something different. But she could not identify what it was.

Together they turned and went into the house.

Oblivious of the activity on the terrace outside the library window, and caught up in an exciting new book he had brought back with him from Oaklane, Philip believed he had made a discovery. The book of sermons at first had looked dull. But the contents of the unknown vicar's collection had proved, in the main, interesting. There was even a hidden treasure to be found somewhere. And from all the clues, that treasure might well be found at Oaklane.

The scandals mentioned in such a disapproving way by the author, and narrated in such full detail, meant little to Philip. He had no interest in lovers, and in fact he did not understand what all the fuss was about. But one of the tales brought up echoes to his own mind. A countess, and a lost treasure. Surely this must be the lady his mother had told about?

And a lost treasure! If the countess in the book were the Bellamy countess, then the treasure was a legacy and the Daltons would inherit, wouldn't they? And Silvester could go to sea, and he with his share could order books, and books.

Thus far in his life Philip had found his own company to be sufficient for most purposes. He held affection for Jess, a sublime disinterest in Althea, and for Silvester a curious feeling made up of mingled idolatry and respect.

Silvester did none of the things that Philip admired. He was not in the least bookish, and made no secret of his conviction that his younger brother was a very odd fish indeed.

But Philip, while accepting his brother's assessment without resentment, nonetheless regarded him in a way that might, in a more articulate person, be described as a kind of doglike love. Silvester did all the things that Philip knew only in books. He rode like a centaur, he was an excellent shot, he was strong beyond his years . . .

And now, Philip believed he had made a discovery that would at least clutch at Silvester's attention. Philip was growing up, even though he did not recognize the process. He had come to a point where solitude was not the answer he craved. There was a queer hunger in him that had not yet been sated, a hunger for even a modicum of attention, a need to be at the center of his family.

He ran his brother to earth in the stables. Silvester was rubbing down Copper Lightning, having come back across the fields from his morning ride at a canter.

"Here," said Silvester when Philip entered, "make yourself useful. Grab that brush. I've nearly finished this side, you start with her neck on that side."

Silvester, not at all an unfeeling young man, eyed his brother suspiciously. It was unheard-of for Philip to leap eagerly to curry a horse, to say naught of coming to the stables at all.

Suppose something had happened while he was gone? Maybe they had all moved back to Oaklane! Silvester set no store whatever in a ghost haunting the corridors of Oaklane. The intruder was undoubtedly one of the estate hands or even a villager coming in to purloin whatever could be carried away.

True, the appearance rather than disappearance of the furniture did not fit his own explanation, but there was none other, given the nonexistence of spirits,

unless Jess had made up the entire tale. Women did
odd things!

Watching his brother's solemn face as he worked on
the mare, Silvester wondered what the effect of all the
ghost talk might be on Philip. Queer little fellow—
always with his nose in a book and clearly not
interested in any human, even Silvester.

The mare rubbed down and furnished with a
favorite gruel, Philip felt it was time to unburden
himself of his great discovery. He followed Silvester
out to sit on the top of the brick wall, a three-foot
boundary to the stableyard. The bricks were warm
beneath him, and the oak leaves over his head
chattered gently.

In spite of the urgent need to impart his momentous
discovery, Philip felt a great contentment. He had
news to relate, news that would do the entire family a
great deal of good, and . . . in a few moments,
Silvester would be, for once in his life, listening
intently to him.

"Did Cousin Ivor toss you out of the library?"
inquired Silvester. "I gather that nothing else would
bring you outside, even on such a fine day?" He
laughed at his own humor, and a slight chill touched
Philip.

"I found something," said Philip.

"In a book, I suppose. What's in a book compared to
the mystery we've got at Oaklane right now?"

"Well," said Philip, squirming on the hard bricks,
"that's just it. The book tells about the treasure."

"We all know about that," Silvester pointed out
impatiently. "And it's not in the ground anymore.
Somebody dug it up after Cromwell was gone. Cousin
Ivor says it was used to build this place." Silvester
waved a hand at the stone pile called Oakminster.

"But suppose there was another treasure? One
nobody knew about?"

"How could there be? The only treasure there ever was is the Cavalier treasure, which was recovered. If nobody knew about another one, then how did you find out?"

Not quite clear on the means by which the countess —if the book referred to the Bellamy countess—might amass a fortune, Philip lost some of his enthusiasm.

"Besides," continued Silvester, more kindly, moved by a vague stirring of sympathy for his brother, "there aren't any secrets in the Bellamy family."

"What about the countess?" persisted Philip. "We never heard about her until Mama told us."

"But Mama knew about it," pointed out Silvester. "It was not a secret—only something kept from us children. We would all have been told sooner or later."

"I still think," said Philip, after a moment, "that there's something hidden in that house."

Silvester laughed loudly. "Not after Yancey went through it and stopped up everything. There's no way anything could be hidden!"

"There was the light Jess saw."

Silvester stared. "How do you know that? You were not supposed to."

"I was not eavesdropping, Silvester," Philip said with dignity, "Besides, I belong to the family too."

Silvester, jarred by an uneasiness he could not define, had no answer. Jess's adventure was to be kept a dark secret, his mother had demanded, to keep fear from engulfing the servants, and also Philip.

"The servants would desert in a body," claimed Mrs. Dalton, "and you know how hard it would be to obtain others. And of course, Philip is too young to know of such things. For once, I am glad Althea is not here. I forbid either of you, Jess, Silvester, to mention this in their hearing."

And now, thought Silvester darkly, Philip not only knew about the strange light appearing upstairs in the night, but he thought he had an answer for the mystery, in the form of the lost legacy from the Cavalier ancestors, a legacy no longer lost.

The only thing Silvester could think of was to destroy any possibility of a legacy, at least in Philip's mind. Silvester closed his eyes for a moment and imagined the scene in the Oakminster drawing room were Philip to come out blandly with a statement that betrayed his knowledge of the eerie happenings at Oaklane. Their mother's eyes would kindle and turn to Silvester, believing he had disobeyed her orders.

There was only one thing to do. "Nonsense, Philip. Whatever you read in some book is nonsense. Don't you think the family would know if the treasure were still hidden in that house?"

Philip watched the death of a small hope. Silvester not only had not listened, but had laughed at him. Philip had proofs at his fingertips, or at least in his book in the library, but Silvester was not interested. He himself *was*, after all, a member of the family, thought Philip with surprising resentment, even though Silvester did not seem to think so. And he, Philip, had as much right to find the treasure as anybody.

He slid down from the wall and moved into the shade, shivering at the sudden coolness. He stood thinking for a moment, until Silvester quizzed him. "Going back to your books? Good idea. That's where you belong."

Silvester was not, contrary to Philip's impression, being contemptuous. He seriously considered Philip a thinker and not a doer. Great deeds were done by doers, and it was only Silvester's own nature that convinced him that doers were worth more in the world's scheme than thinkers.

He was moved to add another tidbit of advice for his brother's edification. "And don't go looking for the treasure yourself. You'd muck up for certain."

He watched Philip walk slowly out of the stable-yard. He felt a pang of compassion for the small boy, his shoulders bent under the weight of disappointment, but it did not occur to him to call him back and ask to hear more about the bookish discovery.

Philip, just now having grown up to the extent of realizing that sometimes company is preferable to solitude, took yet another step toward maturity. Sometimes solitude is preferable to company, he decided, if it is the wrong kind of company!

He had hoped that Silvester would praise him for finding the real answer to the mystery of Oaklane, and that they could together make a search for the treasure, and perhaps lay the ghost. It had not happened in that manner.

Now Philip was filled with a new kind of determination. If Silvester did not believe in the treasure, Philip did. And Philip would find it.

And Philip, having done a great service for the family, would at least be accepted as a Bellamy, and not as a child too young to be out of leading strings.

The realization that he was considered too young to know anything about the untoward experiences of his sister stung him deeply. He believed, from his copious reading, that in many ways he was older than his mother. But her only concern with him—besides, he thought bitterly, keeping him ignorant of everything that was going on—was to see that he did not sit around in wet clothing, and to say now and then: It's not healthy, Philip, to read so much!

Well, so much for expecting help and cooperation! He could not count on Silvester. Nor, to put it baldly, did he want to apply to any other member of the family. Jess would at least listen, but what Philip demanded from his family now was either whole-hearted and vigorous championing or total ignorance.

Perhaps, though, he had been wrong. He had no

more desire than anyone else to make an idiot of himself. He reread the chapter in the book relating to the countess. She had hidden a treasure, somewhere in a secret place, an outbuilding, a tunnel, a niche in the attic. Philip was again convinced, and this time, being on his own, he lost himself in thought.

By midafternoon he was done with thinking and ready for action. He knew what he had to do. Find the treasure, he would, and bear it home in triumph, as great Alexander had brought home his trophies!

Being methodical of mind, he gave consideration to the possibility that Silvester was right, that there was no treasure. This he dismissed. There must be a reason for lights, chairs, and all the other oddments that had plagued Oaklane in recent days.

His mother had denied there was a tunnel. However, the book certainly indicated that there was a private place—something to do with a lover—and it was strongly suggested that an underground means of getting there existed.

But suppose the treasure had already been found? It couldn't have been, for if it had, there would be no reason for the mysterious comings and goings of . . . whoever. Philip did not think "*what*ever." At any rate, if—and this was most unlikely—if the treasure had been removed, at least he would solve the mystery.

Unnoticed, he left the house and set off down the drive on his way to Oaklane. He would start upstairs, in Jess's old room, whence the light in the corridor had emanated. Making his plans, he was halfway to Oaklane when he realized that he had left it until quite late in the day. Doubtless darkness would fall before he returned to Oakminster! He was prophetic in a way he did not know.

He nearly faltered then, not from fear of the coming dark, but because he realized that, mystery once solved, the family would move back to Oaklane and he would find the library excessively inconvenient to visit. Never mind, he would simply continue the practice that he had begun sometime ago, when he first learned they would remove to Oaklane. Already, hidden in a cupboard behind his bed, were two dozen of his favorite books, carefully and individually abstracted from the Oakminster library. He must accelerate his "borrowings," that was all.

The house was closed up, but Philip did not find a locked door any sort of obstacle. The scullery window was especially vulnerable to prying fingers, and in only a few moments he was inside. He paused to get his bearings in the empty house. The curtains were closed, and the furniture, so familiar in the light, now looked like crouching animals, dark and menacing.

The only reaction Philip allowed himself in this unoccupied house, these shadowy rooms where awkward things might lurk in the dusky light, was a hard swallow over a kind of lump that had developed in his throat.

Then, because Philip was only a boy without experience, but not a coward, he set about collecting the supplies he needed.

20

Giles Leighton returned shortly after noon, and promptly closeted himself in the study with Ivor.

Cleo's curiosity grew. "What did he go to London for? He said there was information he must unearth, information that has to do with this mystery. Jess, what could it be?"

"I cannot guess."

Cleo fumed for some time, even at one time standing outside the study door with her hand on the latch, ready to brave her brother's sure annoyance at being interrupted.

Jess stopped her. "You know, Cleo, that's wrong."

"What can be wrong about wanting to talk to my brother's friend? Perhaps he has seen Charles. You cannot mean that I must not ask about my own husband?"

"Cleo, don't play the innocent with me. I know you are merely curious beyond measure to know what Mr. Leighton has discovered in town. But perhaps he found out nothing. Or at least nothing that has to do with our mystery."

"Then why don't they tell us? Those odious men! You're the one frightened out of her wits—and all they say is: I know best! All we women are supposed to do is sit quietly, do as we are told, and never know anything outside of our embroidery!"

Thoughtfully Jess agreed. "You know, I feel much better about our proposed expedition." She moved into the hall and looked through the open door to the terrace. "I think it will be dark in a couple of hours. Probably we should start soon? What excuse shall we make to my mother and Miss Berwick?" She laughed. "I have already worn out the headache!"

"My turn to improvise," said Cleo with good humor. "I have had more practice than you!"

They grinned at each other like the conspirators

they were. Jess said with spirit, "If they will not confide in us, then we will find out for ourselves what goes on at Oaklane!"

The two men closeted in the study had no intention of confiding their secrets to the ladies of Ivor's family. "If what you say is true, Giles," Ivor said, after listening for above thirty minutes to the news that Giles had brought with him from London, "then it is possible that Oaklane has been used as the head-quarters for some activities that I cannot approve of. What use do you think that scrap of paper would be? A list of rebel leaders?"

"At least a list," answered Giles promptly. "That seemed obvious from the beginning." Suddenly grinning, he added, "At least it was clear after your sister explained it to us. But could it not be equally well a list of 'safe' people."

Ivor frowned. "I think I may begin to see my way through this coil. What do you say we lay an ambush? Perhaps we may catch something if we spread our net carefully."

Giles, remembering that he had traveled to London and back and spent a day and a half in pursuing his urgent inquiries, longed for nothing in the world less than sitting all night in a shrub, lying in wait for malefactors.

Nonetheless, he forced a smile to his lips and said, "When shall we start? Before dark, I should think?"

"Well before dark," Ivor agreed. "And no one must notice our absence!"

Neither Jess nor Cleo, giving rein to the wildest of imaginations, nor Ivor and Giles, reasoning with what they considered impeccable logic, could have guessed what was going on at Oaklane at that moment.

Philip was, while his relatives were making their elaborate plans, already on the spot. He stood now in the scullery, in an attitude of listening. The house had felt empty at the start, but now he was aware of odd creakings, as though the house itself breathed.

Now that he thought about it, he remembered having the impression as he plodded down the drive that someone was behind him. He had stopped then and looked behind him, but there was no one in sight. He had sighed and resumed his steady progress to the house.

Throwing off his momentary alarm, Philip had returned in his thoughts to the steps he would take next. The *Sermons on Scandals* had hinted strongly that there was a tunnel leading from the house to . . . to somewhere. His mother had stoutly denied that the tunnel still existed. However, newly aware of the tendency of his close kin to tell him only what they wished him to know, he dismissed everything he had heard, and relied solely on the book.

And, of course, his own reasoning—with which he was as satisfied as Ivor and Giles were with their own solution to the mystery of Oaklane.

Philip opened drawers and cupboards in the scullery, and emerged into the hall supplied with tools enough to undermine St. James's Palace. He paused, looking up the stairs. The dusk was thick now, and the moving shadow he thought he saw could only be his imagination.

His first objective was the room where Jess had slept at first. That room seemed to be the source of disturbance, because Jess had moved out suddenly and taken the room across the hall. Even though no one had explained to him the reason for this removal, he suspected that some untoward incident had occurred to frighten her.

And there was the light—now he had learned about that event. And the light must have come from Jess's former room.

All kinds of possibilities might have occurred to Silvester. But "tunnel" was on Philip's mind, and a tunnel he would search for.

There had to be another entrance, or exit, to the room besides the one into the corridor, and Philip was convinced he could find it.

Laden with a lantern, Mrs. Cross's prized butcher knife, and strong determination, he climbed up the stairs and came face-to-face at last with the wardrobe in question.

Already it was growing dark outside. Inside the house, the curtains closed, the lantern was a necessity.

The wardrobe was a large piece of furniture, already in place before the Daltons moved in. It was suitable for an elaborate collection of gowns, but Philip was not interested in the countess's probable apparel. His sharp eyes noted a curious fact, and he threw the broad beam of the lantern directly on the wardrobe to confirm his suspicions.

This wardrobe was apparently built specifically for the particular corner of the room in which it stood. It had an odd shape, angled into the walls of the room, and even to Philip's untutored eye seemed awkwardly placed.

No doubt, he thought, because that's where the entrance to the tunnel is.

The wardrobe floor, he discovered, was the bedroom floor. Furniture of this kind was often built so that it could be moved, all of a piece, with its floor an integral part of the whole. In that way, the object could be moved across the room, into another room, all without causing disruption to the contents or causing the sides to shake or collapse.

Satisfied with this confirmation of his deductions, he began to probe the back wall of the wardrobe, using the butcher knife in such a reckless way that Mrs. Cross would have screamed in protest. But his efforts were rewarded at last, when the back panel moved, slowly at first, and then with a jerk.

Philip was surprisingly taken aback. It was as though he had claimed a firm belief in trolls, and one appeared at the breakfast table.

To Philip, his book had turned into reality. This

kind of phenomenon had never happened to him before!

Now, holding to both sides of the open door revealed by the sliding panel, he looked into the darkness beyond, aware of the cold dank smell associated with an unpleasantly damp cellar. Flashing the beam from his lantern into the opening, he could see narrow steps leading down until they vanished beyond the light.

Clearly this passage was constructed with purpose, and what better purpose than to steal away to hide the family treasure when the abominable Roundheads approached? It was possible, at least in Philip's mind, that the treasure had never been recovered, and that Oakminster had been built with funds from another source.

Philip was not yet old enough to give any credence to the reported secret lover of the late countess, who had lived nearly a century after the Civil War. What was the sense of running in and out of wardrobes over something that mattered not a groat?

Airily dismissing the passion that is reputed to turn the world on its axis, Philip stepped through the opening onto the first step. Prudently he left the panel open behind him. It might be that he would need to return in a hurry.

He stood for a moment, hesitating. The lantern beam illuminated only the first half-dozen steps. Beyond them was an evil-smelling obscurity. For a long moment Philip stood still. He wished that Silvester had come with him. Indeed, he wished that anyone had accompanied him, at least this far.

With a curious sigh, and a sense—thought Philip, the classical scholar—of understanding Julius Caesar when he fatefully crossed the Rubicon River, he began to descend the stairs.

Even though he counted carefully, with an eye to an urgent retreat, he knew he had reached the bottom of the stairs only when he stubbed his foot on the hard floor. The lantern showed him a clear straight stretch of corridor ahead, and he stepped out with confidence and a fine feeling of triumph.

The walls of the tunnel were rudely fashioned. A kind of primitive shoring up of the earthen sides was still evident, in fairly good shape for having been in the ground for a century and a half. Philip had no doubt that he was at this very moment following along in the footsteps of a Cavalier named Bellamy. This figure in his mind bore a remarkable resemblance to portraits of the dashing Prince Rupert, even to the rakishly tilted plume in his hat. Philip wondered now whether his ancestor's Cavalier plume might not have survived the damage caused by contact with this low ceiling.

The ceiling of the tunnel was held in place by randomly placed beams of oak, most of which had ominous gaps in them. He eyed them uneasily. But a little danger would not come amiss when it came time for him to relate to his family the details of his daring journey through the bowels of the earth.

The floor of the tunnel was remarkably clear of debris, as though traffic were constant along the narrow way. There was no sign of damage to the tunnel itself. At one point the floor slanted downward, and then turned to the left. At the bottom of the slope, water had collected, and Philip stopped to examine the way ahead.

The tunnel turned to his left. It would have helped, he thought, if he had known how far he had come, and indeed in which direction. He wished he had thought to bring a compass. He had guessed that the tunnel was constructed straight out from the east side of the house. Now this diversion to the left must lead toward the river.

He stood still, trying to remember everything he had heard about the famous flood. It was little enough, only that the angry waters had taken some choice farmland and also some small building, the one that his mother referred to as a folly, whatever that might be. Where had the river flowed before that time? For the first time Philip thought that his journey might be futile. If the pavilion had existed, and if that was where the tunnel ended—according to his literary source—then, since the river had taken that pavilion, it might well have distributed the Bellamy jewels downstream for miles.

The possibility that the tunnel might lead directly downward into the river, and the waters swamp the opening, did not occur to Philip.

He held the lantern high, so it lit up the tunnel in this new direction. The construction was much rougher here, but still passable. There might not be any use in continuing, but he was reluctant to turn back.

The puddle collected at his feet was no more than two feet across, but as he looked at it, he discerned the faint outline of a boot sole! Someone had walked in this tunnel, but it was impossible to say how long ago. But the boot owner had been facing toward the house.

And therefore the other end of the tunnel opened somewhere!

Spirits buoyed, Philip started to step across the puddle. He tried to avoid stepping on the bootprint, to preserve it. His foot started to slip, and with horror he knew he was falling into that noisome water. He reached out frantically for support, and struck the tunnel wall with force.

He heard a scraping noise above him, and he looked up, only to see that the roof was disintegrating even as he watched. He threw himself forward, holding fast to the lantern, safeguarding the light.

But when one fist-size rock from the ceiling hit him on the temple, the light for Philip went out.

21

From the moment Jess and Cleo had left the narrow public road for the driveway to Oaklane, they had also left the gravel and walked prudently on the grass verge.

With enormous good luck, they believed, they had managed to leave the manor house without encountering Ivor or Giles, or Mrs. Dalton. Their possession of a lantern would have sounded an alarm had anyone detected them. But somehow their triumphant escape was not entirely a comfortable thought. No one knew where they were.

They stopped where the drive emerged from scattered trees into the clearing around the house. The unmistakable shape of Oaklane loomed ahead of them. The chimneys thrust up against the waning light of the sky, catching the last of the sun. Below the chimneys the roof spread out featureless and black.

The windows were as blank as sightless eyes, and there was no sign anywhere of living creatures. But just the same, Jess recalled the first time she had come here, with Ivor. Then she had felt there was someone in the house, someone biding his time, watchful. Ivor had indulged her fancy then, and they had not entered the house. Now she recognized that same prickling feeling at the nape of her neck. But Ivor was not here. She longed for his arm around her shoulders.

It was that curious time between sunset and moonrise, the mysterious twilight when shadows live and breathe and an owl's hunting cry sounds like a lost spirit.

Jess was no stranger to madcap schemes, though the one afoot at the moment was perhaps the wildest of all. Her agreement to such a mad foray, contrary to all common sense, could be blamed on the insidious influence and clever persuasion of Ivor's sister, Cleo.

Jess had never known her well, even in the days

when she and Ivor were betrothed. That affair had gone on in London, and their relatives had played little part in the business. She had of course met Lady Chichester, and to tell the truth, had been a trifle awed by the elegant lady of fashion, before Cleo had retired to her country home to await her lying-in.

But here, on Jess's home ground, she felt more confident, and Cleo had made good use of their proximity. In each other's pockets! Acquaintance had ripened into affection and trust. That trust had rapidly reached maturity.

Swiftly, as they stared, intimidated for the moment by the somber atmosphere surrounding them, Jess wondered for the first time how she had come to fall in with this mad scheme.

"I cannot see," Cleo had said, "why Ivor had to take over the manor house and move you out. I suppose he had his reasons, but I will tell you what I dislike most about men."

Jess had a few reasons of her own, categorized under the general headings of arrogance and selfishness, but she was curious to know what Cleo, a married woman of some five years' experience, could tell her.

"First of all, they never tell one what they are thinking."

"That is true," agreed Jess heartily.

"Next, they never tell one what they plan to do."

"That," said Jess firmly, "goes without saying. When my grandfather died, we heard not a word from Ivor for *weeks*. And then suddenly here he is and we are moved to a haunted house."

Cleo cast a shrewd glance at her friend. "Would it have helped to know all that ahead of time?"

"No," Jess admitted. "Nor was there any ahead-of-time when we moved back. Ivor conceived there was danger to us, and immediately we are removed!"

"A good idea! I have enjoyed these few days immensely."

"I too. But we could have dealt with . . . whatever it was, by ourselves, Silvester and I. And Cross of course. I did move across the hall to another bedroom, and—can you imagine it?—I did it without asking Ivor's permission!"

Cleo was lingering on at Oakminster for several reasons, not least of which was to see her brother safely betrothed. She had not known Jess well, and thought perhaps Ivor knew best in saying they should not suit.

But in these few days she had taken the measure of Miss Jessamine Dalton, and thought her own branch of the Bellamy family would be greatly enhanced by Jess's adoption into it. Being a woman as determined as her brother, Cleo bent every effort to effect the desired union of minds and hearts.

Besides, she enjoyed Jess's company and found her days of leisure, without a household to run, much to her taste.

She couldn't now be dragged away from the exciting events transpiring around her: the Oaklane ghost, some rumor of buried treasure, though she did not know quite where she had heard of it, mysterious dashes by Mr. Leighton to London and back, secret conferences in the study . . . In truth, Cleo was having the time of her life.

This very afternoon, sitting beside Jess on the marble bench, a capital idea had sprung full-blown from her mind, rather like Athena, the goddess of wisdom, emerging from the brow of Zeus!

But perhaps wisdom was not the best attribute of her plan, thought Cleo now, looking doubtfully across the lawn to the door of Oaklane.

"I don't know what Ivor and Giles are doing," Cleo had said, only hours ago, "but they will not interfere with us, especially if they do not know what we are planning."

"They would spoil our plan if they could," said Jess morosely.

"To be sure, they would. But, Jess, you cannot go on being afraid of that house! Where will you live? You will not, I am persuaded, wish to stay on here if the ghost is not laid."

"Cleo, I really saw somebody in the house!"

"How could they get in?" Cleo had objected. "Yancey closed up all the holes so that not even a mouse could get in!"

"He did say the house was mouseproof," agreed Jess flatly. "But he also said there was no guarantee against ghosts. And my mother swooned away."

"Ghosts! Surely you don't believe in ghosts, Jess? I can see where a superstitious village woman might well look to ghosts to explain some puzzles. But not you, Jess, nor your mother!"

Jess did not answer. She knew there were strange things going on in Oaklane. She herself had seen most of them. And surely Ivor thought there was danger of some kind, or he would not have bundled them back to Oakminster so swiftly.

"If it is not a ghost," said Jess slowly, "then what?"

"Let's find out."

Now, wrapped in deep twilight, carefully dressed in dark clothing so as not to be overly visible at night, Jess recalled her astonishment at Cleo's daring proposal. Equally, and without pleasure at this moment, she remembered that she had been as enthusiastic as Cleo.

The scheme, as Cleo explained it, seemed then, in the bright sunlight, safely seated on a bench, with Fred hoeing his cabbages in the near distance, the most reasonable and logical plan in the world. They would find out what the men in their lives fumbled over without results. The two ladies would lay the ghost to rest for all time, particularly when there was no such thing as ghosts, and the Daltons could return to Oaklane, away from Ivor. Jess was learning that she would never be content under the same roof with Ivor, even though he treated her with the utmost courtesy. Wryly she thought: *because* he treated her with unfailing, and impersonal, courtesy.

The only problem with Cleo's plan to examine the scene of the eerie manifestations, and lay the ghost for good—at least as Jess saw it now—was that it could not be undertaken until sunset.

Now, at the witching hour of sundown, Jess and Cleo began to walk toward the entrance. Jess was gripped by a kind of awe. She had not before seen the house by moonlight. Nor, to be truthful, did she enjoy the opportunity now. Oaklane was not the house she knew.

The building was an undistinguished pile of bricks by day, but in the ghostly half-light the turrets at the corners of the house turned into Gothic towers, and she would not have been surprised—terrified, but not surprised—to recognize a gargoyle or two under the eaves, generated by the uncanny twilight. Cleo clutched at her arm, causing Jess to utter a small scream.

"Quiet!" whispered Cleo fiercely.

Jess, bringing common sense to the fore with an effort, said mildly, "Why? There's nobody here. Except possibly a ghost, and we do not believe in them."

"True," agreed Cleo stoutly. "However, at this moment I see some merit in superstition."

They moved forward, arm in arm, to the broad entrance steps. There was no light visible anywhere, except for a reflection of the sunset in a window upstairs. The grounds around the house were open, clear of trees and shrubbery, and it was obvious that no one else was nearby.

The front door, surprisingly, was not locked. "Ivor will not like this," commented Cleo.

"Who will tell him?" Jess pointed out reasonably. "We'd have to confess we were here ourselves. I should not like that."

"Nor would I," said Cleo with firmness. "We can be as secretive as they. And serve them right!"

Once inside the house, darkness descended on them like a blanket. An odd stale-smelling blanket—the enclosed dusty odor of a house left alone only a few days but already settling into the decay of human neglect.

Jess paused to turn up the lantern she had begged, with threatening injunctions to secrecy, from one of the stable hands at Oakminster, and threw its beam into the corners of the hall. There was only the long table, and one chair, in the hall. Jess was struck again by the sparseness of the furnishings.

"Anything been added?" asked Cleo in a voice she hoped would not carry.

"No, nor anything taken away. Ivor said *that* was when we needed to worry."

"And all the time you were frightened to death!"

"Well," lied Jess, "I am not now. Let's move on."

They investigated the downstairs rooms, even scrutinizing Mrs. Cross's scullery, and found nothing they considered suspicious. They stayed together, unconsciously clutching each other, and conversing sparingly in whispers. But as they moved through the house, and found no traces of intruders—"Although I wonder what signs a ghost might leave. Footprints? Surely not!" exclaimed Cleo—they became bolder and less apprehensive about meeting an Unknown.

Jess in particular was losing the fear that had kept her company for some time, the fear born of the strange light in her former bedroom in the middle of the night. There was nothing in this house to make her fearful, she told herself. Only that unaccountable light—and that, she was sure, must have a logical explanation could she but find it.

"Let's go upstairs," whispered Cleo, "and look at that room where you found the chairs. I am convinced there must be a secret door somewhere in that room."

"But Yancey told Ivor there was none."

"And he believed him? I should expect the man to lie."

"Why should he?"

"Why shouldn't he? Lots of reasons. If he found a secret door, he might be obliged to investigate it. It might even lead to some underground cellar. I think I might lie, if I thought the truth would be uncomfortable."

Jess eyed her in the dim light of the lantern. She had come to know Cleo quite well in the last few days. Seeing the clear gray eyes, so like Ivor's, an eager light of anticipation in them, Jess laughed shortly. "You never lied in your life, Cleo."

Cleo grinned. "Well, my dear, I have never had to." She tucked her arm into the crook of Jess's elbow. "There must be a hidden entrance, and I guess it must be in the wardrobe. I recall something of the sort in a novel by Mrs. Radcliffe."

"And," said Jess suspiciously, "what was beyond the entrance?"

Remembering too late that the scene revealed by opening the secret door had been horrid in the extreme, Cleo, who had never needed to lie, did so now. "I do not recall," she said with an unsuccessful attempt at airiness. "But surely there must be a sliding panel somewhere in the house. Shouldn't we look for it? That is why we're here, after all!"

For all of Jess's stout denials of belief in insubstantial wisps of malign spirit, suddenly she was consumed by a vast reluctance to go upstairs. She was as sure as could be that they were not alone in the house. It was the same feeling she had had the first time she laid eyes on Oaklane.

And that presence was upstairs!

The presence upstairs was not alone.

In fact, the presence upstairs was at this very moment swearing copiously, thoroughly, and almost silently. When at last Ivor could speak coherently, he hissed in the ear of one of his companions, "What has got into Jess? I told her to stay at Oakminster!"

"When did you tell her that?" Giles asked, and added, "If you don't mind, Ivor, you are turning my arm numb."

"Oh." Ivor released his grip on his friend's arm, which he had clutched the moment he realized that Jess and Cleo stood in the hall at the foot of the stairs. "Sorry. I told her when they moved back to Oakminster."

"And she stayed then. I suspect that Lady Chichester has had something to do with this expedition to Oaklane."

The entire conversation was held in whispers, savage on Ivor's part, calming on Gile's. The third person present in the dark corner of the upper hall, present against his will, was wildly wondering whether he could escape from the others and shout a warning to . . . to whoever else might be in the house.

He leaned forward and touched Ivor on the shoulder. "Beg pardon, sir," he said, "but should I just run down and get the ladies out of the house?" And, once away from his master, he would do his best to announce their presence!

"I think not, Acton," said Ivor. "I should not like to reveal our presence in any way." As though unconsciously, he stepped in front of Acton, boxing him into the corner of the hall. In a conversational tone he continued, "If you utter one sound, I shall make sure you regret it the rest of your years."

The words were quiet enough, Acton thought, but nevertheless a chill settled on him, and he abandoned the idea of warning his fellow conspirator. After all, Acton did not know for certain the other person was even in the house, and Sir Ivor at this moment was not two feet away. The odds had shifted, Acton the gambler decided, and he began to believe he had backed the wrong horse. With a hugh sigh, in part of relief, he transferred his allegiance, no longer divided, wholly to Sir Ivor.

With varied emotions the three men, hidden by the darkness, watched the two ladies below. If they came up the stairs, then Ivor would have to divert them, thereby warning all and sundry that Oaklane was occupied this night, and his and Giles's plan of ambush, designed to capture the ghost, or whoever human was playing tricks, must be ruined.

Jess had not the slightest wish to examine the wardrobe, hers or any others. She had a shrewd guess as to what Mrs. Radcliffe had seen beyond her secret door.

It was enough that tonight they had examined the ground floor, and nothing had leapt out at them, rattling chains and making mournful sounds. She had conquered her earlier fears, and here was Cleo wanting to rouse them all up again.

"Why," said Jess in a reasonable way, "would there be a secret entrance upstairs? It makes more sense to have an escape route on the ground floor. Less construction."

Cleo eyed her steadily. "The wardrobe is upstairs. And that table you mentioned? Upstairs. The smell and the coat? Upstairs. The chairs?"

"Upstairs." She and Jess spoke together.

Jess took a long breath. "Upstairs it is, Cleo. You lead the way. I have the lantern and I can throw the light ahead for you."

"We'll go together," said Cleo practically. She had no wish to be left in sudden darkness by the failure of her light-bearer's courage.

They ascended slowly. It seemed to Jess an eternity, and they had gained only the sixth step. Both were watching the stairs, making very sure of their footing in the ill lighting. Thus, the creature who had appeared silently, without warning, and to the amazement of the three men in the dark corridor, remained unseen by the two women. But not for long.

Jess saw it first. Upon her unbelieving mind burst a creature out of myth, born of ghost stories from the ancient past, from the darkest of race memories.

A white, blurred, wavering shape, swaying at the top of the stairs, leaning forward and staring down at them. At least, Jess thought wildly, it would be staring at them had it possessed eyes, or even eyeholes.

Someone very near to Jess screamed and screamed. She realized that the ragged sounds came from her own throat, but Cleo's own screams, on a higher pitch, rent the air as well.

What happened next happened so fast that Jess did not know what she saw. It was only later that she could sort it out. The screams seemed to unnerve the ghostly white figure even more than the apparition had frightened them, for she saw a sort of convulsion seize the blurred shape, and it came toward them!

It had no feet—ghosts do not customarily come with discernible limbs, Cleo though hysterically while she uttered piercing shrieks—and seemed simply to topple forward, like a great oak struck by lightning, all in one piece.

Instinctively Jess and Cleo clung to the banisters, making themselves as small as possible. The figure crashed down the stairway, striking every step with thudding force.

As the terrifying figure passed Jess, it gave a hoarse cry of alarm, even fear, and by chance hit her shoulder. To her horror, she found she was falling in the wake of the ghost. In a second she would be embroiled *with him* in a terrible heap at the bottom of the stairs.

Her whole soul shrank from even touching the creature!

She reached out frantically for a handhold, but there was none. She grasped only air as she fell, until her fingers closed on something—the creature's ephemeral garment?—and felt the unmistakable texture of fine bed linen in her hands.

Then she fainted.

She lay in an unpleasant place.

Around her floated dark and whinnying shapes, with here and there a deep and very pleasant voice sounding like a great bell cleaving the obscurity that wrapped her. If she could just reach that voice . . .

That voice was speaking in her ear. But there were other voices too, loud and sharp and grating. The voice in her ear—it was Ivor's! But how could he be here? And where was *here*, come to that?

Ivor was saying things she had heard once before, long ago, when life was sweeter and the sun shone. "Darling Jess, whatever possessed you . . . come on, open your eyes for me, dearest . . . tell me where you hurt . . ."

In a rush, Jess knew where she was. In Oaklane, where she and Cleo had come to search out ghosts and sliding panels and had been attacked, and where was Cleo? Was she hurt? But most of all, Jess knew she lay in Ivor's arms, doubtless on the floor of the entrance hall, at the bottom of the stairs.

Those same stairs down which had come . . . She would not think of that. She would think of nothing but that she was in Ivor's embrace and he was saying deliriously delightful things to her. She saw no reason to open her eyes, even though Ivor commanded her to. She had not yet heard enough of the endearments she was starving for.

"Dear heart . . ." he was saying. But something gave her away, and he realized she was pretending to be unconscious. Smooth as satin, he continued, "Wake up at once, or I shall drop you on the floor."

Thus adjured, she opened her eyes, to meet Ivor's devilish grin. "It takes," he said softly, "more cleverness than you have to fool me."

Smiling sweetly, she removed herself from his embrace and said to him very gently, "Truly? But you do not know how long I was in a swoon, do you? A very short time, I warrant you."

Pleased to see an expression of uncertainty flit across his face, she got to her feet. Let him wonder how much she had heard. He had said some very revealing things, after all!

But there was work to be done right here. She was still a little dizzy, and she reached out for support to the newel post. The tableau before her was made of the stuff used by Waverley in weaving his macabre tales.

Cleo, apparently unharmed, had recoiled against the opposite stair railing, and stared at the object at her feet. Giles stood idly prodding the object with the toe of an exquisitely polished boot, clearly waiting until Ivor could give his attention to the problem.

The object itself was of keen interest to Jess. It was of course white, but in the light of a large lantern held by Acton, it no longer looked other-worldly, eerie, terrifying. In fact, Jess was conscious of a pang of compassion for . . . whatever it was.

They were soon enlightened as to its identity. The object had found its voice, and gave out moans of pain. The white covering moved convulsively, and Jess recognized it with a start. "That's my mother's sheet! I recognize that mending at the hem. It's my own work!"

With a shaky attempt at normal common sense, Cleo said, "What does a ghost need of your mother's sheet, Jess? I thought they wore cerements. Grave clothes, I mean."

"We know what you mean," said Ivor crustily. "Let's have this sheet off and see who the fellow is. Acton, give me a hand."

The farm manager, now Sir Ivor's loyal man, bent to the task with alacrity. To the last, the creature held the sheet over his face, hoping futilely not to be unveiled. "Leg's broken, sir," said Acton, "so it looks to me. Have to take him out on a hurdle."

When the sheet was finally removed, and the man's features were visible, Jess recognized him with disbelief. She heard someone gasp behind her.

"Henry!" she said at last. "Henry, was it you all the time?"

The man who had promised she would never be hurt, that he would see that she was safe, the man who had asked her mother for permission to pay his addresses to her, had done none of these things. Why, Henry? But it was a mute cry, for Henry was glaring, not at her or at Ivor, but, surprisingly, at Acton.

"You led them here!" he snarled. "You great fool!"

Acton answered, "With respect, sir, I might say the same of you."

Acton straightened and said, "Sir Ivor, shall I summon the men to take him away? We'll need to find a hurdle and a cart." Ivor nodded his permission.

Jess knelt beside the injured man. "Henry, you're the ghost? And you came in and out of the house? And the chairs . . . and the . . . Oh, Henry! Why?"

For a man at the mercy of others, and desperate for a dose of opium to give him remission from the pain in his broken leg, Henry Hartnell was reckless. "For God's sake, Jess! It's none of your business! But I'll tell you what *is* your business! That nosy brother of yours with the book—"

In his avid desire to tell Jess, he moved too quickly, and his leg sent shocking pains through him. He gritted his teeth to withstand the onslaught, but in vain. He managed to say only, "Philip dead. Little fool . . ." before he lapsed into merciful unconsciousness and left his captors eying each other in wild surmise.

22

What nonsense! thought Jess. Philip was tucked away in his room at Oakminster, without a doubt absorbed in a fascinating book. Or in the library. He would have been missed at dinner . . . surely he could not be dead! Henry was merely trying to frighten her.

She glanced at Ivor, Cleo, Giles, and again at Ivor. She saw nothing but the shock that had been there since the ghost's identity had been revealed. Had she heard Henry rightly? Was she the only one who had?

A disturbance at the back of the house interrupted her thoughts. Acton bustled in, followed by several men from the farms. They carried a makeshift hurdle, a derelict barn door, and they started at once to lift Henry onto it. There were a few murmured questions, for it was not every day that the quality got into such high jinks as to leave one nigh dead, from his looks, and the others, even the ladies, looking like they'd all seen ghosts. And likely they had, for everyone knew Oaklane was haunted, what with lights sometimes at night, and all. But the men asked no questions, being reasonable persons and knowing their inquiries would be taken amiss.

Silvester burst into the house through the front door. "What a trick! Ivor, you should have told me you were coming here! You know I should have enjoyed it above all things . . ."

His voice died away as he became aware of the somber atmosphere around him. "What is it? You found the ghost? What was it? The countess?"

His glance fell on the unconscious man being lifted carefully onto the hurdle. "Mr. Hartnell?" Silvester's voice squeaked in disbelief at what his eyes saw.

Jess opened her mouth to speak, but Ivor forestalled her, with her own question. "Silvester, where is

Philip?" Jess had not imagined Henry's terrible news. The others had heard him too.

"Philip? How should I know?"

"Silvester, I swear I will strangle you," said Jess fervently, "if you quote Scripture to me at this moment. I wish to know precisely where Philip is." And whether he lives.

Ivor, touching Jess's arm, said quietly, "Allow me." Then, bending a stern glance on her brother, he continued, "When did you last see Philip?"

All frivolity drained away, Silvester answered honestly. "I had just come in from riding, and he came out to the stables to help me rub Copper down. I didn't think much about it, except that he doesn't like horses very well."

"An unusual event, I take it?"

"Well, yes. And he was spouting some nonsense about something he had found in a book about the treasure . . . well, not the Cavalier treasure, I guess, because that's all dug up now. But some other—"

"And you didn't even listen!" cried Jess hotly.

Ivor glanced at Giles. Raising an eyebrow, he said, "I think we must look into this." Without a word, Giles turned and started up the stairs.

Silvester was to make handsome amends for his neglect of his brother. The next hours flew by in a maze for him, colored as they were by remorse and guilt. He had unfeelingly sent Philip into such danger as he could not imagine. But at least Ivor kept him too busy to brood.

He went after Giles and Ivor, upstairs and into Jess's old room. The wardrobe door stood ajar still, and a quick flash of the lantern beam showed them that the entire back panel was open. Ivor looked through the opening, seeing the same prospect as Philip had seen not three hours since.

Silvester, crowding behind the two men, could not

see clearly, but he saw enough. A dark hole, a flight of stairs disappearing into nothing, tunnel walls like a cellar—he regretted his assessment of a secret opening, a hidden tunnel, as the most romantic, *adventurous* development in the world.

Now Jess's repetition of Henry's statement chilled his bones. If Oaklane were his, Silvester thought, he would either seal the bedroom wall or detonate dynamite in the tunnel so that no small boy could ever be lured into it again!

Cleo took Jess's arm and led her into the salon. "Sit down, Jess, it will not help Philip if we all swoon!"

Just think, Jess remembered, hardly more than a sennight ago she had sat in this same chair, where she could watch both the stairs and the front door, a poker in her hand. The ghost had been real in the end, and while she did not believe she had been in any real danger from Henry, there was still that odd odor of musk-scented soap to be accounted for. Why Henry should move furniture and travel the rooms and corridors of Oaklane without a shred of legal justification, she could not begin to guess.

Nor why he should dress up in her mother's sheets, perfectly willing, if not to harm Jess, at least to send both Jess and Cleo into screaming hysterics, she could not divine either.

"Well, the ghost of Oaklane is laid at last," Cleo remarked.

"I would rather have Philip," said Jess simply.

"You cannot believe odious Mr. Hartnell told the truth? He simply meant to score off you because he was unmasked at last."

Jess jumped up. "I have to see what is going on upstairs. They've been such a long time! You need not come with me, Cleo."

Cleo joined her. "You cannot think I shall stay down

here by myself? Henry may have had an accomplice or two, you know."

"You know, you cannot frighten me anymore."

"More's the pity," said Cleo cryptically, believing that Jess needed to think about something other than Philip's predicament, whatever it might be.

They arrived in Jess's old room to find it empty. One lantern stood on the floor, giving a feeble light. However, the illumination was sufficient to show them the secret door through the wardrobe, and the wall behind it.

"Ivor must be down below," said Jess, as calmly as though she were speaking about a breakfast menu to Mrs. Cross. "I wish we had brought up the other lantern. I'm taking this one."

"Of course you are," said Cleo, resigned, "and I shall go with you. Sitting up here in the dark has lost its appeal."

Gingerly, holding the lantern with one hand and lifting her skirts with the other, Jess started down the stairs. The condition of the surroundings did not improve. The lower they went, the damper the air. She would not have been surprised to see water dripping from the walls.

"I shall never read another romance as long as I live," muttered Cleo. "In fact, I may write one myself."

They reached the bottom of the steps and walked along the tunnel in the footsteps of Ivor and Giles, and possibly Philip, and certainly Henry. And the countess, perhaps, and the unknown lover . . .

Their footfalls made little sound. From time to time Jess stopped, and they listened. There was no real sound, but a kind of whispering, as of voices far ahead —or from long ago.

Once Jess stopped so abruptly that Cleo, hard on her heels, bumped into her. Jess dropped the lantern, and the flame flickered. Don't go out! begged Jess silently, and her prayer was answered. The light flared up again.

Jess turned to her companion. "Cleo, I can't express how glad I am that you are with me."

Cleo saw tears glinting in Jess's eyes. She hugged her close for a moment. "Just remember whose clever idea to lay the ghost brought us to this muddle."

Turning again to the tunnel stretching away into dimness ahead of them, Jess strangled a cry. "Who is that?" The figure running toward them was only Silvester.

He stopped when he reached them. "Jess, what are you doing here? You're not supposed to come—"

"Is there a cave-in," demanded Cleo, "or did that dreadful man imagine it?"

"The whole tunnel is full. The roof fell in." Even as he spoke, small dribbles of earth drifted down from the ceiling behind him. The three of them looked up, features strained in anxiety. "That's probably the way the cave-in started," said Silvester in an odd voice that Jess had never heard before.

"Philip?" Jess whispered.

"We haven't found him. He may be under the debris." Recalling his urgent errand, he said, "Jess, let me by. I've got to get shovels." He showed them his hands, black as the earth around them, except for traces of blood along the knuckles.

"Can't you get men to dig?"

"Ivor says no. Too dangerous. You can't help any. Better go upstairs, so we don't have to dig you out too!"

Scraping past them, he bounded away down the tunnel in the way they had come. After a long moment, Cleo looked down at her bejeweled fingers and said ruefully, "I'm afraid he is right. I'm of no use whatever."

"Nor am I."

Reluctantly they went back toward the foot of the

stairs. Cleo, feeling a need to reassure Jess, and possibly herself also, kept up a running one-sided conversation. "There is nothing to say Philip is buried under there. Granted, it is possible, but not very likely, I should think. You remember that the ceiling dirt came down behind Silvester, so why would it not have been the same for Philip? He is most likely safe and sound beyond the cave-in."

They reached the bottom of the stairs. Silvester was at the top, clutching two shovels, breathing hard. He had run to the stables. "Had the devil of a time finding them," he panted. "Sorry, Jess."

Now was not the time to point out his rough language, she thought. She and Cleo stood aside and let him descend. He held a lantern in one hand, the shovels uncooperative under his other arm.

"Be careful," called Jess after them, futilely. She had no doubt that Philip had been careful. There is no way to avoid a cave-in. "The only remedy," she said to Cleo, as though she had previously spoken aloud, "is to stay out of tunnels. If we go upstairs, at least they will not have to worry about us."

Time dragged. The clock on the mantel in the drawing room had long since wound down, and there was no way of noting the passage of the minutes. The moon had risen, and cast a bright light into the entrance hall.

"They left the door open," said Jess, "when they took Henry out. Cleo, why is all this happening? What did Henry want down that tunnel, anyway?"

Cleo's thoughts traveled along her own track. "I wonder, Jess, why Ivor and Giles were so near at hand? I would not be at all surprised to learn that they were already in the house. They must have planned to lie in wait to capture . . . Could it be, Jess, that they *knew* that Henry was at the bottom of this?"

"We don't even know what 'this' is. Why . . . *why* didn't they tell us what they were doing?"

Ever the realist, Cleo said simply, "Because they are men, and to the last degree prejudiced."

That seemed to sum it up, thought Jess. "No wonder they did not confide in us," she said finally, "for we blunder in—"

"But we would not have done so, had we known they were doing anything about it." After a minute she laughed. "But we would have insisted on accompanying them, would we not?"

"I suppose so. Why don't they come? Why don't they tell us something? Don't you think they must have breached a hole in that wall by now?"

Cleo was not required to answer, for on the heels of Jess's impatient query came noises from upstairs, heavy and rapid footsteps, coming closer. Ivor took the stairs two at a time, and headed toward the kitchen. He found his way barred by his sister and his dear Jess.

"Please let me pass. I have no news."

Jess did not move. "Where are you going, then? To get another shovel? I'll go with you."

"No, there is room for only two to dig at the same time. I think we might do better if we were to come into the tunnel from the outside entrance."

"But we don't know where it comes out." Jess's voice rose. "How can we find it?"

"I think I know," said Ivor. He put his hands on her shoulders to set her out of his way. It proved impossible.

"I am going with you," said Jess.

Ivor sent a glance to Cleo, appealing for assistance. He did not receive it.

"I believe Jess will be better," Cleo said in a low voice, "to be occupied, rather than sitting up here, idle and brooding."

"Hurry, then," he said sharply to Jess. "I left the curricle in the stable."

Ivor strode across the yard to the stables, Jess hurrying in his wake. Very shortly they drove swiftly down the drive, and turned left at the junction with the public road.

Ivor sent the horse ahead at a speed that generated a hard breeze directly in their faces. He did not notice.

Jess hung on to the seat. "Where are we going?" she asked, catching her breath with difficulty. "Do you really know where the tunnel comes out?"

"We'll know in a few minutes," was all he said.

Under other circumstances she would have found the drive delightful. To be tooling through a spring night, next to Ivor, the moon making the road a bright ribbon unrolling ahead of them—what could be more romantic?

Instead of that, they were speeding to a place she did not know, to search for the outside entrance, also unknown, of a tunnel in which her brother quite possibly lay dead. A sob caught in her throat. Ivor heard it. He laid his free hand over hers in comfort. Gradually she felt her fears lessen.

There was much to do: find Philip, learn from Henry whatever secrets he held, close up the tunnel and the secret door once and for all . . . But in the meantime, Ivor sat solid and reliable, comforting, and capable. If anyone could rescue Philip, it was Ivor.

They turned off the road into a lane that, at last, she recognized. When they came to a stop, she could hear the river burbling gently in the darkness beyond the curricle's lamps. Ivor leapt down and tethered the horse to the same sapling as before, and came to help her down to the ground.

"You think—" she began, but instead of releasing her, he drew her to him. He held her close with one arm. He lifted her chin with a finger, so that he could look directly into those eyes he loved, so shadowed in the dimness that he could not tell their color. Dark, anxious pools, they were, and he winced inwardly in sympathy with her fears.

Gently he kissed her, softly, lingeringly. He could feel the tension draining out of her, and at last he let her go.

"Now, darling, we will simply do our best. We can do no more than that."

He threw the beam of the lantern to help her, and she followed him calmly. Somewhere a small boy needed help, and she and Ivor were coming to rescue him. No longer did she believe her brother was beyond help. Ivor held hope for Philip, and so did she.

They walked around the rocks, covered with thick grass, and even a small sprig of bush that sent a tall thin shadow wavering across the grass as the lantern moved.

"There's no entrance," Jess said. "We did not see one the other day."

"Ah," Ivor whispered back, "but this bush intrigues me." There was a good-size bush growing out of the side of the rock jumble, very close to the riverbank. "I do not remember seeing it before."

He took hold of it, intending to uproot it. Exerting his strength, he pulled hard, and nearly fell backward as the bush, clearly without roots, came away.

"Ivor!" cried Jess. "You almost fell into the river!"

Recovering his balance, Ivor looked behind him. The current slid by at his heels. "So I did." He examined the bush in his hands. "No wonder we did not see it before. It is dead, put here to conceal . . . what, I wonder?"

"I have the lantern."

Sending the light to the spot where the bush had stood, they saw a great hole. Large enough, Jess thought, to admit a man into the emptiness beneath it.

So! This was the opening of the tunnel, the other end of which emerged in the wardrobe in Jess's bedroom. The tunnel once used for amorous dalliance between the Italian countess and . . . whoever was the unknown lover. Jess moved back in her mind, back to the time of Queen Anne, when the countess was immured in Oaklane, well-cared-for by servants, but ostracized from family and society. Where would she find a lover? He could not have lived very far away, Jess concluded, for Mrs. Dalton's story indicated that they met often, and secretly.

The lover would enter the folly? There must have been a concealing belt of shrubbery around the small building. He would somehow—through a trapdoor?—descend into the tunnel originally designed as a priest's escape, and make his way in happy anticipation to the house. Upstairs, of course, so the servants would not see him on the ground floor. It all fit.

All but Henry.

Ivor brought her back to the present. "Help me, Jess. Hold the lantern so I can see better."

He had cleared away dirt to make the hole larger. He did not know what lay below. He reasoned that the drop could not be far, for if it were, water would have filled this part of the tunnel. If Henry came and went, then the tunnel was likely not flooded.

Jess held the lantern. Ivor prepared to sit down on the edge of the hole, dangle his feet into space, and then ease down until he felt earth beneath his boots. Bent and slightly off balance, he was unprepared for an eventuality he had not foreseen. The tunnel was occupied.

There was no warning, save for a faint scrambling sound. The man inside the tunnel, knowing there was no other way out, made a desperate lunge forward and upward. It was unfortunate that he caught Ivor at a disadvantage. Like a rocket, the man leapt to freedom, catching Ivor somewhere around the knees and propelling him backward out of the way.

Jess, standing out of harm's way with the lantern, watched appalled as Ivor, making an odd muffled sound, flew backward. The man did not even pause. Jess heard a splash as of a heavy body landing in the river, and then a smaller splash farther out, as though made by a diver arcing in to the stream.

But that first one!

Jess screamed, "Ivor!" even as she sped to the river-bank. Holding the lantern high, she scanned the moving surface, looking for his beloved head. If he had been hurt before he fell in, he might be unconscious. . . .

Somewhere near at hand someone whimpered. She knew the sound came from her, and she forced control on herself. "Ivor!" she called, and her voice seemed normal enough.

Then she saw him. He was quite close to the bank, but he seemed not to move, except with the current. "Ivor!" she screamed again. She set the lantern down on the grassy bank, and without thought for herself, stepped into the stream. The waters tugged at her long skirts, but she paid no heed. She grabbed for Ivor's coat, his sleeve, his collar. But the wet cloth was hard and fit too smoothly—surely Weston had not designed this coat for a circumstance such as this!—for her fingers to catch hold.

She was crying. She felt the tears slipping down her cheeks, or was it the river splashing up into her face? No matter, she had him now.

Each hand held a fistful of wet black hair. She braced her feet in the muddy river bottom and held him against the tug of the river. Finally she was able, step by step, to pull him to the bank. But she could never in this world pull him out of the river.

If she could get Ivor's horse to the bank . . .

She did not know she spoke aloud until she heard a sputtering sound and a snort that sounded much like

Ivor's laugh. She realized that the pull on her arms had gradually lessened, and Ivor was no longer an unconscious deadweight.

In a moment he had risen to his knees, and regardless of water streaming from his face and shoulders, he reached for her. She felt her knees tremble beneath her, and fell against the bank. Ivor's arms came around her, pinioning her to the bank, and his lips searched for and found hers.

The waters rushed by, oblivious of the humans locked in a most satisfying embrace half out of the water. Jess could hear the river chuckling, and far away a horse whinnied.

"A fine figure I made," said Ivor at last, ruefully. "But I had no thought of anyone inside. Did you get a good look at him?"

"No, but I think he got away. I heard him go into the river, but he did not fall in, I believe."

"Probably swam the river. That's not impossible to do. So he got away." Then, in an altered voice he said, "But you're not going to get away again, my darling Jessamine. I'll never let you go."

"Is this an offer?" she asked, her eyes full of mischief.

"An offer? Yes, I suppose it is."

"You know," she said dreamily, "a young lady likes to look her best when she receives an offer of marriage. And look at me!"

He did. He took full note of Jess, her drenched muslin gown clinging like a second skin, her hair draggled and limp. He bent and gently kissed each pointed breast, even relishing the muddy river taste of the cloth.

"Best get out of this water," he said, keeping a tight rein on his emotions, and speaking in a calm voice. "I should not like you to catch cold. You might postpone our marriage."

"But—"

"But me no buts," said Ivor, standing up and pulling her to her feet. "Not now. At least we know the tunnel can be traveled."

She had forgotten Philip! But on second thought, she knew she had not, for even in her ecstasy a moment ago, she was aware at bottom of great sadness.

Ivor lowered himself into the tunnel first. She handed down the lantern, and then slid down to stand beside him on the tunnel floor. The light from the lantern seemed swallowed up in the dark, damp earth that surrounded them. They were in a kind of cave, an enlargement of the tunnel. It was not empty.

A table, a candlestick gritty to Jess's exploring touch, a box-like object she did not recognize. She dared not take time to examine it, since Philip was somewhere in the tunnel, in danger. Without purposeful thought she grabbed the strange object and thrust it deep in her pocket. Dirty the thing might be, but her dress was still sopping, in all likelihood ruined forever, so a bit more grime would make no difference.

"Come on," whispered Ivor urgently, "we'll come back to this."

They moved cautiously along the tunnel. He estimated that the cave-in must have occurred fairly close to this end of the passage. Young Philip had come a long way. Ivor resolved that the small boy must receive a good share of his attention, if he survived this. Silvester must get his commission, and . . .

Even though a part of Ivor's mind was engrossed in planning for Jess's family, he was still aware of his surroundings. He was not reassured by the constant drifting of earth from the ceiling of the excavation, and even from the sides. They must be getting close to the cave-in.

Jess tapped his back. He turned in the narrow passage. "What is it?" he whispered, fearing to dislodge more dirt.

"Listen!"

He put his arm around her while they listened. She was shivering in her wet clothes, and he pressed her close to give her what warmth he could. From a surprisingly short distance away they could hear the regular sharp sliding sound of shovels being thrust rhythmically into earth.

He swung the langern beam ahead. They could see nothing . . . but the apparent emptiness turned into a wall of earth. Something lay like a blanket at the foot of the wall. Jess cried out, and darted past Ivor.

"It's Philip!" she cried.

A handful of earth was dislodged, and fell with a small thud on the hard floor.

"Ssh!" hissed Ivor quickly. He joined her, and ran his hands over the small bundle on the floor. It was Philip, and front the grunting sounds, he was quite alive! He was tied, though, bound at wrist and ankle.

Jess resorted, this time, to gesture rather than sound. She prodded Ivor's shoulder and pointed. There was light coming through the wall! The shovelers had broken through!

After a brief, urgent exchange at the wall, Giles and Silvester glided away back to the house, and Jess led the way hurriedly back to the entrance cave. Ivor carried Philip, now unbound.

"Can you endure it until we get you out of here?" Ivor had asked gently. "I think there is too little time to get you back on your feet."

Philip nodded, tried to speak, cleared his throat, and said, "I'll be glad to get out."

"So be it," Ivor had said, hoisting the small body to his shoulder. Then, noticing how close to the ceiling Philip's head would travel—not room enough for a Cavalier plume!—he carried him in his arms.

In the cave, seemingly less prone to shed its ceiling, they halted. Ivor rubbed Philip's legs and feet, and Jess massaged his arms. Skin on his wrists bore marks from the tight bonds.

"Who did this to you?" demanded Jess, furious.

"A man," said Philip. "I didn't know him. Jess, I think he was the man you saw. He had that funny smell."

"The musk!"

"Did he say anything?" This from Ivor.

"Not really. You see, I was asleep when he came. Something hit me, a stone, I suppose, and when I woke up, there he was. He was angry. But I told him I had as much right as he did to be down here, because this was a Bellamy tunnel on Bellamy land. Wasn't I right?"

"Of course you were," said Ivor. "See if you can stand on your feet."

"Of course, I'm a Dalton, not a Bellamy, but I thought maybe he didn't know that." He took a few steps around the cave. "Yes, I'm all right now."

"You're a Bellamy, all right," said Ivor, relief at finding the boy alive making his voice rough. "We're all one family, and don't ever forget it."

Philip's expression changed little, but his eyes shone with happiness. "Then I guess it doesn't matter if there isn't any treasure."

"Treasure!" echoed Jess, reaching into her pocket "Look at this."

She held between her fingertips a rectangular object that probably had once been a leather case, of a size and style to hold a man's studs and dress jewelry. It had moldered away over the generations until it was hardly recognizable. Suppose there were jewels still in it! There couldn't be! Both Henry and the unknown man would have taken whatever valuables there were. But nonetheless she felt a quickening of her pulse as she opened the case.

It was empty. A collective sigh measured the unlikely hopes of the three of them.

Ivor was the first to come back to reality. "Let's get out of here. Leave the case, Jess, it's falling apart."

She still stared at the lid of the case. "Look," she breathed. "Initials."

The gold was gone from the initials, but the indentations in the leather still could be read, if caught just right by the light. She handed the case to Ivor. After looking at it long and hard, tilting the case to the light, without hesitation he handed it to Philip as an equal in their consultation.

At length Philip, feeling the responsibility of an adult, said carefully, "It looks like a J and an H." He looked questioningly at his companions.

"It did to me too," said Ivor.

Jess said, as though the words were dragged out of her, "Josiah Hartnell. Henry's ancestor."

To their surprise, when they returned to Oaklane to rejoin the others, they found Cleo sitting at her ease in the drawing room, wearing a satisfied smile.

"The canary swallowed?" said Ivor sourly. He still considered Cleo the force behind the female expedition to Oaklane.

"Ivor," said Cleo in a sisterly fashion, "make your manners to Charles."

"Good heavens, Charles! How did you get here? Don't tell me in a coach, for I shall think Cleo is too much an influence on you! But first, you remember Miss Dalton?"

After introductions were made, and a shawl was found to wrap around Jess in her damp, wrinkled clothes, knowledge was shared and experiences exchanged, after word was sent to Mrs. Dalton that her son was safe.

"What Giles had to tell me roused my suspicions, and I decided that these odd circumstances needed investigating," explained Charles.

"You'd never admit that you missed me excessively," teased Cleo.

"Never in this world would I admit that," her husband retorted, but Jess caught the glint in his eye as he contemplated his wife, and knew he did not speak truth.

"Henry must have been after the treasure then," suggested Jess, at the end.

"I think not, Miss Dalton," said Charles, "at least not at the beginning. He was much opposed, you know, to the demands made by the millworkers. He among others used his influence to persuade the government to set spies among the workers to learn their designs."

"In order to crush them before they could become dangerous," added Giles.

"Then that man who soared out of the tunnel was a spy?"

"We think he is Oliver. The man has no other name, known to us, at least. A spy of enormous if misplaced ability."

"I regret that I was not able to hold him for you," said Ivor.

"Never mind, my men will get him eventually."

"Your men? But are you not on the government's side?" This from Silvester, greatly daring in the presence of his elders.

"Not everyone in the government agree on this, as also on other issues. By the way, there is no need for my presence here to be advertised abroad. I shall of course be returning at once to London, if you can give me lodging tonight, Ivor? In recompense, I shall take your sister back with me."

"I like *that*! Just as though I were a left parcel somewhere!"

"I shall be glad if you will stay, Charles. But you and Cleo will of course come back for the wedding!"

"Wedding!" cried his sister, elated.

"I cannot," protested Jess. "I am still in mourning, you remember."

Ivor said, in mock menace, "If you think I am going to wait nearly a year—"

"Well," Jess said happily, "I suppose it must be marriage, then, for you know I am no Italian countess to settle for less!"

Cleo pointed out, "Neither was she. But to think Henry was nearly our cousin—on the wrong side, of course. But he must have thought the jewels should have been his."

"And perhaps he was right. But to begin with, he begged for government help. That list was of names of friends Oliver could call upon."

"Acton," suggested Jess, "and the L could have been the last letter in 'Hartnell'."

"Most likely," agreed Charles. "Now, Cleo, let us be on our way to Oakminster. I do not doubt Mrs. Dalton will be anxious to see her son. Philip, would you like to ride with us?"

Philip scampered out to the coach, and when the Chichesters had got in, the vehicle drove away.

As they traveled, Cleo said, "I shall be hard put not to tell Cousin Elizabeth the good news about Jess's betrothal and approaching wedding. Of course it is Jess's right to do so. I do not think she will be greatly surprised."

Charles kissed her cheek. "Not after you had decided to take a hand in the affair."

At last Jess and Ivor were left alone. She thought: all my schemes to have my revenge on Ivor, and his to make me jealous of Lady Dorine, all of them were nothing but fancies made up to beguile children—the juveniles that she and Ivor had been four years ago.

Ivor's lips on hers, just now, were real, demanding. There would be rocky times ahead, without a doubt, for they were each strong and willful, but at least, whether Ivor was angry, unreasonable, infuriating, even domineering—at least he was here, within reach.

The lonely years, she knew, would never come again.